change of
HEART

ALSO BY NICOLE JACQUELYN

Unbreak My Heart

change of HEART

NICOLE JACQUELYN

FOREVER

New York   Boston

Forever
Hachette Book Group
1290 Avenue of the Americas, New York, NY 10104
forever-romance.com
twitter.com/foreverromance

First Edition: September 2016

Forever is an imprint of Grand Central Publishing. The Forever name and logo are trademarks of Hachette Book Group, Inc.

The publisher is not responsible for websites (or their content) that are not owned by the publisher.

The Hachette Speakers Bureau provides a wide range of authors for speaking events. To find out more, go to www.hachettespeakersbureau.com or call (866) 376-6591.

Lyrics from "Thief and a Liar" © 2012 by Jeffrey Martin. All rights reserved.

Library of Congress Control Number: 2016942582

ISBNs: 978-1-4555-3800-3 (paperback), 978-1-4555-3799-0 (ebook)

Printed in the United States of America

RRD-C

10 9 8 7 6 5 4 3 2 1

*To my sister and brother-in-law, who are the
reason this story was written. You prove every
day that being a parent has little to do with
genetics and everything to do with love.*

Acknowledgments

Thank you to my daughters, who motivate me and cheer me on, even when I'm completely distracted by the characters in my head. I love you guys! To my parents and my sister, who have my back. Every time. Always. I couldn't have done this without you.

To Nikki, who's my right hand and keeps me on track. Thank you a million times for your feedback and, more importantly, your friendship.

To Ashley, who opened a thousand doors for me, Toni for listening to me ramble at one a.m., and to Donna, who I will thank forever for taking a chance on my very first book, thank you.

To my agent Marisa who keeps advocating for these characters like they're her children, and my editor Alex who loves this book almost as much as I do, thank you.

To the readers and the bloggers who have gotten me this far, I owe you big. I'll never forget that.

change of
HEART

Prologue

Anita

Sixteen years old

People always hid the good shit in their bedrooms.

It was like they believed that some invisible force field kept others from finding the huge dildo or the small stash of weed in their top dresser drawer. Wrong. The only things that kept me from snooping were padlocks and Dobermans—and even those could be bypassed.

I never looked for the expensive things. Most of the foster homes I'd lived in didn't *have* expensive things, and even if they did, I had no use for them. What was I going to do, try and pawn stolen jewelry? I wasn't that stupid.

I also wasn't planning on living on the streets. I'd tried that once.

A fourteen-year-old girl who was a little over five feet tall and less than a hundred pounds didn't have a chance living out there without getting the shit kicked out of her by other homeless people who were bigger, stronger, and had been doing it a lot longer than she had. I didn't even want to remember the others, the ones who'd been a little too nice to me.

No, I'd stay in foster care. For the most part, the families I'd lived with weren't so bad. Sure, a lot of them were in it for the money the state gave them for my upkeep, and there might have been the occasional drinking problem or porn addiction, but in the seven houses I'd lived in, there was only one that I'd left on purpose. I'd felt no guilt over calling the police when I found the overly handsy foster dad's stash of heroin. Boom—new foster home for me.

One guess where I'd found that little nugget of escape. Yep, the bedroom.

I smirked to myself as I pulled open the drawer in the nightstand that sat to the right of my newest foster parents' king-sized bed. A pair of glasses, a string of condoms, a broken necklace, a few buttons, a romance novel, and lube greeted my eyes. I shuddered but slammed the drawer closed. Gross, but nothing out of the ordinary.

I'd already searched through the dresser and the matching nightstand and hadn't found anything. Where did they hide the juicy stuff? I needed leverage, dammit.

"What the fuck are you doing in here?" a deep voice said from behind me as I took a step toward the closet.

Shit.

"Looking for the bathroom?" I replied in an overly innocent tone.

I spun slowly to meet the eyes of the guy standing in the bedroom doorway. Jesus, it was Bram. It was just my luck that the jackass adopted twin son of my foster parents had to be the one who'd caught me. The other twin, Alex, would have laughed, put me in a headlock that I was far too old for, and dragged me out of the room.

This brother, on the other hand, was going to be a problem. The two were so different it was amazing that they were brothers, not to mention identical twins. Not that anyone would ever mistake one for the other. Where Alex was fun and happy and smiling, Bram was a total asshole. And I meant that in the nicest possible way.

He was angry and scowling all the time. It was as if the entire world had let him down, and he no longer had the time to pretend to enjoy anything. *Yeah, join the club, dude.*

I stared at his face for a few seconds, wondering if I'd be able to talk myself out of the mess I'd gotten into, when Bram took one fast step forward and grabbed ahold of my wrist, jerking me back out of the bedroom.

Nope. I wasn't getting out of it.

"What did you take?" he hissed, glaring at me as he shoved me back a couple steps down the hallway.

"Nothing," I said back, rubbing my wrist.

I considered myself pretty street savvy, and I didn't think Bram was going to hurt me or anything, but the guy was really freaking intimidating. He was almost a foot taller than I was, with broad shoulders and a five-o'clock shadow that highlighted the fact that he was grown. At nineteen, neither of the boys lived in the house with us, but they shared an apartment in the detached garage, which meant I saw them pretty often.

Too often.

"What are you doing here?" I asked, turning away from him to move toward the living room. Nervousness would look like guilt, and since I wasn't fucking guilty of anything but taking a quick look around, I wasn't going to let him know he intimidated me. "Aren't you supposed to be at work or something?"

I knew he was supposed to be at work. I knew everyone's schedule; that's why I'd thought it was safe to get the lay of the land. I'd only been in the Evans house for a little over two weeks, but everything seemed a bit too good to be true. So when my foster mom Liz took her daughter Katie into town for some Christmas shopping and the guys were at the logging office for the day, I'd thought I was in the clear.

I'd barely gotten to the living room entrance before hands were gripping me once again, halting my movement.

"What the hell did you take?" Bram asked again as I tried to pull away.

He gave me a little shake and jerked me around to face him, and all of my earlier bravado vanished in an instant.

"I didn't take anything," I whispered hoarsely, lifting my chin as I slapped at his hands.

"You think you're the first kid to pull this shit?" he asked harshly through clenched teeth. "My parents took you in, buy you shit, feed you—and you steal from them?"

"I didn't fucking take anything!" I repeated, swallowing hard.

I froze completely as one of Bram's hands dropped from my shoulder and slid down the front of my stomach, sliding around the edge of my hip and across my back. I didn't move away when he dropped to his knees and lifted up each pant leg to check the inside of my ratty dollar store socks, and I barely breathed as he wiggled his fingers into the front pockets of my jeans and then the back pockets.

When his hands moved back up, my eyesight began to grow hazy from lack of oxygen, and just as his palm slid down between my breasts, I took in a large gasp of air that turned into a loud sob.

"Anita?" Bram asked in confusion, dropping his hands as he took a frantic step backward, his hands in the air.

"I told you I didn't take anything," I murmured, staring at him through tear-blurred eyes. "I told you."

"I'm sorry. I—you were in my parents' room," he stuttered, his expression softer than I'd ever seen it before.

I wiped my face with the long sleeves of my T-shirt and moved backward, watching him closely for any indication that he would try and stop me. Then, when I'd finally gotten my breathing under control, I spoke. "If you ever touch me again, I'll kill you."

I turned and ran toward my room, never slowing even though I couldn't hear him following me.

Later, we pretended that nothing happened. He didn't rat me out, and I didn't tell his parents that he'd felt me up. Our silence wasn't a truce though; it was battle lines clearly drawn.

Chapter 1

Abraham

Fourteen years later

Y ou have five grandbabies, Mom. Pretend a couple of those are mine," I said with a kiss to the side of my mom's head.

"It doesn't work that way," she said in frustration, pinching me lightly on the side as she moved past me into the kitchen.

We'd been having the same conversation for the past five years, and my answer had never changed. I didn't want kids. It's not like I didn't love my nieces and nephews—I did. I just didn't want the responsibility of having one of my own. I was happy being the uncle who bought cool-as-hell Christmas presents and took the kids fishing when I felt like it—then sending them home with their parents.

"Why do you keep asking?" a voice called out from the back door, making my jaw clench. "You know Bram will never love anyone as much as he loves himself."

"Anita," Mom scolded with a sour look.

"Interesting, coming from you," I murmured, bracing myself as I glanced at the slender woman walking into the room.

"What's that supposed to mean?" Anita asked, dropping a bag of groceries hard on the table.

"Don't see any kids pulling on your skirts," I snapped back.

Anita's eyes grew wide with hurt for only a moment. "I'm not wearing a skirt," she hissed stupidly, spinning on her heel and almost running out of the kitchen.

I watched her leave, then glanced at my mom in confusion. *What the fuck?*

"Christ, Abraham," my mom said, shaking her head as she pushed past me. "I don't understand why the two of you can't just ignore each other."

I stood there like an idiot for a minute, then followed them toward the living room, stopping just on the other side of the wall as I heard my mom's voice.

"You okay?" Mom asked.

A watery chuckle answered her.

"You know he was just—"

"I don't expect anything less, Mom. I'm fine," Anita choked out. I leaned hard against the wall and closed my eyes. *Shit.* I wasn't sure what was wrong, but I knew she'd been crying. Her voice was normally husky—I'd pointed out more than once that she'd make a good phone sex operator—but it was magnified by a thousand as she brushed off my mom.

"If you would—" my mom said, her words cutting off as Ani spoke.

"I'm fine. Promise."

Before I could move from my spot, Anita was stepping out of the living room, and the front door was opening wide to show my cousin Trevor slipping inside.

"Trev!" Anita yelled, running toward him.

"Hey," he said on a grunt as Ani jumped at him, wrapping her arms around his neck and her legs around his waist.

My stomach twisted.

"What's wrong? You been crying?" he asked softly as he wrapped his arms around her.

Ani's voice was muffled when she answered him, so I couldn't hear what she was saying, but the second his hand started to run soothingly up and down her back I'd had enough. We were in my parents' entryway for Christ's sake, and it looked like he was about to fuck her against the wall.

I snorted, bringing Trev's eyes to me. I ignored the glare he sent me over her shoulder as I turned and left the room.

* * *

"How's that new site coming along?" Mom asked, trying anything to break the silence at the dinner table.

Friday night dinners had become something of a tradition at my parents' house when we were just kids. While all our friends had to be home on Sunday night for dinner, dragging their hungover asses to the table, our parents had decided that making us sit down as a family before the weekend got crazy would be a better way to keep us in line. They weren't wrong. Sitting down at the table with your parents at the beginning of the weekend was a good little reminder to not fuck up during the rest of it.

For a while before we'd all grown up and moved away, there were eleven of us crammed around my parents' dining room table. Mom and Dad, me, my twin brother Alex, my little sister Katie, and from the house next door my aunt Ellie and uncle Mike and their boys Trevor, Henry, and their foster son Shane. Anita didn't move in until after I had already moved out, but before my brother Alex had left for the Army.

I wasn't sure why we always ate at my parents' house, but it had been that way for as long as I could remember. Aunt Ellie usually came over to help my mom, sometimes taking over her entire kitchen while she cooked, but we rarely ate at Uncle Mike and Aunt Ellie's house. Maybe it was because, when we were all home, we didn't even fit at Ellie's dining room table, though getting us all in the same place at the same time rarely happened anymore.

We were all scattered around the country now. My little sister Katie had moved to San Diego years ago and eventually married Shane, who was stationed down there with the Marines. Henry was down there, too, with his own Marine unit. My brother Alex had joined the Army when we were almost twenty and was stationed in Missouri. Trevor, Ani, and I were the only ones left in Oregon with our parents.

We were also the only ones who showed any interest in our family's logging business.

"The new site's going fine," Dad mumbled as he shoveled more food into his mouth. "Everything's on schedule."

"Well that's good," Mom said brightly. "Maybe you guys can take a break when Katie gets here."

My head snapped up, and I saw Ani's do the same. "When's Kate coming up?"

"She said she was going to find tickets for next month. I guess one of the airlines is having a sale or something," Mom answered with a smile.

"She's going to need it with all those munchkins," Trevor said with a chuckle.

"Why do you think we never went anywhere when you were kids?" Dad asked Trevor, leaning forward to grab a serving tray.

"Your dad and I realized early that, if we wanted to take you kids on vacation, we'd have to rent a passenger van and drive you. Too expensive to fly."

"Remember that time we went to see Mount Rushmore?" I asked Trev, grinning.

"Fun trip," Trevor replied, nodding. "Would have been better if Henry didn't puke all over me every two hundred miles."

Anita snorted, and I couldn't help but laugh. We'd had to drive the entire way with all the windows down, it had stunk so badly.

"Poor Henry," Mom said, smirking. "That boy always got carsick."

"And I always had to sit next to him!" Trevor bitched.

"Well, *I* wasn't sitting next to the puker. He's *your*

brother," I said seriously, glancing up from my plate to meet Ani's eyes.

She was smiling, but it was small. The kind of smile a person wears when they aren't part of the joke but are trying really hard not to look out of place.

My mouth snapped shut.

"Well at least none of Katie and Shane's kids get motion sickness," Mom said, leaning back in her chair.

"There's no way Katie's making that drive again," Ani finally piped in, smiling at my mom. "She said, the last time they drove home, it took them twice as long as it should've because they had to stop a thousand times."

"Little bladders," my dad said, making us all chuckle.

I glanced at my watch and pushed my plate back. "Thanks for dinner, Mom."

"You're leaving already?" she asked, raising one eyebrow.

"I've got plans tonight. Couldn't change them," I replied, standing from my seat and grabbing my plate and glass. "I'll clear the table before I go."

My mom grumbled a bit, but sat back and let Trevor and me clear the table around my dad, who was still eating. I always tried to help my mom clean up after dinner, at least when there were so few of us kids there. When Katie or Alex was home, I pretended like I had no idea how to clean up so they'd get stuck with the dishes. They deserved it for getting out of so many family dinners.

"Man, you need to ease up on Ani," Trevor murmured

while we worked around each other at the sink. "She's been off lately."

"You kidding?" I looked at him in surprise. "She starts that shit."

"Just take a step back."

"Barking up the wrong tree, Trev," I replied, drying my hands off on a towel. "She can dish it but she can't take it? Give me a break."

"I'm just saying—ease up a bit. It's getting to the point that you're pissing me off lately."

"You her protector now? Got something going on with Ani?" I asked, turning to look at him. The question was stupid, and I regretted it the moment it popped out of my mouth.

"Would that be a problem?"

"No," I ground out from between my teeth. "Do whatever you want."

"You're such an ass sometimes, Abraham." Trev sighed and shook his head. "I don't have anything going on with Ani, numbnuts. But I'll still kick your ass if you don't fucking lay off."

I walked out of the kitchen before he could say another word. I was pissed. I never started that shit with Ani—it was always her running her mouth. Christ, the woman couldn't go five minutes without sniping at me, and it had been that way since we were kids. Did I care about her? Of course. Hard not to care when someone's been in your life for the better part of fifteen years, but that didn't mean I was going to lie down and let her walk all over me.

I didn't want to think about why the thought of her with Trevor made my gut churn.

"I'm out of here," I said quietly to my mom, giving her a quick hug.

"Well that was a fast cleanup," she replied, patting me on the back.

"Told you I had plans. I'll see you in the next couple of days."

I nodded at Ani and my aunt and uncle, then patted my dad on the shoulder as I made my way through the house. I was going to have to haul ass if I wanted to be on time.

Chapter 2

Anita

I was distracting myself. It was stupid. I knew that I shouldn't be following Bram through the streets of downtown Portland, but when he'd left the house in such a hurry, I was curious.

Okay, I was *dying* to know where he was going.

Bram wasn't exactly social. I could count on one hand the number of friends he had, and he'd never brought a woman home. Sure, I'd seen him leaving with chicks from one of the local bars—but he never actually introduced them to us. So where was he going at eight o'clock on a Friday night?

I let the question roll over and over in my brain, taking my mind off the things I actually *should* be worrying about as Bram parallel-parked across from a dive bar. *What the hell?* There wasn't much else on the street, so I knew that was where he must be headed, but why?

Pulling around the corner, I parked in the smallest parking spot ever made and jogged toward the entrance of the bar. Bram had already gone inside, and when I glanced at the patrons smoking near the entrance, I groaned and looked down at myself. My jeans and flannel shirt were perfect for dinner at the Evans house, but I was going to stick out like a sore thumb if I tried to go inside.

I stepped quickly back around the corner as I unbuttoned my top, making a homeless guy down the street wolf-whistle. *Jesus.* Keeping one eye on the man sitting on the sidewalk, I pulled the shirt down my shoulders and tied it around my waist, leaving me in a black cami. That should work. I bent at the waist and scrubbed my fingers through my short, dark hair, then rose back up as I reached inside my nose and pulled my septum piercing down so it was visible. The retainer was easily hidden when I was around Dan and Liz, and I didn't think either of them even knew I'd gotten it pierced. I loved it—I thought it looked badass, but my old foster parents really wouldn't and I didn't want to deal with their kind but scolding comments about my "pretty face." I'd gotten enough of that when I'd dyed my hair blue my sophomore year in college.

Rifling through my bag, I pulled out a deep purple lip crayon and used a parked car's side-view mirror to color in my lips and smooth my crazy hair a little. *Perfect.* I walked back around the building and made my way to the door as I slid my tongue ring in and twisted the ball on the end a few times to secure it.

The hipsters at the door ignored me as I walked past, acting like their damn clove cigarettes held the answers to the universe, and I couldn't help but snort as I stepped inside. Acting like you don't care doesn't make you look cool, it just makes it look like you're trying too hard. I could practically feel their bespectacled gazes on my flannel-covered ass. *Take a good look, guys.*

"Welcome to open-mike night," a guy called into a microphone as I bellied up to the bar and slid my ass onto a stool. "For those of you who're new here, the rules are simple. We don't want to hear your song about the melting glaciers in Alaska or the time you drove your VW bus to the Grand Canyon. Covers only, folks. You sing an original song, we'll boo your ass offstage."

The crowd laughed, and my lips twitched as I looked at the guy on a small stage across the room. He was tall and lanky with a short beard and a shirt that said, BEER ME. Good looking, if you were into skinny guys.

"Got a friend starting us off tonight while you pussies get up the courage to sign in. Abraham?" the guy called, looking off to the darkened side of the stage.

My mouth dropped open as Bram stepped onstage, a worn guitar dangling from his hand. *What in fucking fuck?*

"Hefeweizen," I called, glancing at the pretty, tattooed bartender who was leaning across the bartop next to me. "A shot of tequila too, please."

She nodded and pulled her eyes away from Bram to get my drinks.

"Hello, Portland," Bram said with a smile, making my stomach do a weird somersault. "Haven't been onstage in a while, so you'll have to bear with me."

"Yeah, 'cause you're an asshole," Tall Skinny Guy called out.

"Yeah, yeah. I'm here now," Bram said, making the

crowd chuckle. "Can I sing, or are you gonna keep running your mouth?"

"By all means," Tall Skinny Guy replied, throwing his
arms out.

"First song, you might not know—"

"No originals!" Tall Skinny Guy yelled as the bartender
slid my drinks over the counter.

Bram went completely still and turned his head slowly
toward the side of the stage while the crowd snickered.

"Fine. Fine. Go ahead," Tall Skinny Guy said over the
crowd.

"Jesus." Bram shook his head. "And I worried I'd be late."

I couldn't help but smile at the way the crowd was eating Bram up. He was working them—Bram, who rarely
got along with anyone and walked around with a perma-
nent scowl—held a crowded bar in the palm of his hand.

"Like I said, you might not recognize this one—but it's
not one of mine so Jay can shut the fuck up and let me do
it," Bram said, leaning into the mike with a small smile
on his face as he settled himself more comfortably on the
bar stool he was perched on. "This is 'Thief and a Liar' by
Jeffrey Martin."

By the noise of the crowd, I guessed they knew who he
was talking about but I'd never heard of him.

The minute Bram began to play, my heart began
thumping hard in my chest. I couldn't tell if it was nervousness or excitement. When his voice came through the
speakers again, I think I stopped breathing.

He sang, his voice a little raspy but seriously good, and
I spun away, taking the shot fast before chasing it with my

beer. My hands were shaking as I pulled the orange off the rim of my glass and dropped it into my beer. I wanted to turn back around and see him, but for the first time since I'd walked into the bar, I felt weird about the way I'd followed him.

It was odd. I was watching Bram do something that he'd obviously not wanted us to know about, but I was the one who felt naked.

After a few moments, I turned back around holding my beer in front of me just so I'd have something to do with my hands...and met Bram's eyes from across the room.

Oh, God. I'd thought that the dim spotlight on him would hide me from view, but when I'd sat at the bar, the lights behind it illuminated me.

"*I am a thief and a liar of the very worst kind. Oh, I sell to the broken and I rob them blind. I will build you a house with my own two hands, and then burn it to the ground as quick as I can.*" Bram's voice didn't falter, not even when he raised his eyebrows, as if to say, *I caught you.*

I swallowed hard and glanced away, bringing my beer to my lips like nothing was wrong as I slid slowly off the stool. I wondered if I could make it out the doors without him catching me. Part of me thought that he'd ignore my departure and keep going, but the other part of me knew that, if I took one step away from my bar stool, he'd be calling me out over the damn speaker system.

As Bram strummed the last chord of the song, the crowd burst out in applause, and he smiled wide, glancing around in front of him.

"Damn, you guys have a lot of energy. I've been up since

four a.m.; I think it's past my bedtime," he said jokingly as he scratched at his beard. "You want one more?"

Whistling and cheering came through the room, and I wondered how often he came to this bar to sing. The people seemed to know him, or at least recognize him.

"All right. One more." He repositioned on his stool. "Pretty sure you'll know this one. This is 'First' by Cold War Kids."

Bram's eyes came back to me, and I fumbled with my empty beer glass, setting it on the bartop behind me.

He crooned the chorus into the mike, slowing down the familiar song. *Holy shit.*

He was going to kill me.

I stood frozen through the entire song, and Bram's eyes never left me. When he was done, he climbed up from the stool, and I calculated my distance from the front door as I pulled a twenty-dollar bill out of my purse and threw it on the bar.

I took one step toward freedom, my eyes on Bram, when his head slowly shook from side to side, warning me to stay put.

"Your turn to entertain me," Bram said, leaning down into the microphone. The crowd cheered, but his words were for me.

"We'll entertain you," a tall girl called out, her arm wrapped around her much shorter friend as they swayed. The entire bar erupted in laughter, and the girl's face dropped as her eyes went wide. She was drunk, but apparently not drunk enough to ignore the fact that she'd just made an ass out of herself.

Bram's eyes went soft as he glanced over, then he leaned back into the mike again and nodded toward me. "Sorry, beautiful, but my girl's waiting for me at the bar."

My mouth dropped open and my stomach flipped as he moved toward me, but before he'd made it through half the crowd, I'd snapped it shut again and was crossing my arms over my chest. He better have been talking about some other woman at the bar. If he thought I was playing along with his bullshit announcement, he was sadly mistaken.

"You di—" The words weren't even out of my mouth before his hand was wrapped lightly around the front of my throat, his fingers and thumb resting at the bottom of my jaw.

"Hey, baby," he murmured, leaning in without any warning and kissing me gently.

I'd been expecting something different. Something punishing. Hard. Maybe a bite. I think that was why, when he went to move away, my mouth followed his.

It was instinct. Nothing more. But the soft brush of lips hadn't been enough.

Bram made a surprised noise in his throat when my arms dropped and wrapped around him. Our eyes met for a split second before he groaned and pushed me back against the bar.

Then his mouth was on mine again, and there was nothing soft about it. He pulled gently, wetly, at my bottom lip, and I opened my mouth, my breath hitching as his tongue slid inside. *Holy shit, Bram could kiss.*

I forgot where we were. I forgot who he was. Hell, I forgot who I was.

Nothing mattered except our points of contact. His hips pressing against my waist, his hard back beneath my palms, one of his hands at my throat and the other setting his guitar on the bar behind me so he could slide his fingers through the short hair at the back of my head.

"I'll put this in the back room," the tall guy's voice said teasingly from behind me, I assumed talking about the guitar.

Bram nodded, still kissing me, and then his hand was on my ass, lifting me as I jumped up and wrapped my legs around his waist.

Oh God, that was so much better. I ground against him as he stepped away from the bar and pulled his mouth from mine. His hand moved around the back of my head, and he shoved my face into his neck as he moved through the bar.

Shit. What the fuck were we doing? I held on tight, my face burning in embarrassment even though it was hidden, and my pussy rubbing against his dick with every step he took.

We were both breathing heavy when we hit the cool night air, and I shivered as he asked me where I was parked.

"Around the corner," I rasped, making him shudder as my lips rubbed against his skin.

He strode down the pavement, never letting me down until we'd rounded the corner and were shadowed by the tall building.

"What the fuck are you doing here?" he asked as he dropped me to my feet.

"What the hell was that?" I snapped back, stumbling a little as I lost my balance.

"If I wanted you here, I would have fucking invited you." He ignored my question, scowling as he gripped my arm to make sure I didn't fall over.

"I didn't know you could sing like that."

"Who do you think taught Katie?" My foster sister Kate was incredible on the guitar, and she'd had a kick-ass voice for as long as I'd known her. I'd never wondered how she'd learned; it had always just been true.

"Oh," I said, sidestepping him.

"Did you follow me?" he asked incredulously, stepping back in front of me. "What the fuck is wrong with you?"

"With me? Yeah, *I'm* the one who fucked up tonight. Right," I said back sarcastically. "You just kissed me!"

"That's the way you want to play it?" he murmured, shaking his head as he scratched at his beard. "Sure. I was getting the barflies off my back and used you to do it, but the rest of that shit was you."

"Me?" I screeched, making the homeless guy down the street start yelling about waking him up.

"Shut the fuck up," Bram yelled back at the guy, making him go silent.

"I didn't do shit!" I hissed, my hands fisting at my sides.

"That wasn't you, grabbing me and pulling me into you—giving me fuck-me eyes?"

"Fuck-me eyes?" I screeched again.

"You're still fucking doing it!" Bram yelled back, leaning down.

We both went silent for a long moment, glaring at each other.

I'm not sure which one of us moved first, but all of a sudden, Bram's mouth was back on mine, and he was pushing me against the brick wall of the building behind me.

"When the fuck did you get a tongue ring?" he gasped into my mouth as he slid his thigh between mine, lifting my body slightly as he pressed up.

"A couple years ago." I moaned and rocked against him.

"I've never seen it." His hands moved over my torso, reaching up to grip my breasts over my cami.

"I know." I slid my hands under his T-shirt and dug my fingers into the warm skin at his sides.

A familiar wolf whistle came from down the street, making us pause.

"Keys," he whispered before pressing his mouth to mine again. "Keys. Now."

I fumbled with the purse hanging over my shoulder and pulled out the keys to my SUV.

The second Bram heard them jingle, he was stepping back and grabbing them from my hand. Without a word, he gripped my fingers and walked me over to my car. When we reached it, he paused and turned his head to look at me.

I held my breath as he clicked the remote, unlocking the driver's-side door.

Then he clicked it again, unlocking the rest, and opened up the door to the backseat. He stood there, not moving, letting me make the decision. I could have snatched the keys out of his hand and moved around the front of my SUV. That would have been smarter.

Instead, I slid past him and climbed into the backseat.

I was making a really bad decision. I knew that. I think we both knew that. Nothing good could come of messing around with Bram. At best, things would be even more awkward between us later. At worst, we'd actually hate each other instead of the halfhearted bickering we'd been doing before.

But I didn't care.

This wasn't real life. I knew that, once Bram climbed back out of my Toyota, whatever was happening would be over. But in three days, I was going to have to deal with more real life than I wanted to, so I pushed back all the doubts in my mind.

The backseats in my car were pushed down because I'd been hauling shit for my house that week. So when we got inside the dark car, we had a wide expanse of room to move. That didn't mean it was easy though. Bram hit his head and cursed as he climbed in behind me, locking the doors with a loud honk. I got a rug burn on my elbow as I rolled to my back and scooted across the rough carpeting.

Then, finally, there we were.

I was on my back, my knees spread wide around Bram's hips, and he was coming down on top of me, bracing himself on his elbows.

"I can't see shit," he said as our eyes adjusted to the dark.

"You know what I look like," I whispered back, my nerves making my voice a little shaky.

"I don't know what these look like," he argued, dropping one of his hands to slide it over my breast, his fingertips finding my nipple through my cami.

Well. It seemed as though the lack of sight didn't hinder him in the slightest.

His lips came down on mine, and I groaned into his mouth as his tongue slid across my tongue ring, playing with it for a second before he was pulling away slightly and sucking my bottom lip into his mouth.

"You had Hefeweizen," he commented, running his lips down my jaw.

I couldn't stop the giggle that burst out of my throat.

"What? It's my favorite." He moved his mouth to my neck, and I arched back as he sucked at the skin there, moving to my shoulder as his hand gripped the strap to my cami and jerked it down my arm.

"Shit," I groaned as his lips moved down my breast and pulled my nipple into his mouth.

"You're so tiny," Bram murmured, making me freeze.

I wasn't shy, and I wasn't unhappy with my body. I was small. Small hips, small breasts, small ass, short legs—the works. But no man had ever had the balls to say something like that to me before, especially while he had his mouth on me.

"Don't be an idiot," Bram scolded, biting down on my nipple as he felt me stiffen. "Look at that sweet little nipple. Perfect size for my mouth."

"Bram," I groaned as my entire body flushed. I reached down and pulled at the back of his shirt, pulling it up and over his head. When it reached his arms, it got stuck between us, and what little sight I'd had completely vanished as the shirt covered my eyes.

"No blindfolds this time," Bram murmured, leaning up on one arm and then the other to pull the shirt off. *This time?*

As soon as he was bare chested, I dove for his skin, licking at his nipples and biting at the skin near his collarbone. He tasted so good. Clean, with the tiniest hint of salt. It must have been warm under the bar's spotlight.

"Stop," he said softly, then again louder. "Stop."

"What?" I jerked back, hitting my head against the floorboard.

"No biting," he said, not meeting my eyes as he pulled down the other side of my cami so both breasts were on display. "You can scratch the hell out of me, suck anywhere you want, but no teeth, all right?"

"Okay," I stuttered.

"You like it?" he asked as his head dropped to my breast and his hand found the button on my jeans.

"What?" My hands had dropped to my sides when he'd told me to stop, and I wasn't sure what to do with them. I was feeling . . . off. The unselfconsciousness that had fueled my movements had completely disappeared, and I was afraid to do something wrong.

I was never self-conscious about sex. I figured if a guy had worked hard enough to get me naked and was still interested, there wasn't a whole lot I could do to change his mind at that point. I could howl like a cat or shake like I was having a seizure, but if the guy was still getting laid, it wasn't like he was going to stop.

"You like it when I bite you?" Bram asked again.

I wasn't sure what the correct answer was, but I couldn't stop the small sound that rumbled from my throat as he bit down gently on my nipple again.

"Yeah, you do." He gently ran his tongue over the abused skin and leaned back to tear my shoes off. My jeans were already unbuttoned, and he jerked them hard down my hips and off one leg. My underwear quickly followed.

"You still with me?" Bram asked softly as he leaned back down, his hand sliding down my belly.

"I'm—" I laughed uncomfortably and flapped my arms a little. "Can I touch you, or—"

"Are you joking?" Bram snapped, jerking his head back.

"You already told me to stop, so I—" My voice was sharp as I tried to hide my embarrassment.

Bram froze above me, then scoffed, reaching for his shirt.

"What are you doing?" I asked, snagging his shirt in my fist before he could grab it.

"This was a mistake."

"No." I shook my head. "What?"

I wasn't ready to go back to real life. It wasn't time yet. I was lying there in nothing but a camisole wrapped around my waist for God's sake. I needed to change my tone. I needed to get him back with me.

"Can I have my shirt?" Bram asked flatly, still hovering above my body.

"No," I blurted, making him jerk in surprise.

Without conscious thought, I pulled my knees high up

on his sides, and he inhaled sharply as the skin on my thighs rubbed against his ribs.

"Jesus, you're wet," Bram murmured, his head drooping as if it were too heavy for his neck. He pressed his body farther into mine and slid his belly against me.

"Oh shit," I murmured as his happy trail of hair brushed against my clit. My hands flew to his back, and I pulled down hard, trying to re-create the movement.

"You're such a fucking pain in the ass," Bram gasped, pressing against me as he kissed me hard. "Maybe if I just keep your mouth occupied . . ."

"Shut up," I bitched, letting go of his back with one hand so I could grip his hair in my hand. "Please, just—" My words cut off on a strangled groan as he shifted and slid a finger inside me. No buildup. No hesitance.

"Damn, you're tiny everywhere," Bram stuttered in surprise, making me chuckle, then gasp.

"Pants," I said frantically, my hips moving against his hand as my mind blanked. "Pants. Off."

My hands went to his jeans, and he sighed against my face as I rubbed my hand down the length of him.

"I'm so hard, not sure if I can get them off," he said half seriously, pulling his finger from me in a slow glide.

"I have an X-Acto knife in the console," I whispered back, our hands tangling as we pulled at his jeans.

"You're not getting anywhere near my junk with a knife," he hissed back, moaning as his jeans finally loosened and he pushed them down his hips.

"Commando?" I muttered as my hands hit warm skin.

"Need to do laundry."

I laughed lightly as he leaned back to sit on his heels, grabbed his wallet out of his pocket, and pulled out a condom.

"Hurry," I murmured as I reached down and wrapped my hand around his dick. *Holy shit*. Bram was packing. My lips turned up in a grin. "We're working on borrowed time here."

Bram's head snapped up as he rolled on the condom, and he looked out the windows, making sure no one was nearby. "Shit."

He looked down at me, then up at the windows, then down at me again before gripping my hips and yanking my lower body up so high that most of my weight was resting at the tops of my shoulders.

"What the—"

I let out a high-pitched sound that I'm pretty sure I'd never made before in my life when his head dropped between my thighs and his mouth opened wide over my pussy. His beard rubbed softly against my thighs and the undersides of my ass cheeks, and I shuddered.

"Oh my God," I gasped, squeezing my eyes closed as his tongue licked up my center, curling around my clit. The wet sound of his mouth opening and closing and licking and sucking filled the SUV, partnered with his groans and my heaving breaths.

At first, it just felt really, really good, but then he focused in, rubbing over and over my clit with his tongue, bringing me closer and closer to orgasm. My body locked, and I clenched my teeth against the urge to scream.

Then he stopped and lowered my hips back down.

"No, no!" I lifted my hips frantically against his hands. "Don't stop!"

"Shhh," Bram murmured, coming down on top of me as I slapped at his shoulders. "Knock it off, Ani."

I froze at the raspy sound of my name on his lips.

"You're small," he murmured, lifting my knee high until it was wedged between his arm and my ribs.

He pressed against me slowly, and my entire body relaxed to let him in. I rolled my hips slightly as he moved, and he pulled back out a fraction before pushing forward again. Doing it over and over until our bodies were completely locked together.

Wiping a hand over his beard, he shuddered, then leaned down to kiss me sweetly. "If I woulda waited until you came, you'd be too tight for me to get inside," he said with a soft chuckle. "This way's better."

Then he began to move, shifting his hips just barely back and forth as he ground his pelvic bone against my clit.

My nails dug into his back as he pushed up until his arms were fully extended, and looked down to watch my face. I didn't know what expression I was making, and for a split second, it bothered me that he was watching me so intently, but then it began to build again. Faster and harder than before.

My muscles began to tighten and flex, and unable to control it, my leg that he'd been pressing up into his side shot straight down, my thighs wrapping around his hips like a vise as I came, making the fit of him inside me even more snug.

"Holy shit." He snapped his hips forward hard as I pulsed around him, pulling back quickly and shoving forward again, over and over until my muscles went limp.

"Knees up," he murmured frantically, leaning back to grip my jelly-like legs beneath my knees. He pressed them to my chest and then began to really move, pulling out almost completely and sliding back in hard three or four times before his movements went clumsy and he jerked, groaning deep in his throat.

He fell down to his elbows above me and rested his lips against my shoulder as we each caught our breath.

But as my breathing slowed, my heart began to pound.

What the hell did we just do?

Chapter 3
Abraham

I fucked Ani.

Ani.

The words ran over and over inside my brain as I lay there on top of her, her body still clasped tightly around mine.

I needed to pull out. I really did.

I didn't want the condom to come off or leak or something—not that I saw that happening anytime soon since I seemed to still be hard as a fucking rock.

I'd just come so hard I'd practically blacked out, and I was still hard.

Jesus.

I couldn't tell if I should be dancing a jig or crying into a beer over the fact that I'd just had the best sex of my life in the back of a Toyota 4Runner with my foster sister.

But was she really my foster sister anymore? I mean, she had been at one point, but that was years and years ago.

I'd never even lived with her, if we were going to get technical about it.

I groaned as I felt her hands run tentatively up my back and then slide into the long hair at the nape of my neck, and I couldn't stop myself from canting my hips forward, making her squeeze my dick in response.

Out of the corner of my eye, I saw a shadow move, and when I glanced up, the homeless guy who'd been hassling us earlier was standing a few feet from the back window.

"Motherfucker," I hissed, pulling out of Ani quickly and ripping the condom off my dick. "Get dressed. We've got company."

I buttoned and zipped my jeans as Ani squeaked and pulled frantically at her tank top. Shit, I hadn't even taken it off all the way. Her hands were shaking as she tried to pull her jeans up her legs.

"Hey, it's fine. You've got tinted windows," I assured her, reaching out to help her. She was freaked the fuck out, and I felt like an asshole for fucking her on a public street where anyone could have seen her.

"I've got it," she barked, slapping away my hands as she got the jeans around her hips. "Just go."

I rocked back and stared at her as she found the flannel she'd had tied around her waist in the bar and pulled it up over her arms.

"Go," she said again, pushing my shirt into my hands.

For less than an hour, I'd forgotten what a bitch she was, but within minutes of getting her off, I remembered exactly why I couldn't stand her. At least I didn't feel like an asshole anymore.

I picked up and tied off the condom I'd dropped on the carpet, then used my other hand to find the keys I'd set in the armrest, unlocking the doors when I found them. I watched in satisfaction as our Peeping Tom noticed the lights flashing and raced back to his spot down the street.

"Don't get out, just climb over the seats," I said to Ani as I climbed out of the backseat, still holding her keys. I didn't want that dumbass seeing her get out of the car. Usually, I could keep my temper at bay, but I knew if the fucker said anything, I'd go over there and beat his ass.

There was something vulnerable about a woman after sex. A softness that I didn't want anyone seeing on Ani that night but me.

I closed the door and walked around to the driver's side to open her door and hand her the keys.

"Ani—" I called when she wouldn't look at me.

"It didn't mean anything," she blurted, glancing at me and then away. "Don't worry. I won't tell anyone about your weird little hang-up with biting."

I was trying to be nice. I was trying to be a good guy. But the moment those words came out of her mouth, any fondness I'd felt about her and the sex we'd just had completely vanished. There was nothing wrong with asking someone not to bite you during sex—but I knew she must have caught on that it wasn't just a preference. It made my damn skin crawl.

"Thanks for the fuck," I spat back, feeling nothing but satisfaction as she flinched at my words. I tossed her keys into her lap and slammed the door shut. *Fuck her.*

I didn't turn back around as I walked away, but I listened closely for the sound of her SUV starting and pulling away. I wasn't about to leave her ass in the middle of Portland after some guy had stood next to the car listening to us have sex.

I rounded the corner and almost ran straight into my friend Jay.

"What the hell are you still doing here?" he asked in surprise around a lit cigarette. Then he pulled the cigarette from his mouth and inhaled deeply through his nose. "Never mind. Know exactly what you were doing. Might want to clean the pussy off your beard if you're goin' back inside."

"I'm not," I replied, inhaling Ani's scent. Fuck, I was going to have to smell her for the entire hour-long drive home.

"Who was—"

"Ani."

"Oh. Shit."

"Pretty much."

"Was it—"

"Best I've ever had."

"In her car?"

"Yep."

"Damn."

"Call you later."

"Will do."

Jay nodded as I moved past him, taking a deep drag of his cigarette. He was probably my best friend if I didn't count my twin brother Alex and my cousins, and with

just a few words from me, he'd known how completely I'd
fucked up.

Ani and I had never gotten along. I didn't know if it all
stemmed from the fight we'd had when I thought she was
stealing shit from my parents' bedroom or if our personal-
ities just clashed—but I couldn't remember a time when
we'd ever agreed on anything.

No, that wasn't true. A little over a year ago, my sister
Kate had gone through some major shit when she was
pregnant with my youngest niece, and she'd been completely inconsolable. Ani and I were on the same side
then—we'd both wanted to cut Shane's dick off.

But I couldn't remember any other time over the last
fourteen years that we'd gotten along at all.

Ani was opinionated and rude and pushed her nose
into everyone's business like she had a right to be there.
Tonight in the bar had been a perfect example. She'd been
curious about what I was doing, but instead of asking me
or just leaving it the fuck alone, she'd followed me all
the way into Portland. It wasn't some spur-of-the-moment
idea, either. It took almost a full hour to drive from my
parents' house to Jay's bar. She'd had plenty of time to
turn around, but she hadn't.

My hands clenched around my steering wheel as I
pulled onto the highway.

If she would have just turned around, I wouldn't still
be hard as a rock thinking about the way her cunt had
clamped down on my dick when she came.

I tapped my fingers on the steering wheel, turning up
the radio in my truck.

It didn't matter—that's what she had said. Like I was going to get clingy or some shit. It was fine as fuck with me. I wasn't going to repeat that shit anytime soon.

I remembered the feel of her teeth against my skin and shuddered, my dick growing softer at the memory of the sensation.

Never again.

* * *

Monday mornings always blew. I had a ton of paperwork to go through before I headed out to talk to our side rod—the guy who was in charge at different logging sites. I was tired, pissy, and I never got as much done as I thought I would.

When I walked into our small office, I was already in a completely fucked-up mood before I'd even realized that there was no coffee in the pot and the place was completely silent.

"Hello?" I called out, gripping my thermos tighter as I moved toward the offices. The door had been unlocked when I walked in, so someone must have been there.

"In here," my uncle Mike called, then cursed as I heard a loud rustling.

"Hey, where is everyone?" I asked, watching as he picked up unopened mail from all over the floor.

"Your dad is with your mom today, Trev is at that meeting he had with Mark from the mill, and Ani called in sick, which is why I'm trying to open up this mail," he answered, grabbing letters by the handful and dropping them back on top of his desk.

"Ani called in sick?" Was she fucking avoiding me? That was real goddamn mature.

"Yup. Looks like it's just you and me today."

"I've gotta head out to some sites and meet—"

"Nah, Trevor can do that today if you want. He's already out there."

"Yeah that works," I said distractedly, tapping on his door frame. "You need anything?"

"Nope, I'm gonna handle this mail and then head on home. Ellie's making me lunch."

"It's seven in the morning."

"Your point?" he asked, raising one eyebrow.

"No point." I lifted my full hands in the air and backed out of his office.

My dad and uncle had started our logging business over thirty years before and were mostly retired now. When Trev and I had begun taking over, they'd balked a bit, but they were glad now for the extra time to spend with their wives and sit in front of the television.

They weren't the type of men to go golfing.

In Oregon, the logging business is really close knit. Everyone knows everyone, and your business's reputation and the reputation of the loggers you hire play a huge part in how many jobs you get. That meant, at first, the old-timers at the mills wanted little to do with Trevor and me, even though we'd been working on crews for years and they knew us. Thankfully, our dads had stayed on for a while, and eventually we'd earned a good enough reputation that we were bidding on and winning jobs pretty frequently.

It helped that Ani ran our front office, and half the men that came in and out of there had a damn crush on her.

Where the fuck was she?

I settled down into my old computer chair and scrubbed my fingers through my beard. This was ridiculous. If she couldn't handle seeing me at work, how the fuck was she going to be able to sit through Friday night dinner when everyone was there?

I pulled my cell phone from my pocket and called her, grinding my teeth together when she didn't answer and I got her voicemail.

Fuck it. I had shit to do, and I didn't have time to baby her. I hung up without leaving a message and started going through the files on my desk. I had jobs to bid or my guys weren't going to have any wood to cut.

* * *

The week passed by slow as hell. We were busy, so there was a ton of stuff to do, but Ani hadn't come into work all week and it was messing with my head. Every time the front door to the offices opened, my stomach churned with nerves until one of the guys passed by my office. I was getting to work early and staying late—but Ani didn't stop by once.

It was driving me insane. I was barely sleeping, and when I did, it wasn't deep. Part of me thought it was a good thing that she'd taken the week off; it gave us some time to get our heads straight before we had to deal with each other. But the other part was fucking dying to see

her. I wanted to know where we were at. Were hostili-
ties at a standstill or were things worse than they were
before?

She needed to grow a pair and just face me already.

I walked into my mom and dad's a little late Friday
night, dragging ass. I hadn't wanted to go to dinner. I just
wanted to head home, grab a beer, and sit in front of the
TV in my underwear—but I wasn't going to be the one
who didn't show up.

I'd been where I was supposed to be that week. I wasn't
going to be the one who flaked out on family dinner.

"Hey, Mom," I called as my mom came out from the
kitchen.

"Dinner's on the table," Mom said with a smile, looking
me over closely. "You're late, and you look tired."

"I am tired," I replied, kissing her head as I reached her.
"Long week."

"Well, let's fill you up and then you can head on home."

I followed her to the dining room and let my eyes sweep
over the table. Dad, Trevor, Aunt Ellie, Uncle Mike. I
tried to keep my face blank as I realized Ani wasn't there.
I was fucking pissed. She didn't even show at family dinner?

I stewed as we started dishing up the homemade mac
and cheese. My aunt must have cooked that night because
mac and cheese was her specialty, not my mom's.

"Where's Ani?" I asked when I couldn't take it anymore. I immediately wanted to bite back the words.

"She had some other stuff planned tonight," my mom
said with a shrug, like she hadn't guilted me into changing

any set of plans I'd ever made that would land during family dinner.

"She wasn't at work all week," I said, staring at my food like it was the most important thing I'd ever seen. "She go on vacation?"

I glanced up at my suddenly quiet family and looked at their faces around the table. "What?"

"She had some stuff to do this week so she took some sick leave," Trevor said flatly, not even looking at me as he spoke.

"Sure she did," I said under my breath, shoveling a forkful of food into my mouth.

"What?" my mom asked, turning to me.

"Nothing." I shook my head, then looked quickly at my aunt. "This mac and cheese is good, Auntie."

"Thanks, honey," Aunt Ellie said with a smile, turning to my dad to talk about...whatever it was they'd been talking about before I interrupted.

I couldn't focus on anything happening around me. My skin felt tight, and my head was beginning to throb at my temples from clenching my jaw so hard.

"I'm gonna head out, Mom," I finally said when I couldn't sit there a minute longer. I was being rude, and I *always* stayed to help with cleanup, but I was so wound up I knew there was no way I was going to be able to stay at my mom's for another hour to do the dishes.

"Okay, you go home and get some rest," she said, reaching out to rub my back and making me feel like an absolute dick for pretending that was why I was leaving.

I said my good-byes and headed out the door before anyone else had stood from the table.

Then I drove across town to the little house Ani had bought six months ago. It was a fixer-upper, built in the 1930s, but what it lacked in looks and function, it more than made up with charm. It was actually kind of perfect for her since she had four men in her life that were good with their hands and willing to pitch in. The first thing she'd done was paint the outside, which didn't make any sense whatsoever but she'd said she wanted to come home to a pretty house, even though the floors inside had been covered in olive shag carpeting and she'd had no appliances in the kitchen.

I pounded hard on the door, and the minute it opened, I started railing.

"You don't show up for work all fucking week and then you bail on family dinner? What? Are you avoiding me now? Let's just be adults—" My words faded out as what I was seeing finally sunk in. "What the fuck is wrong?" I asked, immediately taking a deep breath when it came out sharper than I'd intended.

Her hair was wet like she'd just gotten out of the shower, but her face was pale as a ghost except for dark circles under her sleepy eyes, and she was hunched over a little like an old lady. She looked like shit, and she was wearing flannel pajamas at seven o'clock at night.

"Hey, I'm not feeling well," she said, giving me a crooked smile. "Can we talk about this in a few days?"

"No," I replied stubbornly, stepping forward so she was forced to move farther into the house. "What's wrong with you?"

She sighed and winced, motioning for me to close the

door, then turned and started hobbling toward her bedroom.

"Hey." I reached out and grabbed her arm, stopping her
halfway down the hallway. "What the hell is going on?"

"I had to have surgery—not a big deal, okay?" she said,
pulling her arm out of my grip. "I'll be back at work next
week, but right now I feel like shit. So could you just go?"

I followed her as she shuffled into her room, and
watched as she sat gingerly down on her bed.

She looked up in surprise when I shut the door behind
me, then her lips twisted in a wry grin. "If you're back
for a repeat, I'm not really up for it," she said sarcastically,
smoothing her hand down the wispy dark hair that was
beginning to dry.

"What kind of surgery?" I asked roughly.

Why hadn't anyone told me she'd been in the hospital?
I was so fucking confused that my mind was racing. Was
she really so pissed at me after we'd fucked that she told
them not to tell me? We were family, our lives were en-
twined, hell we even worked together, and no one had
thought it was important to let me know what the fuck
was going on?

"None of your business, Abraham," Ani answered flatly.

"That's bullshit." I looked her over trying to find where
the hell she'd been cut open—I grew nauseous at the
thought of that—but I couldn't see anything except the
pajamas that she was practically swimming in. "You had
surgery, and no one fucking told me?"

"Because *it's none of your business*."

"Fine," I snapped, pulling my phone out of my pocket.

"What are you doing?"

"Calling Katie. Maybe she'll tell me what the fuck is going on." I had just pulled up my contacts list when my phone was slapped out of my hand.

"She doesn't know, and she doesn't need to know," Ani hissed, glaring at me as she leaned forward, her hand braced gently against her belly. "Just go the fuck home, Bram!"

I lost it. Before she could step away, I was unbuttoning the first button on her pajamas and moving quickly to the next. "I have to find it? Fine." My hands were shaking so bad I could barely unfasten the second button.

"Bram," Ani finally said gently when I'd reached the fourth button. "Bram, stop."

I paused, clutching the sides of her top in my hands, and glanced up at her, my heart racing. What the fuck? What the fuck was wrong with her? Did she have cancer? Did they have to take something out of her? Her appendix? That wasn't a huge deal. Or was it something worse?

"Just tell me," I ordered, working hard to keep my voice steady.

She stared at me for a long moment, then finally spoke.

"Oh, you know, routine hysterectomy." She tried to say it jokingly, but on the last word, her voice broke, and she started to cry.

My stomach rolled. "Aw, baby. Don't," I murmured, the words coming without any thought. I leaned down and slowly lifted her into my arms as she sniffled, trying to get herself under control.

"I'm sorry," she murmured as I laid her down on her

bed. "It's *not* a big deal. At all. I don't know why I'm crying." Even as she said the words, her voice hitched and more tears ran down her face. "I just took a pain pill— Vicodin makes me weepy."

"Shhh." I stepped away from the bed and turned out her bedroom light, leaving the room dark except for the moonlight coming through the window.

"Thanks for turning out the light," she said, sniffling. "I'll see you Monday, okay?"

I nodded my head as I kicked my boots off.

"I'll even bring coffee since I know you're too lazy to make it yourself so you haven't had any all week."

"All right," I replied as I pulled off my shirt and dropped my jeans to the floor.

She sniffled again as I rounded the bed, and sobbed once as I climbed in behind her, curving into the shape of her and wrapping my arm around her chest so I wouldn't touch her incision.

The dam broke then.

She moaned as her sobs burst out of her mouth, and I pulled a pillow in front of her so she could press it against her belly as she curled into a ball. I didn't know what to do for her. I thought about calling my mom, but I knew that Ani must have sent her home or she would've already been there hovering.

"I'm sorry," she whispered as her sobs finally seemed to calm. She hiccupped and groaned, and I placed my hand over hers on the pillow, holding her steady against me.

"Nothing to be sorry for," I said softly, kissing the back of her head.

She went quiet. She didn't say anything for so long that I thought she'd fallen asleep until she spoke again. "I can't have babies anymore," she said sorrowfully, her hands clenching into fists against the pillow.

I wanted to tell her that it wasn't a bad thing. I wanted to ask why the hell it mattered. Why she was so upset about it. Why she'd even want to bring kids into our fucked-up world in the first place.

But I didn't.

Instead, I just ran my fingers lightly over her hands until they relaxed and gripped mine. "I'm sorry," I said simply.

She nodded, and a few minutes later, she fell asleep with her fingers threaded through mine.

Ani wasn't a crier. She didn't show a ton of emotion normally, preferring to mask any discomfort or sadness with a sharp tongue and a sarcastic remark. I understood that about her, because she and I were a lot alike in that respect.

I used my chin to smooth the hair at the back of her head out of my face and closed my eyes, refusing to think about why I wasn't hopping out of bed and getting the hell out of there.

Chapter 4
Anita

I woke up around three in the morning and knew two things simultaneously.

I needed a pain pill, and Bram had stayed.

His arm was still around me but had moved up my torso, his palm resting on my collarbone and his forearm pressed between my breasts. It felt good. I couldn't remember the last time I'd spent the night with someone. Sex—yes. Sleepovers—no.

But as nice as having Bram's arm around me felt, I needed to move it so I could get out of bed and grab some pain pills from the top of my dresser across the room.

"Hey," Bram rasped as I tried to lift his arm off me. "You okay?"

"Yeah," I whispered back, suddenly feeling awkward. "I just need to take a pill."

"Oh!" He sat up behind me, and I immediately missed his warmth at my back. "Where are they? I'll get 'em."

He stood from the bed as I tried to protest, but my

words were cut off on a giggle as he stumbled around trying to get his balance. I'd heard about Bram's wake-up clumsiness, but I'd never actually seen it. "Are you drunk?" I asked, watching as he braced himself against the wall.

"No," he shot back defensively. "It just takes me a minute to wake up."

"That's the cutest thing I've ever seen," I said seriously, sitting gingerly up in bed.

"Shut up."

"No really, you're like a newborn giraffe. It's adorable."

"I can't fuck with you right now, but you know I have a good memory, right?"

"All wobbly legs and bewildered expression," I teased, grinning as his expression became even more disgruntled.

"It's dark in here, and I don't know my way around," he argued, taking a few tentative steps forward.

"It's not that dark."

"Then you have eyes like a fucking bat," he mumbled. "Where are your pills?"

"Top of the dresser. I have a cup of water there too."

He stumbled over to the dresser and grabbed my little orange bottle of pills and my cup from the hospital, but his steps became steadier as he came back to the bed.

"You found those pills pretty easy in this super-dark room," I needled as he handed me the small bottle.

"Shut the fuck up," he replied, handing me the water and crawling over the foot of the bed to climb back in behind me.

I snickered as he got comfortable, then took my pill,

lying back down when I was finished. I wasn't sure how to position my body. Bram was lying on his back with his hands behind his head, but I didn't want to just assume he wanted me to snuggle into him. However, lying on my side with my back to him seemed kind of rude. Was that against bed-sharing etiquette? Whenever I saw a couple like that in a movie, it was when they were fighting—not that we were a couple or anything.

Finally I just lay down on my back next to him, even though it wasn't exactly comfortable, and rested my hands on my stomach. That should work. Super nonchalant.

"Why did you have the surgery?" Bram asked quietly once I was settled.

"I have—had these things called fibroids. They're painful, and I've had them for years, and it finally got to the point that I just couldn't take it anymore," I answered as simply as I could. I didn't explain the long periods that left me feeling drained and depressed or the few times when it had hurt to have sex. I wasn't going to go into the fact that I'd debated it in my head for over a year before I'd finally elected to have the surgery. How the thought of never carrying a baby had been completely abhorrent for a long time. That I'd finally come to the decision on my twenty-ninth birthday that I couldn't keep dealing with the pain on the off chance that, at some point, I'd have a husband and I'd want children. That I'd cried about it for the two weeks leading up to the surgery, and even while they were putting me under, I'd wondered if I was doing the right thing.

"Is that—" He paused for a second. "Is that cancer, or—"

"No. Not cancer." I turned my head to look at him, and found him staring at the ceiling.

"But they've been hurting you?"

"Yeah."

"I didn't know that."

"Why would you?" I asked in confusion.

"Well, at least you won't have to deal with that any-more, yeah?" He tilted his head down and met my eyes, his jaw tight.

"Yep," I said quietly, nodding my head.

How did I explain that I almost wanted it back? It wouldn't make any sense to him. Shit, I didn't know if it would make sense to anyone.

"Come here," Bram called, reaching out to grab my hand and pull it so that I rolled into his side, my arm around his waist. "That okay? It doesn't hurt or anything?"

"No." I shook my head before laying it on his shoulder. "They went through my vagina so I have some little in-cisions from the laparoscopy on my belly but most of it is—" My words cut off as I realized how absolutely still Bram was.

"Bram?"

"They—" His body shuddered. "They were—they cut you—"

"I'm fine," I tried to reassure him, but his body didn't relax. "Bram, seriously, they do it all the time."

"They don't do it to *you* all the time."

"Thank God for that. Shit hurts."

Bram shuddered again, and his hand swept down my back, pushing me closer against his side.

"Let's just go to sleep," he said roughly, pulling the sheets up and over us.

My skin prickled. "What, are you grossed out now?" I said sharply, embarrassed at his reaction. "I didn't ask you to stay. You can go at any time. Wouldn't want to gross you out or anything with the surgery I *just* had, that I wasn't even really sure I *wanted*, and—"

He cut my words off with a wet kiss, one that probably wasn't appropriate considering the fact that I wouldn't be able to have sex for a long time while I healed.

"I don't like the idea of someone with a fucking scalpel up inside you, okay?" he hissed into my mouth, his hand coming up to tangle in my hair as he was careful to keep his weight off my body. "Can we just fucking drop it?"

His breath was ragged, and I could feel his heart racing where my face pressed against his chest. He was *really* freaked out. I could see it even though I didn't understand it. By the look on his face, he didn't understand the reaction, either.

"Okay," I finally whispered with a nod, kissing his chin softly. "We can drop it."

He nodded back, inhaling deeply as he pulled his fingers through my hair and then smoothed it away from my face.

His muscles relaxed as he leaned back to rest his head on my pillow, but his arm never released the tight hold on my back.

* * *

The next time I woke up, Bram was gone. I wasn't surprised. He'd never struck me as a wake-up-the-next-morning-and-make-breakfast kind of guy. No, what surprised me was that he'd even stayed at all the night before.

I groaned as I leaned over the side of the bed and grabbed my pills and water cup from the bedside table. The cup was one of two that I'd brought home from the hospital with me, with a lid and a straw that had kept me from tipping it over and spilling it as I'd fumbled for it the first couple of days home. I leaned forward a little bit and paused with my lips around the straw.

The cup was cold and so was the water inside it. I shook it a little and heard ice cubes clicking against the plastic. I smiled. Bram had gotten me fresh water before he took off.

After another pull of the water, I set it down and lay back on my pillow. My pain was significantly better than when I'd first gotten home from the hospital, but I was still pretty sore. I wanted to give myself a few minutes before I tried walking around the house.

My eyes were just starting to grow heavy again when my foster brother Alex's voice came from my phone somewhere near my pillow.

"*Pick up the damn phone, Ani. Pick up the damn phone, Ani. Pick up the damn phone, Ani.*" Jesus, I should have deleted the app that let people record their own ringtones.

"What do you want?" I answered when I finally found my phone inside a pillowcase.

"A stripper. Blond hair, blue eyes, and massive—"

"You called the wrong number...again," I replied drily.

"Wait, are you sure?"

"Why exactly are you calling me at nine a.m. on a Saturday?"

"How you feeling?" Alex asked.

"Like I lost my ladybits," I said, sighing as I relaxed back into the blankets.

"Oh, shit. You had the sex change at the same time? Your dick better not be bigger than mine or we can't be friends anymore."

"Do they even make dicks as small as yours anymore?" I smiled as Alex started laughing.

"You wish you had a dick as big as mine," he guffawed.

"Nah, my balls are bigger."

"Yeah, they are," Alex said, his tone completely serious. "How are you, really? Everything okay?"

"Yeah, I'm good," I reassured him. "Less sore today than I was yesterday."

"What about, you know, emotionally?" he asked uncomfortably.

"Are you joking?" I snickered.

"Oh, shut the fuck up," he replied.

We talked for another twenty minutes about everything and nothing before finally hanging up. I loved that guy.

When I'd finally decided to have the surgery, Alex was the first person I'd called. I'm sure that would be weird for most people, but it had made sense to me. I'd needed a friend who could look at the situation unemotionally, and I knew that Kate and Liz wouldn't. They'd see it from a woman's perspective. They would have known how hard it was for me to relinquish the right to ever carry a baby, to lose that part of myself.

I'd needed a friend who would tell me that it was okay without bursting into tears or smothering me with questions. Alex had been that friend.

I rolled out of bed and shuffled into the kitchen to make a cup of coffee, stopping dead as I noticed a familiar flat cardboard box sitting on the middle of the counter. I moved closer and found the top had been written on by what looked like a black marker.

Didn't know what kind you liked.

I pulled the lid off the box and found a variety of donuts stuffed inside. Maple bars and chocolate bars and bear claws and glazed donuts and every other kind that the donut shop down the street carried.

I was twenty-nine years old, and a box of donuts may have been the sweetest thing anyone had ever done for me.

I glanced around the kitchen trying to spot anything else out of place as I picked up a maple bar and absently took a bite. God, that was good. Groaning, I took another bite as I started a cup of coffee.

I didn't have anything to do since it was Saturday, but I could feel the nervous energy pumping through my veins. After spending almost a week in bed, the thought of crawling back in there to watch another movie sounded like complete crap. I was used to being busy, either working at the office or working on my house. I didn't ever have downtime—I liked it that way—and the forced inactivity was beginning to wear thin.

I finished my donut and grabbed my cup of coffee, leaving my work-in-progress kitchen to head into my work-in-progress living room. After six months of working on my place, it didn't seem like I was any closer to finishing it. Yes, the ugly shag carpeting was gone, and I now had a refrigerator and stove in the kitchen, but the old hardwood floors were still unfinished, and my countertops belonged in a '70s porno complete with bow-chicka-wow-wow music.

I loved my house. It fit me, and I liked the fact that it was built so long ago. It had a history. Coming from foster care, I didn't have much that had survived intact from childhood. Moving so much and living with different kids with all different problems meant that a lot of things were lost. Stolen. Broken. Forgotten.

I'd managed to keep ahold of two things. A backpack that I'd carried from home to home, and a pillowcase that I'd needed to sleep with when I was little. That was it. That was the extent of my family heirlooms. Walking around a house that had survived family after family for almost a hundred years was comforting. It wasn't a cookie cutter in a new development. It was unique and built to last.

I glanced around my living room as I sipped my coffee. The walls were painted a light gray—I'd finished those the weekend before my surgery. The fireplace was one of the few things that hadn't needed to be redone but I'd painted the mantel white. There wasn't anything on the scuffed floor but a drop cloth and the paint I'd used on the mantel. I'd gotten enough to paint the trim around the windows and the baseboards.

I tilted my head as I looked at my brand-new windows. They'd cost a shit ton because the old windows had been a weird size, but I was happy with how the new ones had turned out. Now they just needed some nice white trim.

I looked back at the floor where my can of paint was stashed.

I could totally sit on a chair and paint the trim. I wouldn't be exerting myself. If anything, it would be relaxing.

With my decision made, I walked into the kitchen and grabbed a little paint stick thing and a small brush from the tiny pantry. I'd paint for a while and then take another nap.

* * *

"What the fuck are you doing?" Bram's voice boomed behind me, startling me into almost falling out of my chair.

I fumbled with the paintbrush in my hand, but eventually got it under control and turned to look at Bram as I dropped it on the stack of newspaper at my feet. Oh shit, I was sore. I couldn't remember the last time I'd had a pain pill.

"What time is it?" I asked, ignoring his question as I set the lid back on the paint can and started to seal it with a hammer.

"Gimme that," Bram muttered, taking the hammer from my hand and closing the paint with three hard whacks. "It's almost three."

No wonder I felt like shit—I hadn't had a pain pill all day...or lunch, for that matter. Once I'd started painting, I'd fallen into a little bit of a trance. I liked working on the house. It relaxed me to know that I was building something that was unique. Something that was mine.

"Looks good, huh?" I said proudly, looking back at the lower half of my windows. I hadn't painted the top halves because I'd known I should probably stay off my feet. Not that it mattered. I still felt like complete shit now that I'd stopped.

"You painted half the windows," Bram answered flatly, crossing his arms over his chest.

"Why aren't you a detective? Because that was seriously observant." I climbed to my feet and tried to hide my wince. Yeah, I needed a pain pill.

"Why the fuck did you paint half the windows? Aren't you supposed to be taking it easy?" Bram asked, stepping forward like he was going to help me.

"I was bored." Shuffling around him, I took a deep breath. Pills first, then food.

"You were bored," Bram growled as he followed me into my room.

"Yeah, I was bored." I opened up my pills and forced myself to take only one. Two would be better, but I didn't want to fall asleep and I knew they'd completely knock me out.

"How'd that work out for you?" Bram asked, leaning against my doorway.

"Great," I replied stubbornly, lifting my chin. "I got half the windows done."

"They look like shit."

"No they don't. They look *halfway finished*." I pushed past him and made my way back to the kitchen, eye-balling the donuts still sitting on my table. I wondered if I could get away with eating another one. Oh, fuck it. It's not like I ever gained weight anyway. Even when I was trying to put on a few pounds, I couldn't. I didn't bitch about it—I knew people would kill to be able to eat whatever they wanted and not gain an ounce—but it wasn't like it didn't irritate me. Maybe I *wanted* boobs. Maybe I *wanted* a little junk in my trunk. Maybe I didn't want old ladies to make comments at the grocery store about me starving myself.

"Thanks for the donuts," I called, stuffing a glazed one in my mouth.

"You're welcome," Bram replied, coming to a stop at the entry of the kitchen.

I wanted to ask him why he was there. I didn't understand his sudden need to visit my house and feed me. Was it nice? Sure. But we'd had sex one time. It wasn't like we were together. Our relationship was the same as it had always been.

I grew irritated as he stood there silently watching me eat. I hated not knowing what to say or where to look. We were in *my* fucking kitchen. My comfort zone. My sanctuary.

When the silence finally became too much, I wiped my hands on my pajama pants and took a step forward.

"Look, I'm pretty tired, so—"

"Sure," Bram cut in quickly, nodding his head as he scratched at his beard. That's when I noticed that he was as uncomfortable as I was. He was fidgety. Awkward.

"So, I'll see you Monday, right?"

"Yeah. Monday." Without another word, he spun around and walked out of my house, closing the door quietly behind him. Then I heard him locking the dead bolt, reminding me that he had one of the spare keys to my place.

I had a key for his town house, too. I'd never needed to use it, but I had it.

The weight of our intertwined lives hit me with the force of a sledgehammer as I made my way back to bed.

We not only shared the same family, but I worked with Bram. I saw him every single day. Sure, we didn't really speak to each other unless it was work-related—but I still saw him. When my best friends came to visit, he was there. When I went to see Liz and Dan, he was there. When I needed help on my house, he showed up with Dan, Mike, and Trevor, complete with a tool belt and a truck full of power tools.

For the first time since we'd met, I was nervous around Bram. My snarky mouth seemed to suddenly disappear when he looked at me, when before his presence was all I'd needed to smart off. After fourteen years of living parallel lives, we'd intersected, and now I had no idea how to get us running parallel again.

And the shittiest part of the whole deal was that there

was no way I could avoid him, and I was pretty sure that there was going to be no way to avoid the fact that I'd held his dick in my hand, either.

* * *

I lied.

Apparently, it was super easy to avoid Bram.

To be fair, I wasn't sure if I was avoiding him or he was avoiding me or we were both avoiding each other—but I'd barely seen him since the day in my kitchen when I'd pretty much kicked him out.

It had been almost four weeks. When we had family dinners, he was quiet. Not that that was unusual for Bram, but for obvious reasons, I noticed it more. He didn't talk directly to me, and all signs of our ongoing verbal warfare had disappeared.

I knew that Trevor suspected something. Maybe Liz and Ellie, too, but no one said anything. They just watched us closely as we orbited each other, never getting close enough to actually interact. It drove me nuts. He needed to act normal if we were ever going to put that night behind us without alerting the whole family that we'd bumped uglies in the back of my Toyota.

I was lying.

I needed to get my shit together. Me.

Our dynamic was practically set in stone. I made the first comment. Always. I'd say something, then Bram would say something back, and then we'd trade jabs for as long as we were together.

But for the life of me, I couldn't give him shit. I just couldn't. I'd open my mouth to make some comment, and I'd snap it shut again at the memory of him crawling into bed behind me. I'd like to think that I could have moved past the fantastic sex, but it was the *caring* that shut me up quicker than a republican during a gay sex scandal. I'd look at him, remembering his soft words in my ear, and I just couldn't make myself antagonize him.

"You're quiet tonight," Aunt Ellie said quietly as we sat down at another Friday night dinner. "Everything okay?"

"Yup," I chirped, trying not to wince or look at Bram. They were going to know. I'd gotten through three weeks of family dinners, and I felt like, at any moment, the tension in my limbs was finally going to snap, and I'd stand up from the table and tell them that I'd fucked grumpy Bram on a side street in downtown Portland.

"Feeling okay?" she murmured, passing me a bowl of biscuits.

"Yeah. Went to the doctor yesterday and I'm all healed up. She said to take it easy for a while longer but I'm mostly back to normal now," I replied quietly, passing the bowl to Trevor on my left.

"Really? That seems fast," Ellie said, giving me a small smile as I shrugged. "Well, I'm glad you're feeling better."

She leaned over and patted my leg a couple times before getting back to her dinner, and I was reminded of the fact that Ellie had never been able to carry a baby, either. I wasn't sure what the problem had been, and I'd never felt it was my place to ask. She and Mike had eventually become foster parents and adopted Trevor and Henry, but I wondered if she'd ever had regrets.

I shook myself out of those thoughts. Ellie hadn't had a choice. I knew that much. Our situations weren't the same.

"Two more weeks," Liz sang out across the table, diverting my attention. She rubbed her hands together in glee. "I can't wait to hold my grandbabies."

"Is Shane coming up with her?" Trev asked, leaning forward to blow on the hot chili in front of him. "He's got a deployment coming up, doesn't he?"

"Yep," Uncle Mike answered, leaning back in his chair. "He's taking leave so they can come up here, then he'll have about a week at home getting shit at the house ready before they start gearing up to go."

"I don't know how Kate does it," I said, shaking my head as everyone's attention landed on me. "'Hey, why don't you go play in the sand for a bit while I take care of everything back home, and then, when you get back, I'll jump into your arms like I haven't just killed myself for the last six months.'"

"Are you fucking joking?" Bram rumbled, glaring at me from across the table.

"No. I mean, I get it—"

"Obviously, you don't," Bram snapped, dropping his spoon into his bowl with a splat. "He's carrying a gun over there. People are shooting at him. Blowing up his friends. You think he wants to leave his family for six months at a time?"

"Bram," Liz said, glancing between us, "knock it off."

My jaw clenched as I tried to hold back my anger. If he had let me speak, I would've said that I knew it was hard on Shane, too. That it was dangerous and scary. I understood it. I did. I just wouldn't ever be able to do it.

"Please, Bram," I hissed through my teeth, "tell us all about how much you know about the military from all your time cutting wood in the fucking forests of *America*."

"Is everything a fucking joke to you?" His voice rose. "You tell Alex how much you respect his sacrifice? How about Henry? I'm sure he'd love to hear your opinion on that."

"Oh, fuck you," I shot back, getting to my feet.

"Sit down, Anita," Liz ordered.

"I'm going to go—wouldn't want Bram here to get fucking indigestion," I sneered, glaring at Bram across the table.

"Sit the hell down!" Dan roared, dropping me to my seat without conscious thought. "We don't talk politics at the fucking table."

"It's not politics. It's—"

"Bram, I swear to Christ if you don't shut up I'm going to lose it," Dan warned, breathing deeply as Liz laid her hand on his arm and rubbed it softly.

My heart pounded as I stared at my chili, and I could feel tears building at the back of my eyes. I could count on one hand the amount of times Dan had lost his temper in my presence—but he'd never lost it at me. He was such a mellow guy. He loved his wife, his kids, his company, and food—in that order. There wasn't a lot of shit that got under his skin. But talking about the military—or fighting about it the way Bram and I were—was enough to completely wipe the look of perpetual calm off his face.

I didn't like being yelled at. I really didn't like it.

I sat there, swallowing against the sob building in my throat, my hands trembling in my lap while everyone at the table was silent.

"There's no one at this table that disrespects the sacrifice our boys have made for their country," Dan said roughly after a few moments, his voice at a normal level. "I wouldn't let them in my goddamn house."

I bit the inside of my cheek, refusing to look at anyone. When I saw Ellie's hand reach toward me, I flinched away, and she dropped it.

"Ani knows better than to make light of what Shane does," Dan said. I didn't know if that was a warning to keep my mouth shut or his way of saying that he knew I wasn't being disrespectful.

"Sorry, Dad," Bram said quietly.

Dinner resumed, and the family started talking again, but I couldn't move my eyes from my bowl. I was still shaking. I couldn't get it under control.

For so long, I'd used my smart mouth to keep people from getting too close. I'd done it my entire life, starting before I'd ever been taken from my mom. It worked. I didn't seem like I took anything seriously, and I liked it that way. It made me funny.

I was the funny girl, not the sad foster care girl.

When I'd moved to Dan and Liz's, my personality was already set. I was irreverent. I made jokes at funerals and laughed in people's faces. But the Evans family seemed to like me anyway. That, in turn, had made it worse because I felt comfortable being myself there. They didn't care if I jokingly called Trevor our token black man. They didn't care when I told people that pretty Henry was born a girl or convinced them that Alex and Abraham only spoke Spanish, then watched them try to converse in Spanish as the twins looked at them in confusion. They didn't care when I called them fat—even though they weren't—and said I ended up with the wrong family because I was so much smaller than they were. They didn't care when I referred to the logging business as Dan and Mike's little hobby.

Because they knew that every time I teased and every time I made fun, it wasn't malicious. I loved the family that had taken me in. I'd kill for them. And every time someone looked at our family, with slender me and curvy Kate, and blond Henry, and identical Hispanic Alex and Abraham, and dark-skinned Trevor, I made a joke of it.

Because it didn't matter to me. I wasn't making fun of them—I was making fun of the world. The society we lived in. The people who stared. The people who cared how much we weighed and how successful the logging company was. The ones who asked questions with their noses turned up.

If I had a dollar for every time someone asked me what nationality I was, I'd buy a fucking Dutch Bros. coffee trailer just so they could make me an iced Caramelizer whenever I wanted without having to wait in line. *Actually, you fucking busybody, I have no idea what nationality I am because I have no idea who my father was.* None. My mom was fucking so many men that she had no idea, either. For all I knew, I may have been filling out forms wrong that asked if I was Native American for my entire life.

I inhaled deeply through my nose.

I was hard to take. I knew that. But I'd never felt judged by these people. They'd never taken me at face value—they'd always read between the lines. They'd heard what I meant, not what I said.

But all of a sudden, after fourteen years, I didn't feel safe in the Evans house. I felt like I was coming out of my skin. Like they hated me. Like they didn't understand me. Like I didn't belong.

I lifted a shaking hand to my spoon and stirred my chili, trying to control my breathing as the voices droned on around me. I needed to leave. I needed to get away from them. But I was afraid of calling attention to myself by getting up from the table.

What if Dan yelled at me again?

I was twenty-nine years old and afraid of getting scolded like a child. I clenched the hand on my lap into a fist and shuddered.

"We gotta head out, Mom," Bram said as I continued to stir my food.

"We?"

"Yeah, I told Ani I'd take her to Jay's bar." I jerked in surprise as I heard Bram say my name, but I didn't lift my head.

"But, you just—"

"We'll see you later." He was quiet for a second, and I

could picture him kissing the side of his mom's head the way he always did. "Thanks for dinner."

I sat frozen as he came around the table, but climbed to my feet when his hand reached out. I gripped it as he pulled me out of the room while I successfully avoided everyone's eyes.

"Shit!" Dan roared in the kitchen as we were walking out the front door.

I couldn't stop the sob that bubbled out of my mouth, and I instantly slapped my hand over it.

"Hey," Bram said quietly.

"It's fine. Fun dinner, huh?" I said jokingly, taking a couple steps toward my car without looking at him. "I figure it's a success if I can piss off the guy with the lobotomy. I mean, really. That's skill."

"Ani," Bram cut in warningly.

"Just another day of being me—pissing off war veterans and their children. It's a gift."

"Anita," Bram called.

"What?" I snapped back, raising my eyes to meet his.

"Where are you going?"

I looked at my car, then back to Bram. "Uh, home?"

"You don't want to go to Jay's?" he asked gruffly.

"Wait, that was a real thing? I thought you were just getting me out of there—thanks for that by the way—"

"Do you want to go or not?" he asked in irritation.

I looked at my car again, then back at Bram.

"Sure, okay," I finally answered.

"Then get in the fucking truck."

I scowled, then stomped past him.

"You have to bring me back to get my car tomorrow. I'm sure as shit not coming back here tonight," I ordered, moving around the hood of the truck.

"Fine."

"Fine." I turned on my heel and ran back to my car to grab my purse as Bram grumbled behind me, climbing into the truck and honking the horn as he started it.

What a fucking gentleman.

Chapter 5

Bram

I'd never been so pissed at my dad in my entire life.

When we'd moved in with Dan and Liz when we were kids, I was weary. That was probably the best word. Alex and I had been moved from home to home, never staying anywhere for long since we'd gone into the system at age seven. I'd known even then that our moves were my fault.

Alex was cute. He was funny. He got along with everyone and was perpetually happy.

I was the problem. I was the one who had an attitude and didn't seem to connect with anyone. Who brooded and sat silently in the corner of the room during Christmas and birthday parties.

If it hadn't been for me, Alex probably would have been adopted right away when our mom died. Fortunately for me, the state hadn't been comfortable separating a pair of identical twins, because if they were, I would've never seen my brother again.

So yeah, I'd been angry, pretty much all the time.

Angry with our mom, and the foster care system, and the world in general, but since we'd moved in with Dan and Liz, I'd never been seriously angry at either of them.

I'd chafed at their restrictions as a teenager, but the love behind the rules hadn't let me stay mad for long. I'd been irritated as fuck when Dan didn't want to hand over the company to me—even though he'd been talking about it for years—but I'd understood it.

But watching him yell at Ani that night had busted something loose in my chest, and I'd wanted to reach across the table and knock him out of his fucking chair.

That shit scared me. I'd learned to hold my temper within two years of coming to live at the Evans house— and in thirty seconds all that self-control had completely evaporated and I'd wanted to hurt him.

I glanced over at Ani. She was sitting with her head tilted back, her eyes steady on the road in front of us. She hadn't said a word since we'd pulled out of my parents' driveway.

The fucked-up thing about the whole situation was that I'd started it at the kitchen table. Shit was getting worse and worse between Ani and me, and everyone was noticing. We weren't arguing. We weren't even looking at each other.

So when she'd made that crack about Shane playing in the sand, I jumped on it. It had given me a reason to snap back at her the way I usually did. It worked.

What she'd said was irritating as hell, but I'd known that Ani wasn't implying that Shane's job was unimportant— hell, we all knew that—but I'd just needed the excuse to get her going.

I hadn't anticipated her trying to leave or my dad losing his shit. But I should have seen it coming. I knew how Dad felt about the military—especially his sensitivity to deployments and discussions about going overseas. He'd been a Marine in Vietnam. But I'd been so glad to finally get her bitching at me that I hadn't stopped while I was ahead.

When she'd dropped back down in her seat, and her chest rose and fell frantically as she stared at her lap, I wanted to pick her up and drag her out of there. It hadn't gone the way I'd planned.

I think I might have hurt her—or at least opened her up to be hurt—and that had never been my intention.

Fuck.

"You wanna grab something to eat?" I asked as we drove through town. "You didn't eat."

"Not hungry," she said back quietly. "Thanks though."

"I didn't mean to—"

"Forget about it, okay?" she said, turning to look at me. "It wasn't a big deal. I just don't like to be yelled at."

"I yell at you all the time," I argued, for no reason except to make sure she kept talking, if only to contradict me.

"Yeah—but it's different with you."

"Oh, yeah? Why is that?" I asked as I changed lanes so I could go over a bridge that would bring us downtown.

"Because I'm usually yelling back," she replied with a snort.

"True."

"Can we just drop it?" she asked tiredly. "I just want to go, get a beer, and watch you sing. You're singing, right?"

"Yep." I cursed as a bicyclist cut in front of me with no sense of self-preservation whatsoever.

"Jesus, does that guy have a death wish?" Ani asked, rolling down her window to yell at the bicyclist stopped at the light in front of us. "Hey, jackass! Watch where the fuck you're going!"

I laughed as the bicyclist flipped her off, and locked the doors quickly as she tried to climb out of the truck.

"Just stay inside, psycho."

"That dick just flipped me off!"

"Yeah, after you called him a jackass."

"I could take him."

"You probably could," I agreed as we watched the spandex-wearing bicyclist take off at the green light, "but he's got about fifty pounds on you, and you'd never catch him on foot."

"Chase him in the truck?" she asked seriously.

"Nah, don't want to be late. Jay likes me to kick off the open-mike night."

"Fine," she pouted, and suddenly the night was looking up.

It was looking up until we parked across from Jay's bar and Ani immediately started fucking stripping.

"What the hell?" I blurted, my voice coming out a lot higher than it had been since I was fourteen.

"What?" she asked in confusion, pushing her jeans down her thighs and off her feet.

"Put your damn pants back on," I ordered, turning the truck off.

"No way. I'm not wearing those in there."

"Why the fuck not?"

"Because they're my at-home jeans. They're ratty, and they sag at my ass."

I stared as she flipped down the visor and slid a tongue ring in expertly, then delicately pulled the septum ring down and out of her nostrils.

"You're not going in there without pants," I argued as she turned her head to smile at me.

"Sure I am." She jumped out of the truck before I could stop her.

"Anita!" I yelled, making her grin as I rounded the hood.

"You're yelling," she said.

"Sorry." I grimaced.

Ani laughed, and then adjusted her shirt.

Jesus. It was a tank top, but she'd pulled it down to just under her ass cheeks, the lace at the bottom giving just a couple inches more length.

"See—it's a dress."

"It's not a fucking dress." I swallowed hard as she adjusted the thin straps at her shoulders.

"Sure it is. Let's go."

I followed her across the street, trying not to stare at her small but perfectly rounded ass as it moved underneath the thin material.

"Are you even wearing underwear?" I asked, glaring at the idiots smoking by the door.

"Wouldn't you like to know?" she teased as she entered the dark bar.

Jesus.

"Can I get a Hefeweizen?" Ani asked as she stepped up onto the bar's foot rail and leaned up against the counter, making her shirt rise up the backs of her thighs. I stepped quickly behind her so she wouldn't flash the bar, and she instantly leaned back against me, her elevated height making her ass nestle right into my crotch.

"Fuck," I hissed, my hand coming up to grip her hip.

Ani's smiling face turned toward me. "Actually, make that two."

"I'm going to fucking kill you if I have to get on that stage with my dick hard," I warned, pulling her tighter against me.

"Then you should probably back up," she retorted, standing up straight so her back was pressed up against my chest and her weight was resting against me.

It would be so easy to run my hand around her front and slide my fingers into her cunt without anyone knowing. The way we were pressed against the crowded bartop hid her from just below her ribs, and the tank top was so high on her thighs I wouldn't even have to move it.

"Two Hefs," the bartender announced, smiling at me.

"Thanks, Rach," I replied, pulled out of my fantasy. I pulled a twenty out of my pocket and set it on the bar.

As soon as the bartender had moved away, Ani spun around so she was facing me, leaning back on her elbows and making it infinitely harder not to fuck her right there in the bar.

It was getting ridiculous. I didn't know where the hell it was coming from, but the sudden attraction was almost overwhelming. I'd always thought Ani was pretty—she was pretty by anybody's standards. Her features were small, and she had pouty lips and clear blue eyes, and even though she was tiny, she was rounded in all the right places. But I hadn't wanted to fuck her until that stupid fucking kiss almost a month ago when I'd been trying to protect the bruised ego of a drunk girl.

Apparently, I'd opened Pandora's box. And by the way her eyes were dilating as she stared at my mouth, I'd opened it for both of us.

Jay started his usual spiel about only singing covers and I cleared my throat, making Ani's gaze meet mine.

"I should get up there," I said roughly. How the fuck I was going to walk with the hard-on from hell tenting my jeans, I had no idea.

"Yeah."

"Stop with the fuck-me eyes."

"You really want me to stop?" she asked quietly, leaning forward a little.

I cleared my throat again, my hand tightening at her hip. "Fuck no."

Her lips tilted up in a smile, and she leaned forward even farther, taking my bottom lip into her mouth and sucking on it gently. The tide broke.

I slid my leg between hers and leaned down farther so I could slide my tongue into her mouth as her hands came up to rest against my jaw.

I didn't understand what the fuck was happening, but

I hadn't lied. I didn't want her to stop looking at me like she was. I didn't want her to stop kissing me or driving me fucking insane with her tight little body.

I knew I was fucked, but in a crowded bar in Portland, an hour from our homes and almost completely anonymous, I just wanted to keep kissing her and feeling her little tits pressed up against my chest.

"Abraham, come on, man!" Jay's annoyed voice broke through the fog of lust in my head.

"Shit," I complained, pulling away.

"Go," she said back, pushing at my chest.

I glanced down her body while Jay gave me more shit from up on the stage. "Stay right here, all right?"

"Where would I go?"

"I don't fucking know, but I don't want anyone messing with you."

"Bram," she said in annoyance, rolling her eyes.

"You're in nothing but a tank top, and I'm already on the fucking edge after that shit tonight," I warned, taking a step back.

"That shit tonight?" she growled back, stepping down from the foot rail.

"You think I didn't see your face when Dad—"

"Bram—let's go!" Jay yelled into the mike, making it squeal.

"Fuck. Stay here," I ordered, turning around to make my way through the crowd.

I was anxious as fuck to leave her to cross the bar, but I'd promised Jay I'd open up for him. Usually people weren't in a hurry to sign up at open-mike night. They came wanting to get up onstage, but it took a bit for them to gather up the balls to do it. That's where I came in. I'd been playing in Jay's bar for the past couple of years, and I was pretty comfortable up there. I made it look easy. Simple. I wasn't great, but I wasn't bad, either. By the time I was done with one or two songs, people had usually filled in the open spots on the sign-up sheet.

"Hello, patrons of Jay's," I said, leaning into the mike as I took Jay's guitar from him and set the strap over my shoulder. "How drunk are you?"

The crowd cheered, and I smiled, looking over to Ani.

She was sitting at a bar stool with her legs crossed, her ass almost hanging out of her tank top as she sipped from her beer, her eyes on me. Her lips were turned up around the rim of her glass, and I couldn't help but smile back.

What the fuck was she doing to me?

* * *

"You did so good tonight," Ani said sleepily from the passenger seat later that night.

"Thanks," I said quietly as we finally pulled into the little subdivision I lived in.

My town house wasn't much, but I owned it outright, and the homeowners' association took care of the yard and shit so I didn't have to. When I'd started looking for a place a couple years before, all I'd found were three- and four-bedroom houses in our little town. Homes for families. I didn't really want or need that much space. So when they'd started building town houses on the edge of the city limits, I'd jumped on one. My house was a place I crashed—nothing more, nothing less—and I didn't want the hassle of trying to keep up with the yard and maintenance and shit.

"You're not dropping me at home?" Ani asked, a small smirk on her lips as I pulled into my one-car garage.

"Just noticed that, huh?" I joked, shutting off the truck and pressing the garage door remote on my visor. I'd passed the turnoff to her place more than a mile back.

"I'm not very observant," Ani mocked, jumping from the truck to the cement floor.

As I rounded the truck, she stepped in front of me, reaching for the door to the house. She probably would have made it, too.

But she hadn't put her pants on when we'd climbed back into the truck, and as she'd sat in the cab, the bottom of her tank top had ridden higher and higher. By the time she reached the doorway to my house, the bottoms of her ass cheeks were peeking out of the lace along the bottom edge of her shirt.

By the sway in her hips, she knew it.

"You like teasing me?" I murmured in her ear as I wrapped my arm tightly around the front of her body, stopping her in the open door.

"You like it," she replied with a small laugh, arching her back.

"Floor, wall, kitchen table, or bed?" I asked, pushing her ahead of me into the dark house without letting go of her.

"The couch isn't an option?"

"You want the couch?" I pulled the garage door closed behind us and locked it.

"Not really."

"Bed, it is."

"Well that's not very original."

"Always busting my balls," I muttered, spinning her around and pressing her up against the wall. "That foreplay to you?"

"If it is, we've been practically fucking for the last ten years—"

I laughed against her mouth as I leaned in, and within seconds, she was laughing with me, wrapping her arms around my neck as she hopped up. I grabbed her bare ass in my hands and groaned, finding the smallest piece of underwear known to man nestled between her cheeks.

I stomped toward the stairs as she rubbed her lips against mine, and thank fuck I didn't have a ton of furniture and knew my way around in the dark or we would have fallen ass-over-elbows as she ground her pussy against my stomach.

I stumbled slightly as she sucked my neck between her teeth, and I had to brace myself against the wall as I moved up the stairs. Jesus. I couldn't remember ever wanting anyone the way I wanted her—and that was so fucked up I couldn't even wrap my head around it.

I felt drunk, and I'd had only one sip of the beer she'd ordered me at the bar before she finished it off.

I dropped her on my bed as soon as we entered my room, and as soon as she hit the sheets, my mind remembered the last time I was in bed with her.

I completely froze. "Oh, fuck," I hissed, looking at her in horror.

"What?" She hopped off the bed like it was on fire, looking frantically around the room.

"No. No," I stuttered. "Are you okay? I didn't hurt you, did I?"

How could I have forgotten? Shit, she'd just had surgery, and I was throwing her around and slamming her into walls, and, oh fuck. I'd pressed her belly up against the bar.

"I'm fine," she said in exasperation, falling stiff as a board straight back onto the bed. "All healed up."

"Are you sure? Shit!"

"Yes, I'm sure. I think I'd know."

"Well maybe—"

"Maybe what? I was just so overcome with your good looks and *charming* personality that I was willing to overlook any discomfort or pain in order to get one more look at your ginormous cock?" she cut in sarcastically, pulling her tank top over her head as she said it.

"You're such an asshole," I mumbled, staring at her perfect tits. "Why the fuck do I even like you?"

"Aw, you like me? Tomorrow can we make daisy chains to wear in our hair and paint each other's toenails?"

"For some reason, your mouth is moving but I can't hear anything past the sight of your nipples."

"That doesn't even make any sense," she replied as I tore my shirt off and ripped open the front of my jeans.

"Made perfect sense to me."

"Okay, well . . . ," she murmured as she turned over and

pressed her chest to the bed, pulling her knees up until her ass was perched high in the air. "Does this help? Can you hear me now?"

I wanted to fall to my knees and fucking worship her. Instead, I tripped, cursing while I pulled the rest of my clothes off, and she giggled.

I leaned forward and bit her ass.

"Oh, shit," she moaned, her back arching even closer to the bed.

"You just keep talking," I said against her skin, sliding my fingers up until I could grab the thin strings at her hips and slide them down over her ass, snapping them once against the smooth skin there. "Giving me so much shit all the fucking time." I pulled the underwear down to her knees and gently helped her raise her legs so I could take them off. "But when I get you like this, it all goes away, doesn't it?"

"Yes," she said breathily as I smoothed my hand down her back.

"You'd do whatever I wanted—"

"I wouldn't go that far—" Her words cut off on a sharply indrawn breath as I bit her ass again, this time a little harder.

"You smell good," I murmured, pulling her thighs farther apart.

I licked my lips as I stared at the pretty, dark-pink skin between her legs, then noticed a small hand inching down over her clit.

"Nice try," I laughed, reaching under her to grab her wrist before her hand made any good contact.

Then I opened my mouth and ran my tongue from her clit to the small opening that was already weeping for me.

Ani yelled out my name as I pressed my tongue inside her, and I felt like fucking Superman.

My dick was so hard it hurt. Hell, it felt like I'd had an erection the entire night, from the moment she'd taken off her pants in the truck. Ani's hips started rolling against my face, her legs trembling, and I pulled back fast before she could come.

I wanted in there before she did.

"I fucking hate you," she moaned against my comforter when I wiped my face and got to my feet.

I chuckled as she toppled to the side, looking up at me through dazed eyes.

"You're gorgeous," I said quietly, bracing my hands on the bed so I could lean down and kiss her hip. "Come here."

I pulled her to her knees on the bed and brought her face to mine. Why the hell did I want her so bad?

As soon as her mouth met mine, I groaned. Sliding my tongue into her mouth, I grabbed her ass in both hands, jerking her against my body. It had been a month since I'd felt all that smooth skin, and I wasn't even sure where to start.

Falling onto the bed, I pulled Ani with me. When her legs had settled on each side of me, she pulled away from my mouth, leaning back until she was straddling my hips.

"Ride me," I ordered hoarsely.

"Condom?" she asked, reaching down to wrap her hand around my dick.

I almost shot off the bed it felt so fucking good.

"I'm clean," I told her, searching her eyes.

Maybe I was a dick. Insensitive, or whatever. But for the entire ride home, I'd been really conscious of the fact that there was no way to get Ani pregnant. I could fuck her any way I wanted to, come inside her at any time, and there was no way for my worst nightmare to happen.

I didn't have to worry about a broken condom or faulty birth control. It was like Christmas.

"So am I but..." She looked off to the side for a moment, squeezing her lips together. "Okay, yeah."

"Yeah?"

She didn't answer me again with words, but instead, pulled my cock away from my belly and ran it through the wet lips of her pussy. She kept doing it, rubbing it back and forth for a long time.

"Sorry," she laughed humorlessly, and shook her head. "I'm nervous all of a sudden." Her cheeks grew pink as she tried to play it off, but I could see how uncomfortable she was by the tilt of her head and the way her jaw clenched.

I knew her. I knew all of her tics, most of her expressions.

"Hey," I called quietly, sitting up so our faces were close. "That's why you're on top." I reached up and gently pushed her hair away from the sides of her face. "Go at your own pace; it hurts—we stop."

"This is stupid," she replied, notching my dick at her opening and barely pressing me inside. "The doctor said I'm healed."

"Then stop fucking around," I said shortly.

"You're such a dick," she gasped, pressing down harder against me.

"I'm thirty-two years old. I stopped dry humping when I was seventeen—" My entire body jerked as she suddenly forced herself down. "Oh, fuuuck."

I'd known that pissing her off would get her out of her head, but I hadn't realized how little it would take to make her forget her fear.

"It feels different without a condom," she whispered into my ear, running her hands into the back of my hair and fisting it tightly as she rolled her hips.

"No shit," I gasped out. "Fuck, that's good."

"It doesn't feel *different?*" she asked hesitantly. The word came out tentatively, and I knew she didn't mean *different*—she meant *bad*. Why she'd ever think that, I had no clue. But it was so far from the truth it was laughable.

Her words hit me hard. I don't know if it was the vulnerability that normally she would have killed to keep hidden or the fact that she'd trusted me with it, but in that moment, I felt more tenderness for her than I'd ever felt in my entire life.

"Better," I whispered, kissing her jaw. "It's better."

She pulled back to look in my eyes, then didn't look away as she lifted up and slid back down. I caught her smile as my eyes drifted closed and my head tilted toward the ceiling.

A sexy woman was fucking me raw, tight as hell and wet as fuck, and there was no way I could get her pregnant. It may have been the best moment of my life.

"Best moment of my life."

"Jesus, it doesn't take much, does it?" Ani laughed.

"Did I say that out loud?"

"Sure did."

I pulled her hands from my hair and fell back on the bed, my hands rising to grip her waist. She was so slender that I felt like I could wrap my fingers all the way around her if I tried. I'd have to come back to that later.

"Go," I ordered, lifting her up and dropping her back down. "Stop fucking around and do it."

Ani smiled and fell forward, sucking my bottom lip into her mouth, pulling on it as she leaned back again.

Then she braced her hands on my chest and ground down hard. Within minutes, she was bouncing above me, and one of her hands had slid down her torso to press against her clit. Every time she rose up, I could feel the tips of her fingers against my dick, rubbing and pressing.

She came first, thank God. But I was right behind her.

Chapter 6
Anita

So, sex without a condom meant a very messy cleanup and a wet spot on the bed. Good to know.

"Shower with me?" Bram asked as he pulled me up off his bed.

"What happened to postcoital cuddling?" I asked when he didn't wait for my answer and tugged me into the bathroom. "Is that not a thing anymore?"

"It's a thing," he answered as he turned on the shower. "But I have a beard."

I tilted my head to the side as I waited for him to continue, but that was all he said.

"And?" I finally asked as we climbed into the shower.

"And it smells like your pussy," he said, his lips pulling up in a satisfied grin. "I like it."

"Then why are you washing it off?" I asked, stepping into the spray nonchalantly like my cheeks weren't on fire.

"Because I have to help Trev up at his place in the

morning and I don't want him smelling you," he replied simply.

"Pretty sure he wouldn't know it was me."

"Doesn't matter."

I nodded as he stuck his head under the water and then grabbed his shampoo and started lathering his hair and beard.

"Shit, I forgot to take the rubber band out and now my fingers are too fucking slick," he sputtered through soapy lips. "Can you get it?"

He turned away from me, and I took a second to take in his long, lean back. It was muscular without being too much. Perfect really, and that wasn't a term I'd ever thought I'd associate with Abraham Evans. I reached up and slid my fingers through the knotted hair at the back of his head, gripping the ponytail there and pulling the band out as gently as I could. His hair wasn't super long or anything, but it was longer than mine. He wore it in a knot at the back of his head most of the time, and I'd barely ever seen it down. The guys we worked with gave him so much shit for it that I didn't know why he kept it long, but he just took their jokes and laughed it off.

"Why do you keep it so long?" I asked as I set the rubber band on the ledge of the tub.

"Just do, I guess. Don't have to get it cut as often." He dipped his head under the spray and began rinsing.

"And people don't confuse you with Alex anymore."

"They didn't really confuse us before," he said with a shrug, grabbing some body wash as he pushed me back under the spray.

"No?"

"Nah, not really."

"Do you miss him?" I asked as he poured the soap into my hands.

"Every day. He likes what he's doing though."

"You think he'll ever come back home for good?"

"Not until after he retires," Bram replied with a shake of his head.

"Shit, that's like ten years away."

"A little less than eight," he argued.

"Counting the days, huh?"

"Hell yeah."

We were quiet for a few minutes, each cleaning up and rinsing off until the water finally ran clear around us.

"Spend the night?" he finally asked, reaching out to slide his hands up my torso as he met my eyes.

"Don't you have to help Trev?"

"I'll drop you off at your car on my way," he said easily, leaning in to run his tongue up my neck.

"What are we doing here?" I asked, tilting my head to give him better access.

Bram completely froze with his face still close to my neck. "What do you mean?" he asked.

"You and me. What is this?"

"What are you getting at?" Bram said darkly as he jerked his hands away from my hips.

"Oh, Jesus Christ," I snapped, immediately irritated. I shoved hard at his belly. "Get off of me."

"What the fuck is your deal?" he shouted as I scrambled out of the bathtub, grabbing a towel off the rack. I didn't think it was clean, but at that point, I didn't really care, either.

"Is this a onetime thing?" I asked, throwing open the bathroom door and shivering as I let the cold air in. "Back to normal tomorrow?"

"I fucking doubt it!"

"Well then, what the fuck are we doing?" I asked in irritation as he grabbed a towel under the sink and began rubbing it over his face and hair. "Is this a secret?"

"You really want everyone to know that we're fucking?"

"Is that all this is?"

"What the hell do you want me to say?" he bellowed, pulling the towel from his face. "Just tell me. I'm not dealing with your high school drama bullshit. You have something to say—then just fucking say it!"

I took a deep breath and shook my head. "Fuck you. How about that? That work for you?"

"Christ, Anita."

I turned and made my way into the bedroom, picking up my tank top and underwear on the floor by the bed and quickly pulling them on. I was still fucking freezing, and I wished I had worn more clothes. My jeans were all the way downstairs in the truck. Shit.

"Is there a reason you're acting like a crazy bitch right now?"

"Nope, no reason."

"Ani—" I lifted my hand to cut him off. I just wanted to go home and crawl into my own bed. I hated that we were fighting about our relationship status. What a joke. I wasn't trying to tie him down. Hell, half the time

I didn't even like Bram. I was just curious what the parameters of this little attraction were. We'd just had sex without a condom. Did that mean we were exclusive? Were we going to be super careful to keep things quiet, or was it not a big deal that we were sort of seeing each other?

"I like hanging out with you, and I want to fuck you," he finally said quietly as he pulled on a pair of boxer briefs. "Probably not what you want to hear, but that's what I've got."

"You couldn't have said that before, instead of completely freezing up and acting like a pussy?" I yelled back, crossing my arms over my chest. God, I was freezing, and my wet hair was dripping down my back.

"I'm the one acting like a pussy?"

"I just wanted to know what we were doing! I wasn't angling for a fucking marriage proposal."

"Good," he replied flatly, bracing his hands on his hips. "That's never going to happen."

I didn't want to marry Abraham. Not even a little bit. But the way he said those words, so matter-of-fact and emotionless, felt like a punch to the gut.

"Right," I murmured, looking away from him.

"I'm not marrying anyone. Ever," he said, his voice softer than it was before.

"Not my business," I said cheerfully, pulling myself back together as quickly as I could. I liked fighting with Bram. I actually enjoyed pissing him off. But our conversation was hitting topics a little too serious for my taste, and I just wanted it to be over.

"Shit, you're freezing. Come here," he called, grabbing a shirt from his dresser.

"I'm fine," I replied, taking a few steps forward.

"Here, put this on." He started to pull one of his flannel shirts over my shoulders, then stopped and cursed. "You're soaking wet."

I stood there motionless as he pulled my tank top back over my head and used the towel hanging over his shoulder to dry my hair and back. When he was finished, he put the flannel back on me, his hands sweet and gentle as he pushed my arms into the sleeves and buttoned two buttons on the front of the shirt.

"Better?" he asked, tossing the towel toward the bathroom door.

I nodded.

I was afraid, if I spoke, that my voice would come out weird. He was so fucking confusing. He could make me feel like complete shit in one minute, then take care of me like I was a baby the next. He didn't want me for more than sex, but was concerned when I was feeling chilly.

"Stay the night?" he asked, cupping my face and lifting it toward his.

"Fine," I grumbled, making him laugh.

He pulled me back into bed, avoiding the wet spot as he pulled my underwear back down my legs. I expected him to pull the flannel off, too, but as soon as he'd thrown my underwear off the edge of the bed, he was rolling me to my side and crowding in behind me.

Spooning. He was spooning me.

Then his hand slid down my hip, pushing his flannel out of the way so he could press his fingers between my legs. I whimpered when his fingers moved over my clit and tried to widen my legs, but one of his legs moved to trap mine together.

"No, don't move," he said quietly, his mouth near my ear. "You're tired, I'm tired."

His fingers played while I lay there stuck, and after a few seconds, one slipped inside me, making my hips jerk. He pulled out slowly then pushed in again, before his hand completely stopped moving.

"Sleep," he murmured, using the hand curled up near his head to press my hair away from my face.

"I can't sleep with you inside me," I argued, tightening the muscles around his finger.

"Sure you can."

"No, I really can't."

"Then I guess you won't sleep," he said teasingly, gently squeezing his hand cupping my pussy. "Just relax, baby."

He called me baby. It shouldn't have mattered, but it did.

I closed my eyes and tried to relax but it wasn't happening. I was getting wetter by the second, and it took everything I had not to move my hips against his hand. I breathed deep, clenching my hands in front of me as Bram's body grew heavier behind me.

When I realized he was falling asleep, I made myself ignore the finger still inside me. If I could wait just a few minutes without moving, I could crawl away once he was finally passed out. Finally, when his breathing grew deep and even, I braced myself to move.

And that's when his finger began thrusting again. In and out.

Then another finger. He curled them forward as he jerked his hand up, and my back arched involuntarily, a small sound bursting out of my throat.

"You fucking sneak," I breathed as he did it again.

I felt a light kiss on my ear as Bram pulled his fingers from me, then he was sliding into me from behind in one long push.

"You really thought I could leave my fingers in you and sleep?" he asked in amusement, thrusting slowly. "While you were dripping down my hand?"

"Yes," I hissed, reaching back to grip his hip. "And it was one finger."

He chuckled and grabbed my hand at his hip, pushing it forward until he'd trapped it against the sheets in front of us. "Slow," he murmured.

I could barely move, and as much as I wanted to fight him on it, I couldn't deny that I really liked having him control the way our bodies moved together. He'd get me there if I was patient.

I gritted my teeth as he just barely sped up his thrusts.

"Better?" he asked.

"Not even a little bit," I moaned, making him chuckle.

"How about now?" He thrust harder but didn't speed up.

"No."

"Now?" His hips moved faster, and my eyes drifted shut.

"No," I said again stubbornly.

He pulled back and slammed in hard, our bodies inching across the bed.

"Yes," I gasped without him even asking.

"Wanted some sleepy sex," he groaned into my ear, his hand leaving mine on the bed so he could slide it underneath the flannel shirt and pinch one of my nipples between his fingers. "But I'll take this."

His hand moved south and I cried out as two of his fingers slid around my clit, barely pinching it as he slid them back and forth with his thrusts.

"Shit," I moaned as I came, shuddering as my muscles tightened against his hold.

"Oh fuck. Yeah, I'll take this," he groaned, thrusting again before his hips began to jerk against my ass.

His weight rested against me as we breathed heavily in the aftermath.

"Stay still," he said quietly as he slid his hand from between my thighs.

He pulled his leg from the top of mine and moved backward, pulling out of me slowly. I heard him get off the bed behind me, then pause.

"That's so fucking sexy," he said, leaning forward to run his finger over my pussy from behind. I shuddered against the movement, and he groaned. "Every time you tighten up, my cum drips out. Jesus. I think I'm having a heart attack."

I snickered as he kissed my ass cheek and then stepped away from the bed and moved into the bathroom. When he came back out, he was carrying a wet washcloth, and without any warning, he leaned over me and cupped it between my legs.

"Roll over," he ordered, cleaning me up as I followed his instructions.

"Thanks," I mumbled quietly when he pulled the wash-cloth away.

"No problem. You ready for bed?"

He walked back into the bathroom, and I could hear the sink running for a minute before he came back empty-handed.

"Actually, I'm wide awake now," I answered brightly, sitting up cross-legged. "And hungry."

"I'm going to be worthless tomorrow," Bram complained, looking at the alarm clock on his nightstand. "Come on, I'll feed you."

He pulled me up from the bed and dragged me down-stairs, lifting me up to sit on the counter when we got to the kitchen.

"Ooh, ice cream," I ordered when he opened up the freezer door. "That's what I want."

He handed me the carton and a spoon, then leaned against the counter across from me, watching as I dove in.

"You want some?" I asked around the spoon as I shov-eled a bite into my mouth.

"No." He smiled.

"Fine. But it's really good."

"I know. It's mine," he said drily.

"So what are you and Trev doing tomorrow?"

"I'm really sorry about tonight," he said at the same time.

"Huh?" I asked in confusion.

"All that shit at dinner," he clarified, running his hand over his beard.

"Not your fault," I said quickly, shaking my head.

"Yeah, it was."

"Just drop it."

"He shouldn't have yelled at you like that," Bram pressed. "If I would have known—"

"*Abraham, drop it,*" I said again, grabbing the lid to the ice cream and shoving it back on.

"I'm trying to fucking apologize!" he barked, pulling the ice cream out of my hands and throwing it back in the freezer.

"Fine, you're forgiven," I shot out, tossing the spoon into the sink.

"Sometimes I wonder how the fuck I've dealt with you for the last fifteen years," he growled, glaring at me. It was closer to fourteen, but who was counting?

I looked him over, my eyes catching at the long, wild hair barely resting at his shoulders, the brown eyes that were almost black, and the arrow-straight nose with the small bump on the bridge. God, he was attractive. Even more so when he was scowling.

"Because I'm cute," I finally chirped back, smiling wide as I tilted my head to the side, "and because instinctively you knew that I could suck dick like a Hoover."

Bram's face continued to scowl for as long as he could hold it, then suddenly he burst out laughing. My smile grew impossibly wider.

"Really?" he asked, raising one eyebrow.

"Only one way to find out."

I shrieked as he came at me, slinging me over his shoulder as he practically ran out of the kitchen and up the stairs.

* * *

"You go. I'm sleeping," I grumbled as Bram tried again to shake me awake.

"Oh, hell no. You kept me up all fucking night, and I'm the one who has to help Trev put up new gutters all fucking day," he growled, shoving his hands into my armpits so he could force me to sit up. "Get dressed. We gotta go."

"You loved it," I said as I threw my legs over the bed. "I rocked your world."

"Yeah, you're the best I've ever had. Now get the fuck up. I was supposed to be at Trev's twenty minutes ago." He sat next to me on the bed and started pulling his socks and boots on.

"Really, the *best*?" I sang, clasping my hands together under my chin as I tiredly batted my eyelashes at him.

"You're such a fucking pain in the ass," he laughed, shaking his head.

He pulled me out of the room and down the stairs, and I was kind of disappointed that he'd already been up for a while by the time he'd woken me up. I wanted to see sleepy, stumbly Bram again. That Bram was my favorite.

"Ah, there they are," I said to myself as Bram opened up the door to the garage and I saw my flip-flops discarded carelessly on the cement step right outside.

We climbed in the truck, and I shimmied into my jeans as he pulled out onto the highway.

"I left my tank top and my underoos at your house,"

I said as we got closer to Dan and Liz's house to pick up my car.

"You can just grab 'em the next time you're over," he said easily, turning down the long gravel driveway.

"Ooh, I get another ride?" I said sweetly, turning my head to look at him. "When?" I clapped my hands in front of my chest.

"When I call you."

"You're so *dominant*," I murmured breathlessly. "Are you going to spank me if I call first?"

"I fucked you all night, and you're still busting my balls?" he asked incredulously, coming to a stop next to my Toyota.

"It's cute that you thought anything would change," I mocked, reaching out to tap his cheek with my fingers, then pulling away quickly as he snapped his teeth at me.

"Thanks for the ride!" I sang as I climbed out of the truck.

"Which one?" he asked as I slammed the door closed behind me.

I jogged around to the driver's seat of my car as Bram turned the truck around, and just as I'd started up the car, Dan opened up the front door of the house and took a step outside.

I pretended I didn't hear him call my name as I quickly backed up and turned around. I didn't want to deal with that shit yet. Not yet. Not until I could look him in the eye without feeling like a bug under the microscope.

And not until I was dressed in my own clothes and not braless and commando under one of Bram's favorite flannels.

Bram. I sighed and smiled as I pulled out onto the road,

and for a few minutes, I was almost giddy at the tenderness between my legs. Then, without warning, I thought about the night before, and my smile turned to a scowl. I pulled over to the side of the road and pulled out my phone to text him.

If we're having sex without a condom, you're not fucking anyone else.

I wanted to write a long-winded text about how I didn't care if he wanted to see other people but I wasn't going to take the chance of him giving me some STD, but I didn't want to give the impression that I was protesting too much. Even though the thought of Bram with anyone else made my stomach churn. I stared at my phone for a full five minutes, periodically glancing at the empty road ahead and behind me, then finally saw that he was typing a response. I braced.

You aren't either.

Well.
My lips curled up as I pulled back onto the road.

* * *

"Hey, asshole!" I yelled, answering my phone the next day. I was covered in paint and sweaty as all hell, but I'd finally gotten all the trim painted in my living room, and it looked magnificent.

Good word. Magnificent.

"How's it going, Anita Bonita?" Henry's voice came through the speaker as I set my phone down on a stool and started stripping off my paint-splattered clothes.

"It's going. Just working on the house today. What about you? Anything new?"

"Nah, not much. Same shit, different day. I'm doing some training in a couple months though—that should be pretty badass."

"Oh, yeah?" I asked, rolling the clothes into a ball and stuffing them into a garbage bag. They weren't even worth keeping.

"Yeah. I'm thinking about heading up with Shane and Katie when they come up in two weeks. I've got the leave—I just need to get it approved."

"Sweet!" I yelled, doing a little dance.

I loved it when everyone came to visit. We were all so spread out that it didn't happen often. The last time we'd all been together was Katie's thirtieth birthday party in San Diego almost a year before. This time, the only person missing would be Alex.

"Can I stay with you? I think Katie and Shane are staying at Aunt Liz and Uncle Mike's, but I don't want to stay with the 'rents."

"You're not bringing skanks to my house," I warned.

Henry started laughing. "Wouldn't dream of it as long as you don't give me shit for not coming home like my parents or Trev would."

"I can honestly say that I don't give two flying fucks where you sleep at night, Henry dear."

"Perfect."

I smiled at the relief in his voice. Oh, to be young, gorgeous, and single . . . wait. I was young, gorgeous—sort of—and single. I didn't feel that way though. I felt like I was forty-five.

"So Mom said you had surgery?" Henry asked, then paused. "Oh shit. I wasn't supposed to know, was I?"

"Christ, no, it's fine. I had to have a hysterectomy. It's all healed up, the end." I walked toward my bedroom.

"Wait, why? So you can't have kids, right?" Henry went silent again. "Motherfuck, Ani. That was a shitty thing to say."

"You're fine." I smiled sadly, sitting completely naked at the end of my bed. "No, I can't have kids. It is what it is though. No worries."

"Well, I've completely fucked up this entire conversation," Henry groaned. "When I stay at your house, you can shave one of my eyebrows off when I'm sleeping. Fair?"

"I was going to do that anyway," I said, wiping at my wet eyes. "It's the only reason I said you could stay."

"Me and you, Anita Bonita. We're going to party like its nineteen ninety-nine."

"Do you even remember nineteen ninety-nine?" I snorted, sliding beneath the covers on my bed.

"Yes." Pause. "A little." Pause. "Oh, shut the fuck up."

I started laughing while Henry grumbled.

"Let me know what day you'll be here and I'll make sure to get you a key," I said after I'd stopped laughing.

"Sounds good."

"I'm really glad you're coming up, dude. I miss you like crazy."

"Yeah me too. Should be fun to have the kids all together again."

"Except for Alex," I said, suddenly really missing my best friend.

"That's what he gets for joining the Army. Pussy."

"Don't be a dick," I ordered, smiling.

"Hey, you're not going to be bringing home guys from the bar either, right? I really don't want to hear that shit."

My mouth pulled up in a devious grin, and I had to bite my lip to keep from laughing. "What shit?" I asked innocently.

"Uh, you know." Henry cleared his throat uncomfortably. "Moans and shit."

"Oh!" I nodded my head even though he couldn't see me. "Like, *oh God, stranger from the bar, your dick is so huge. Oh, please, stick it in, stick it in!*" I made my voice as breathy as I could and finished off the sentence with a high-pitched moan.

"You. Are. A. Dick," Henry commented when I was done, every word enunciated like it was its own sentence.

"You're welcome."

"That's how you sound when you have sex?" he asked seriously. "I thought it would be hotter."

"Fuck you!" I laughed.

"I'll call you in a couple days and let you know when I get in."

"Get in," I snickered, making him chuckle, too.

"Bye, Bonita Anita."

"Bye, asshole."

I dropped the phone on the bed and snuggled farther underneath the blankets. It was nice to hear from Henry. He'd been such a cute kid when I met him. Fourteen and skinny as a rail, he'd been the only one in either of the families that was anywhere close to my size. He'd bulked up as he'd gotten older, but he was still pretty small compared to his brothers and cousins. He'd hit on me back then, so sure that he was smooth.

I'd shot him down faster than the words could come out of his mouth.

The little cutie-pie. I'd wanted to just reach out and pinch his cheeks, but I was pretty sure, if I'd done that, he would have died from mortification on the spot.

I sighed. I needed to go get him a key for the house—or maybe I'd just see if he could borrow Bram's, even though I was pretty sure Bram would say no. Take away his key and give it to absentminded Henry? No way in hell.

I hadn't seen Bram since he'd dropped me off the morning before, but I wasn't really concerned about it. I'd been busy napping and then working on my living room long into the night, before crashing and waking up early again to finish it up. Now that the walls were completely done, I needed to refinish the floor in there, and just the thought of it made me groan. I was so freaking tired.

I closed my eyes and relaxed into the bed. It was Sunday—I could nap if I wanted to.

* * *

"You waiting on me, gorgeous?" a soft voice whispered into my ear a few hours later, making me smile. *Bram.*

"I'm pretty sure the front door was locked," I replied drowsily, opening my eyes as Bram's body slid in behind me. His hand smoothed up my hip and around my belly as his body curled into mine.

"I have a key," he whispered in my ear, his fingers running lightly up my ribs and over my breast.

"I was really too trusting when I handed those out."

"Why you sleeping in the middle of the day?" he asked, ignoring my comment as his lips met my bare shoulder.

"Because I was tired?"

"Living room looks good. You got a lot done."

"Yeah, now I need to refinish the floors and finally put some furniture in there." My voice grew husky as Bram's fingers ran slowly down my torso and between my thighs.

"I'll do the floors," he argued gruffly, gripping my thigh to spread my legs wide, one resting over the top of his. "Look at you, wet already."

"Look at you, hard already," I teased back, pressing my ass against the very hard cock behind me.

"Shit, I was hard as soon as I saw you were naked," he said with a small laugh, reaching down between my legs to position himself.

I moaned deep in my throat as he slid slowly inside me from behind. As soon as he was buried to the root, he pushed my leg back down so my thighs were pressed tightly together. Then I breathed deeply through my nose as he began rolling his hips in a smooth, slow rhythm.

"There's the sleepy sex I wanted," he murmured against the side of my neck. "Feel good?"

"I've had better," I ground out as he ran a finger lightly around my nipple.

"No you haven't," he argued with a small chuckle.

I started to arch my back, and Bram's hand was immediately at my belly, stopping the movement.

"No. Just relax," he ordered.

"I don't want to relax," I replied, reaching up to clench his hair in my fingers.

"Shh. Close your eyes, Ani. Just let me get you there," he said sweetly, running his fingers up and down my belly.

I wanted to flip over and ride him into oblivion. The emotions clogging my chest were becoming really uncomfortable. Instead, I took a shuddering breath and relaxed my hand, letting it slide down to wrap around the side of his neck.

He rewarded me by slipping a finger between my tightly pressed-together legs, running it over my clit.

When my orgasm hit, it rolled over me in small waves, and it went on for freaking ever.

* * *

"I talked to Henry earlier," I said a while later, running my fingers through Bram's hair as I rested on his chest.

"Oh, yeah? What's he up to?" Bram asked, his arm wrapped around my shoulders and his fingers tickling my back softly.

"He said he's coming up with Katie and Shane, and

he wanted to know if he could stay here." I snorted. "He doesn't want to stay with Trev or his parents because he wants to whore it up."

"What? Why didn't he ask me?" Bram bitched, his fingers pausing on my back.

"I don't know—maybe because you're a dick and he doesn't want you running off his conquests?" I laughed and pulled Bram's hair lightly.

"I'm not a dick."

"You're *such* a dick." I laughed again.

"So he's gonna be bringing chicks here? That makes a lot of sense," he grumbled.

"Aw. Are your little feewings hurt?" I teased, leaning up so our faces were close together. "Are you sad your best fwiend didn't ask to stay with you?"

"I think my balls just shriveled up into my stomach when you started talking," he replied, grimacing.

"And no—he won't be bringing anyone here. He can fuck them at their houses," I said with a scowl. "I don't want that nasty at my house."

"He does realize that you have no fucking furniture, right?"

"Looks like we need to do the floors tomorrow so I can get a couch," I mused.

"Shit," Bram said under his breath. "I'll rent a sander tomorrow after work."

"I'll go with you. I need to buy the finish stuff anyway," I said, pulling away so I could climb off the bed.

I went to the kitchen and made some sandwiches, bringing them back into the room with a couple of sodas.

"Dinner is served," I announced, meeting Bram's eyes as he leaned back against my headboard.

"Stop," he blurted, his gaze roaming up and down my nakedness. "I think I'm having an out-of-body experience."

"Shut up."

"You're bringing me sandwiches. Naked. You might be the perfect woman."

"These sandwiches are mine, fuckface. Feed yourself," I replied as I climbed onto the bed.

"And the fantasy is gone," he replied sadly, then grunted as one of the sodas hit him in the stomach.

"I *am* the fantasy," I said as I got comfortable across from him, setting the plate full of sandwiches on the bed between us. "I'm bendy like an acrobat, cook like Julia fucking Child, and can do most home improvement shit myself. I'm the whole goddamn package."

"Yeah," Bram mumbled, grabbing a sandwich while he eyed me. "But you also know how to load and shoot a gun—that works against you."

I snorted and grabbed a sandwich for myself. "What do you think the kids would say if they saw us together like this?" I asked, biting into my sandwich.

"Katie would scream and dance around the room. Shane would walk away without saying anything. Henry would stare at your tits. Trevor would close his eyes and start trying to discuss the situation, and Alex would fucking high-five me," Bram said with no hesitation.

My mouth dropped open at his very accurate assessment. He was totally right. Katie would be excited as hell. Shane wouldn't want anything to do with the mess. Levelheaded Trev would try to make sense of what he was seeing. Henry wouldn't care except that he'd get to see me naked, and Alex would be stoked as hell that his two best friends were together.

"So you don't think Shane would want a good look first?" I asked after a minute.

"Of course he would," Bram said mockingly while shaking his head.

"He should be so lucky."

"Amen," Bram said, giving me a small smile. "So I'm thinking we'll get the sander and shit tomorrow—then we can take Tuesday off and get the floors done."

"I can't take any more time off," I answered, shaking my head. "I just took a whole week, not that long ago."

"I've got shit on Monday, but Tuesday's pretty clear. You're fine. It's one day."

"I can't, Bram," I argued.

"Yeah you can."

"No, really."

"No, really, you can. I'll tell Trev and the dads not to let you into the office on Tuesday."

"I'll junk-punch you."

"No you won't. You need me to help you with the floors."

Chapter 7
Abraham

Y ou're such a fucking pain in my ass," I barked, stomping toward where Anita was standing in front of the Harris and Evans Logging office Tuesday morning.

"They locked me out!" she shouted incredulously, pointing at the office door.

"I told you I'd meet you at your house."

"I told you I wasn't taking a day off work!" she screeched back.

"Looks like you don't have a choice."

"This is ridiculous," she bitched, shaking her head as she moved toward me. "Who forces their employee to take a day off?"

"You're also family," I reminded her, throwing an arm over her shoulder and steering her to my truck. "Come on, you can ride with me, and we'll get your car later."

I glanced up as she was climbing in the passenger seat, and noticed my dad at the glass front door, his arms crossed over his chest and a shit-eating grin on his face.

Crap. I narrowed my eyes at him and watched him laugh as I closed the door behind her.

"Thanks for doing this," Ani finally said after almost fifteen minutes of silence.

"No problem. Today would have been a slow day for me anyway."

"Exactly," she murmured as we came to a stop in front of her little house. "You could have had a slow day."

"You need the floor done, right?" I asked, turning off the truck but staying inside the cab.

"Yeah, but—"

"Well, let's get it done then."

Ani's eyes met mine, and her lips pulled into a shy smile. "You're good to me," she said softly. "When the hell did that happen?"

Her words made me squirm. Did she think we were in a relationship? It was sex. Fucking great sex, but nothing more than that. We didn't have a relationship; I didn't do relationships. The thought of anything long-term made my skin crawl.

"When you started letting me fuck you," I said with a nervous laugh.

I pretended I didn't see her smile fall as I climbed out of the truck.

* * *

We didn't talk much as I sanded the floor—the machine was too loud for that—but Ani stayed pretty close while I worked, using the smaller sander on the edges and corners of the room. By the time we were done, the room was covered in a fine layer of dust, and we were both sweaty as hell.

"You have the rags?" I asked as I came back in from dragging the sanders to my truck.

"Yep." She tossed me a rag and went to work, wiping down the walls and windows with her own blue rag.

The silence between us was uncomfortable as I dropped to my knees and started wiping down the floor. I wasn't sure what to say to get things back to the easy way they'd been before. Should I apologize? Somehow I thought that would make it worse.

It was a relief when Ani's phone started ringing in her pocket. I didn't even know her phone could ring—usually when it went off, it was someone's voice telling her to pick up the phone.

"Hello?" she answered behind me. She didn't say something for a long time after that, so I turned to check if she was still there.

Her head was bowed as she held the phone to her ear, but after a moment, she looked up, and her face was completely void of color. For a second, I thought she was going to tip over.

I got to my feet quickly, but before I could go to her, she started shaking her head and lifted one finger to ask me for a minute. When I nodded, she left the room.

I dropped back down to my knees and started wiping down the floor again. I had to make sure that all the dust was completely gone before we could put the finish on, or the entire floor would look like shit and we'd have to start over. My arms still felt numb from pushing that vibrating machine around the room, and I sure as fuck wasn't planning on doing that again anytime in the near future...at least not until Ani was ready to do the hallway and bedrooms.

Twenty minutes went by, and then thirty, and by the time Ani got back to the living room, I'd gone through three rags, and the floor was almost wiped clean.

"What's up?" I asked slowly, coming to my feet as she paused in the middle of the room.

"Uh." Her eyes searched blindly around the room, then finally came to rest on me. "My sister's having a baby," she said, shaking her head.

"What? Kate?" I asked in confusion.

"No, my real sister."

I almost argued about that statement but decided that was a conversation for a different time. "You have a sister?"

"Yeah." She reached up and scratched at her hair with both hands, making it stand straight up in some places. "She's fifteen."

My stomach rolled. "Oh, fuck."

"I have two little brothers too," she went on. "All still live with my mom. She got her act together, at least enough that CPS didn't step in with them."

"Jesus Christ." That had to fucking *kill* her. Alex and I had never dealt with that kind of family shit. Our mom had died when we were little, hit by a car when she was walking to work one day. It sucked big time, but we hadn't been taken from her, she'd been taken from us.

"So yeah, fifteen and having a baby. Mom's doing a fucking bang-up job. Obviously."

I took a step toward her but froze when she held up a hand to stop me.

"I need a shower," Ani muttered after a minute, looking down at her clothes. "So do you."

She turned and left the room, peeling off the tank top she was wearing as she hit the hallway. "You coming?" she called over her shoulder as she paused to shove her jeans down over her ass.

"You wanna talk about it?" I asked after I'd stripped and climbed into the shower behind her.

"Not especially." She wasn't crying, but her eyes seemed almost blank as she grabbed a bar of soap and lathered her hands.

"You sure?"

"Yeah, it is what it is," she said, reaching forward to run her soapy hands over my forearms.

"I didn't know you had siblings," I said quietly as her hands moved to my chest.

"Yeah, I found my mom when I turned eighteen. It was stupid to even look for her nasty ass—but I found out then that she'd had more kids. I keep in touch with Bethy and the boys, but they live in Seattle."

My breath caught as her fingers moved farther down my chest, and I reached out to push her wet hair out of her face. I didn't say anything because I had no fucking idea what I was supposed to say to that.

"They have *B* names," she scoffed, lifting her hands from my chest and turning to face the spray. "I'm Anita, and they're Bethy, Ben, and Brayden." She shook her head, her shoulders so tight they were practically pressed up against her ears. "The second wave. Her second goddamn chance—and she still fucked it up."

I couldn't stand it anymore. She looked so small with her arms crossed over her chest in the spray of water, her back curved inward enough that I could count every vertebra up her back. I reached around her and pressed my hand to her smooth belly, pulling her back against me.

"It's a good thing you got out then, yeah?" I whispered into her ear, wrapping my other arm around her chest. "She didn't get any better. You're the lucky one."

"Yeah," she replied hoarsely, resting her chin on my arm as her body relaxed into mine. "But if I had been there, I could have watched out for them—"

"You were a kid, Ani—you couldn't have done shit," I said flatly.

"She's fifteen, Bram." Ani sniffled, her whole body shuddering. "Jesus."

"Come here," I ordered, turning her in my arms so I could see her face.

Her eyes were red and so was her nose, but she wasn't crying. She was keeping it together for some reason, even though I'd seen her bawling her eyes out before.

"You got out, baby," I said gently, watching as her eyes closed and her chin dropped. "You're feeling guilty for something you couldn't control. You know how many kids wanna go back to their piece-of-shit parents? But it's not up to them and it wasn't up to you. That wasn't your choice to make."

"She started over again," Ani choked out. "Like, 'oh,

fucked up with the first one, better try again.' Who does that?"

My throat knotted around any words I might have said. How long had she been feeling like that and saying nothing? Had she talked to Katie about it? Alex? I wasn't sure if anyone even *knew* that she had younger siblings. I'd never heard anything about them.

"Pieces of shit," I finally ground out, cupping her face in my hands. "Look at me."

She opened her eyes and almost brought me to my knees with one look.

"It's her loss. I know that sounds too simplistic. I know that." I brushed her hair away from her face as I struggled to speak. "She lost out *big* with you, all right?"

Ani nodded and pressed her lips together tightly like she was holding in the words that wanted to pour out of her mouth.

I leaned down and kissed her gently, running my lips over her stiff ones until they softened against mine. Running my hands down her neck, I stopped at her shoulders, pressing my fingers in lightly until the muscles beneath her skin began to relax a little at a time.

"You don't have to be nice to me," Ani murmured against my lips as I crowded her against the wall, running my hands over her breasts as she slid her tongue over my top lip, then sucked it into her mouth.

I pulled back slightly. "Yeah, I do."

"I'm already a sure thing," she argued, wrapping her arms around my neck and lifting one leg so that I'd pull her up my body.

"I'll be a dick to you later," I assured her as her legs tightened around my waist.

"But what if I want your dick now?" she said with a small laugh against my mouth.

"If you insist," I grumbled jokingly. "You good?"

"Fine," she said with a nod, like our entire conversation since we'd jumped into the shower had never happened.

* * *

"What the fuck are you doing here?" I yelled in surprise a week later, opening my front door in nothing but a pair of white boxer briefs and a huge grin.

"Thought I'd surprise you. You're welcome."

I took a couple steps back and let my brother inside, barely waiting for him to drop his bag on the floor before I was wrapping him up in a bear hug.

"It's good to see you," I said gruffly, slapping him hard on the back.

"Yeah, you too, brother," he replied, tightening his arms around me. "You look like Grizzly Adams."

We both pulled back at the same time, and I got a good look at the grin that looked so much like the one I knew I was wearing.

"All the kids together again," I said with a laugh, picking up his bag so I could carry it into my spare bedroom.

"That was the idea," he said with a nod, following me farther into the house.

"How the fuck did you get here? I woulda picked you up from the airport."

"And miss the look on your face when you came to the door? No fucking way. I rented a car."

I smiled as I opened up the spare room and tossed his bag on the bed.

Thank Christ, Ani had already left before Alex showed up on my doorstep. We'd seen each other almost every day for the past week, but she hadn't stayed over and neither had I. She was dealing with some shit, so I left her to it, even though I'd gotten a little used to the overnights.

"How long are you here for?" I asked as we made our way back to the kitchen, grabbing a couple beers from the fridge.

"Week. I couldn't take more than that."

"Katie, Shane, and the kids will be here in the morning. Henry too."

"Yeah, I bet Mom's flipping out, huh?"

"Jesus Christ, she's gonna have a heart attack when she sees you," I joked, grabbing my T-shirt that Ani had left on the counter earlier and pulling it over my head.

"You start cooking in the buff since I've been gone?" Alex joked as he watched me.

"Nah, took it off earlier before I got in the shower," I muttered, turning to grab a dish towel from the counter and putting it on the handle of the stove.

I knew, if he got a good look at my face, he'd know I was lying and he'd start asking questions, and if he started asking questions, I'd be fucked. Why the hell hadn't I thought of that before? Alex knew me better than anyone—he was going to see exactly what was happening the minute Ani and I got in the same room.

Fuck.

"So I can't decide if I want to show up before Katie tomorrow so Mom can calm down before she and the kids get there or if I should show up right after she gets there and steal her thunder," Alex said seriously, taking a long pull of his beer.

I met his eyes as I took a drink of my own.

"Steal her thunder," we both said at the same time, bursting into laughter.

God, I was glad he was home.

* * *

"I was wondering why the fuck Henry was staying with Ani instead of me," I blurted, shaking my head a couple hours later and seven beers in.

"Aw, did it hurt your feelings?" Alex asked with a grin, lying back on my couch with his bare feet propped on the coffee table. That was almost exactly the same thing Ani had said. God, sometimes they were so alike it was uncanny. Like they shared a brain.

Though most of the time I thought Alex was funny and Ani was a bitch.

"It didn't hurt my feelings, asshole," I replied, making Alex laugh. "It was just weird."

"Eh, they're buds. I'm not surprised," Alex said with a wave of his hand. "I am surprised she had room for him— how far is she on the house?"

I shook my head and relaxed farther into my recliner, grabbing a new beer off the floor. "Not far. I helped her get the floors finished in the living room so she could buy a couch for him to sleep on."

"I have no fucking idea how she's lived there for so long with only bedroom furniture," Alex said with a small laugh.

"She's got her TV and shit in her room so she just hangs out in there," I replied without thinking.

"Oh yeah? You've been hanging out in Ani's room?" Alex joked, watching me closely.

"Yeah," I deadpanned, my palms going clammy. "I go over there to watch TV while she sucks me off."

Alex froze for a minute, then broke out in gut-busting laughter. "The only way Ani would put your balls in her mouth is if she'd already cut them off and was planning on eating them," he choked out, his face turning red from laughing so hard.

I snorted like I knew he expected me to, but couldn't stop the memory of Ani during a seriously good blow job the day before. My balls had definitely been in her mouth at one point. My dick hardened in the sweatpants I'd grabbed earlier when we came into the living room.

"Shit, I'm beat. I'm gonna head up," Alex said as he finished laughing. "Wake me up in the morning?"

"Yeah, no problem."

I locked up the house and cleaned up the beer bottles before following Alex upstairs. He was already snoring through the closed doorway to the spare room, and I couldn't help but smile.

I loved it when Alex was home. He was literally my other half. The better half. When our mom died, he was

the only thing I'd had to hold on to in a drastically changing world. I may have been the tougher twin, but he'd
always been the strongest. Where I jumped to conclusions
and went off half-cocked, Alex was slower to react. He
watched and waited, covering up his feelings with humor
until he was ready to let loose.

Few saw the serious side of Alex. He rarely showed anyone the guy who worried over his sister and parents almost
maniacally. They didn't see him angry. They rarely saw
him quiet.

Alex was the life of the party—always—and he planned
it that way. Sure, his personality was a pretty cheerful one,
but no one was in that great of a mood all the time. Other
people didn't notice but I always knew.

I could read him as well as he read me.

I stripped naked and climbed into bed, bracing my
hands behind my head as I stared up at the ceiling.

I loved that Alex was home, but it freaked me the fuck
out, too. He'd see shit that the rest of my family didn't.
My fingers itched to pick up the phone and text Ani not
to come over, but I knew that was ridiculous.

She wasn't going to show up at my house after she'd
already left for the night. It wouldn't happen. But still,
my stomach churned with anxiety as I lay there in bed. I
didn't want to ruin the surprise for her, but I sure as fuck
didn't want her accidentally telling the entire family that
we were fucking like bunnies.

My heart thumped hard as I thought about what Alex's
reaction would be to the fact that Ani and I were sleeping
together. I'd told Ani that he would high-five me, but I

knew even while I was saying it that it was far from the truth.

Alex would be livid.

He knew me.

He'd know what it was.

And he'd be pissed as fuck that I was screwing Ani with absolutely no intention of being in any type of relationship with her.

Chapter 8

Anita

Holy shit, she's huge!" I called, running toward the front of Dan and Liz's house and the woman standing there with a toddler in her arms.

I'd successfully avoided having any type of conversation with Dan since he'd lost it on me at family dinner, and I'd timed my arrival perfectly so that I wouldn't be alone with him before Katie and Shane showed up with the kids. I was kind of a genius that way.

"Language," Katie sang as I wrapped my arms around her and Iris, leaning down to give Iris a kiss on the back of her head. The one-year-old hadn't seen me in months and had no idea who I was, so she was hiding her face in Katie's neck.

"You look good, dude!" I said, taking a step back so I could look at her.

She was wearing a pair of brightly colored leggings with flip-flops and a tunic, her hair in a bun on top of her head and long, dangly earrings hanging from her ears. Comfortable but gorgeous, as usual.

"Yeah, yeah," she griped, shaking her head. "My ass is still huge."

"Turn around," I ordered.

She turned her back toward me and shook her booty as she looked at me over her shoulder. "See? Huge."

"It is pretty massive," I replied, nodding my head while she scoffed. "But dudes dig chicks with ass. No joke. Tits and ass is a thing. Fat-bottomed girls and all that."

"You're lucky that's a Queen song or I'd punch you," she laughed as she turned toward the driveway. "Oh! Bram's here!"

I swallowed hard as she began to wave at the truck pulling up the driveway.

I'd barely seen Bram except to fuck him for the last week. After his confusing signals the day we'd worked on the living room floor, I'd been keeping my distance. I wasn't sure what to make of his sweet words followed by his standoffishness. It kept happening, so I decided to pull back a bit so he could figure his shit out.

We were circling each other, Bram and I. Pushing together and then, when things got a little too serious, pulling apart again.

"That mother-effer!" Katie hissed beside me, covering Iris's ear with her palm.

"What?" I turned toward the truck, and my heart turned over in my chest.

Bram was climbing out the driver's side, and Alex was dropping down from the passenger seat.

"Alex!" I screamed, jumping off the porch and running full tilt toward him.

"Surprise," he called with a huge-ass smile on his face just as I jumped him.

"I can't believe you didn't tell me you were coming!" I yelled, hitting his arm before hugging him tightly.

It was an odd thing, hugging your lover's twin. His body was really similar to Bram's, though their muscles were made from different kinds of work and were shaped differently as a result. His voice was really close to Bram's, and Alex's smile was almost identical even without the beard.

I'd never mix the two of them up though, even with the physical similarities.

Alex didn't smell the same. He wore cologne. He didn't smell like deodorant and sawdust and the outdoors like Bram did. He didn't breathe in the same cadence as Bram, or move his hands the same way.

He'd never made my heart race or my nipples pebble.

As much as I loved Alex, he just didn't do it for me.

"You asshole!" Katie screeched, making me turn my head as she charged toward us. She must have set Iris inside because the baby wasn't with her as she ran down the steps. "You stole my thunder!"

Alex set me down and pushed me to the side since it seemed as though Kate wasn't going to stop running at us.

Bram caught me as I stumbled, squeezing my hips hard before quickly letting go. Yeah, we were going to have to be careful while everyone was home because that small touch had lit me up in a way that I knew would be easy to notice.

"Alexander?" Liz called from the front door as Katie tried her hardest to wrestle Alex to the ground.

"I'm going to hurt you," Kate announced as Alex laughed, moving defensively against her but never over-powering her the way I knew he could.

"Aren't you happy to see me, Katiebear?" he asked through his chuckles.

"Oh, fuck you!" she sniped at his teasing, curving her fingers in a way that warned me of the epic pinch she was going to land somewhere on his body.

"Jesus, you've turned into a psycho!" he yelped as her fingers made contact.

He jerked her arms out to the side, then bent at the waist, throwing her over his shoulder.

"Put me down!" Kate yelled, kicking her feet.

"Nope," Alex answered. Then he took a few steps away from the truck and started to turn.

"Oh, shit," I said to Bram, my own laughter coming to a stop.

"Yeah."

"I'm going to puke!" Kate yelled as Alex began spinning in the middle of the driveway with Kate over his shoulder. She'd been kicking her legs at one point, but she'd frozen completely when he began to move, and now the only thing on her body that wasn't holding on for dear life was her long, auburn hair.

"Knock it off, you two!" Liz yelled, coming down the front steps. "I swear, you act like you're twelve years old."

"She started it!" Alex yelled, coming to a stop and stumbling slightly.

"Put her down before you fall down," Kate's husband Shane ordered from the porch.

I felt Bram stiffen next to me as I glanced at the porch and noticed everyone in the house had made their way outside.

Alex and Katie were both finally laughing, and I felt a grin tug at the corners of my mouth just as I caught sight of my niece and nephews milling around on the porch.

"Your auntie is here!" I announced loudly, stepping away from Bram. "Come to me, minions!"

Keller let out a war whoop as he jumped down the stairs and ran for me, Gavin and Sage following closely behind him with shouts of their own. Damn, I loved those kids.

They hit me hard in a tangle of arms and legs, and I felt Bram behind me once again to steady me on my feet.

"I missed you guys!" I laughed as all the kids started talking at once, telling me about the airplane and school and a million different other things. "We're missing a couple." I glanced at the porch where Dan was holding Iris. "Where's Gunner?"

"He fell asleep on Grandma's couch," Sage said with a roll of her eyes.

"Well, we better not wake him up," I said seriously with a wicked smile on my face.

"Don't you dare," Kate warned, coming up behind me to throw an arm over my shoulders. "He's been up since five this morning. If he doesn't nap, I'm sending him home with you."

We made our way into the group of family, and Henry

pulled me into a hug as the kids raced off to God knew where.

"No dramatic hello for me, Anita Bonita?" he asked, wrapping his arms around my waist and lifting me into the air. "I'm hurt."

"Aw. I missed you too, Hen," I mocked, nodding my head. "I missed you most."

"Damn right, you did." Henry smacked my ass and let me down as I met Bram's angry eyes over his shoulder.

"Hey, now. None of that," Alex ordered, pulling me into his side. "We all know Ani missed me most."

"Nuh uh!" Keller yelled as we went into the house. "She missed me the most!"

Gunner started crying from the couch.

"Son of a bitch," Katie said under her breath, glancing at Shane before going to pick up their wailing son.

I laughed hard as chaos reigned around me.

* * *

"Stop staring at me," I hissed at Bram hours later as we unloaded stacks of soda out of the back of Aunt Ellie's SUV.

"I'm not staring at you," he argued, stacking up four cases and lifting them into his arms.

"Uh, yeah. You are," I argued quietly as I picked up another case.

"Why the hell is Henry all over you?" he asked, making my eyes grow wide.

"What? What the hell are you talking about?"

"He had his hands on your ass."

"That's probably the seventy-millionth time he's slapped my ass since I met him," I replied incredulously. "He slaps everyone's ass!"

Bram glared at me and opened his mouth to reply, then snapped it shut again as Alex came around the side of the house.

"At each other's throats again? Jesus," Alex said jokingly. "Why don't you just fuck already and get that shit out of your systems?"

My body completely froze, and beside me Bram dropped four cases of soda at our feet.

"Oh, no fucking way," Alex breathed, looking back and forth between us. "You didn't."

I couldn't make myself deny it. My tongue felt too thick in my mouth, and I knew my eyes were wide as saucers.

"You're an idiot," Bram finally replied, leaning down to grab the soda cans that were busted and fizzing and probably completely unsalvageable.

"You fucked Ani?" Alex asked incredulously.

"Hey!" I hissed, offended.

"No offense."

"Your tone was pretty fucking offensive!"

"Oh, my tone was offensive?" Alex asked, his jaw tightening. "My tone was offensive but you letting Bram fuck you, even though he can't stand you, isn't?"

My jaw dropped as hurt seemed to seep into my skin.

Before I could reply, Bram's fist was sailing out and clipping Alex on the jaw, causing him to stumble back a few steps.

"This was fun," I said woodenly, gripping the case of soda still in my arms.

I turned on my heel and walked toward the house, my entire body singing with humiliation.

"Ani, you know I didn't—" Alex's words cut off, but I didn't turn around to see why.

"Oh, good, you got the soda. We never buy any at home, and I've been craving it all day," Kate called out as I made my way in the back door.

She was standing in the kitchen making sandwiches, and I could hear the rest of the family in the living room talking loudly over one another as they caught up.

"I fucked Bram," I said baldly, setting the case on the kitchen counter.

Kate almost dropped the butter knife in her hand and scrambled to catch it.

"Say again?" she asked, looking at me like I had two heads.

"I fucked Bram. A lot. All over his house...and my house. A lot—"

"Yeah, I get it," she cut me off, her face pulled up in disgust.

"Alex just figured it out, and he has a big fucking mouth, so I'm telling you before he does." I nodded once for emphasis.

"Why the hell would you sleep with Bram?" she hissed, glancing over my shoulder to make sure no one was eavesdropping.

"Because he's sexy." I shrugged nonchalantly, hiding the way my skin crawled over our conversation. "And because he's got a big—"

"Ew! Jesus, Ani!"

"So now you know," I said, opening up the soda and carrying it to the fridge. We would have had to use the cooler for all of it, but since Bram had essentially ruined four cases with his butterfingers, we'd have room in the fridge.

"So are you guys together now? Why didn't anyone tell me?"

"We're not together," I replied before she could start dreaming up fairy tales in her head.

"What?" she said, her voice growing hard.

"Leave it, Katie. We're not together."

"But—"

"Did I give you shit when Shane was fucking you around?"

"Yes."

"Exactly." I ignored her affirmative answer. "So drop it."

I finished unloading the soda in the bottom of the fridge and got to my feet as Kate stared at me.

"Ani—" Bram called as he stomped in the back door. His eyes met Kate's for one second, and that's all it took. "Motherfuck," he hissed, turning to me. "Thought we weren't spreading that shit around."

"It's Katie," I argued dully.

"And we fucking agreed—"

"Alex was going to tell her anyway!" I said, wrapping my arms around my waist as he glared at me.

"I just spent the last ten minutes talking Alex into keeping his fucking mouth shut!"

"Charming," Katie drawled, snapping our attention to

where she was watching our conversation with a pissed look on her face. "It's a secret then?"

"Yes," Bram said immediately, while I bit the inside of my cheek.

"Why, Bram?" Kate needled snidely. "You doing something you shouldn't be?"

I inhaled sharply at her tone.

"Don't act like I'm the asshole here—"

"If the boot fits," Kate cut in.

"—we both agreed we were going to keep it quiet."

"It's fine, Katiebear," I said, setting my hand on her back as she grew even more worked up. "We both agreed that we weren't going to tell anyone."

"That's bullshit," she argued. "I'm your best friend—"

"It's just sex." I shrugged.

"Well, what if you got pregnant or something? It's never *just* sex—"

"Not sure how I could knock her up when she's missing most of her parts," Bram said snidely.

I closed my eyes in defeat and dropped my chin to my chest.

"Oh, fuck," Bram muttered quietly into the suddenly silent room.

"What?" Kate asked in confusion beside me.

"Ani—" Bram called, his voice dripping with apology.

"It's nothing. I finally had the hysterectomy," I said, opening my eyes and waving my hands in front of me. "Go me!"

"You did?" Kate breathed, her eyes filling with tears. "Why didn't you say anything?"

"That," I said sharply, pointing to her eyes, which had begun to overflow. "That's the reason. It's fine, Katie. I'm fine. Stop crying."

Kate's mouth trembled as she searched my gaze, then her breath hitched as she pulled me toward her, wrapping her arms around my neck and pulling my face into her shoulder.

I shuddered as I felt my own tears rise to the surface. *This* was why I hadn't told her. She made me weak when I wanted to be strong, because I couldn't hide from her. Kate knew just by looking at me what I was feeling, and she wouldn't let me brazen my way through acting like the whole thing wasn't a big deal.

It was a big deal, and she knew it. She wouldn't pretend like it wasn't.

"I'm so sorry, Ani," she whispered into my ear. "That sucks."

"I'm fine."

"I'm still sorry."

"I know."

She held me close for another minute, and when she let me go, Liz and Ellie were standing in the doorway and Bram was gone.

"So you finally told her," Liz said with a small smile, swatting us as she pushed by us to get to the fridge. "Good. We don't need secrets in this family."

I looked up, meeting Kate's narrowed eyes, and barely held back the nervous laugh that was bubbling up inside me.

* * *

"Look, I got you a pretty new couch to sleep on," I announced later that night, leading Henry into my house.

"Aw, I hate *pullouts*," Henry complained jokingly.

"Wear a condom and you don't have to," I said back, making him laugh. "Sorry, I don't have any other furniture, and there's no TV out here."

"No problem, I'll probably just crash here anyway. I've got plans with Trev and the 'rents pretty much every day."

"Oh good. I didn't want you all up in my shit all the time anyway," I mumbled.

"Aw, don't worry, Anita Bonita. I'll have plenty of time for you," he shot back, ruffling my hair as he passed me. "We'll go out this week and hit the bar. I won't be up in your shit...unless you're into anal."

"Shut the fuck up," I choked on a laugh.

"No really, I'd be down for anal."

"Not happening."

"My heart is broken."

"I'm going to break your dick in a minute."

Henry cupped his junk in his hands in fear. "Fine, no anal."

"Jesus," I muttered, shaking my head as I moved toward the kitchen. "You want a beer?"

"Sure," he called back as he riffled around in his bag. "Where's your—"

His words cut off as someone started knocking on my door.

"Who the hell is that?" I asked, even though I didn't

expect him to answer. I carried the two open beer bottles to the front door and swung it open.

"For me? Thanks," Alex said as he stepped in my front door, snagging a beer out of my hand. "Love what you've done with the place."

"What are you doing here?" I blustered as Bram followed him inside, taking the second beer from my hands.

"What the fuck?" Bram snarled as he moved past me.

"What?" I spun around as I closed the door and saw Henry standing naked in my living room. "Are you out of your fucking mind?" I screamed, covering my eyes.

"I was getting fucking pajama pants on! *You're welcome!*" Henry yelled back.

"Dude. No one wants to see your baby junk," Alex laughed.

"You couldn't change in the bathroom?" I practically screeched with my hands still covering my eyes.

"You were getting beer. I thought I had time to change real quick," Henry snapped back. "You can uncover your face, asshole."

"Seriously? You couldn't even keep underwear on?" I sniped as I dropped my hands, very aware of the way Bram was glaring as he chugged the beer he'd stolen out of my hand.

"I don't wear underwear," Henry said flatly.

"Oh, hell," Alex gasped, his face getting redder and redder as he laughed. "This shit just keeps getting better."

"Fuck all of you. I'm going to bed." I threw my hands in the air and stormed to my room. I really hadn't wanted to see Henry's closely shaved blond pubic hair or frank and beans. If I'd had any inkling that I was going to have to deal with that shit, I would have told him he couldn't stay with me. I shuddered.

Before I could slam the door to my room, making my point even more firmly, Bram was pushing in behind me and closing us in.

"What are you doing?" I asked incredulously as he pushed us farther into the room. "Henry doesn't know, jackass."

"He's about to," Bram replied roughly, pushing his hands into my hair.

"Uh, no," I muttered, dodging his lips.

"What, you won't kiss me now?"

"Not when you're being a jackass," I mocked. "Henry was being Henry—this jealousy bullshit is misplaced."

"Jealousy?" Bram barked out a laugh. "Henry's hung like a twelve-year-old."

"Actually—"

"You really don't want to finish that sentence," he said darkly.

I scoffed. Stupid boys and their appendages. It was all ridiculous.

"I've been with you all day," Bram said in annoyance, tightening his hands in my hair. "And I haven't been able to touch you once."

My entire body seemed to soften at his words.

"Oh," I sighed, reaching up to rest my hands on his forearms.

"The kids know—"

"I'm sorry I didn't realize that you'd keep Alex quiet," I apologized, grimacing.

"—so I'm staying the night."

"Wait, what?"

His mouth covered mine, and I groaned as my hands slid off his arms and went straight to the bottom of his shirt, sliding under it so I could feel the soft, warm skin of his stomach.

"You're so fucking sexy," he said against my lips as my fingers found his nipples, making him shudder.

I lifted my arms above my head so he could pull off my T-shirt, and before the fabric had even hit the floor, my bra was gone, too.

"I hate it when you wear a bra," he grumbled, making me giggle.

"T-shirts require a bra—even for me," I informed him as he tore off his own T-shirt.

"Bullshit," he argued with a grin. Then he tackled me to the bed, making me laugh. "You're missing a few things," he said suddenly, pulling his face from mine.

"What?" I looked down at my bare chest and denim-covered legs.

"This," he murmured, tickling my nose as he pulled my septum ring down until it was visible. "And this." He slid a finger into my mouth, rubbing it over my tongue, his hips jerking as I sucked.

"Tongue ring is in my purse," I said after he'd pulled his finger away. "In the living room."

Bram paused for a second, then a small smile pulled at his lips as he yanked me off the bed. Before I knew what he was doing, his T-shirt was being pulled over my head and my jeans were whisked down my legs.

"Now go get it," Bram ordered, his gaze roaming up my body and pausing at my hard nipples beneath the thin cotton.

"Are you serious?"

"I wanna feel that ring tonight," he said huskily, making my stomach clench in need.

"Okay," I whispered back.

I took a deep breath and opened my bedroom door as Bram started unbuttoning his jeans. *Jesus, he was hot.*

As quietly as I could, I walked out into the living room, where Alex and Henry were spread out on the sofa bed drinking my beer and chatting. I was hoping to make it to the entryway where I'd left my purse without notice, but Alex caught me sneaking by and a wicked grin spread over his face.

"Nice shirt," Alex called out, catching Henry's attention.

"Good color on you," Henry said, nodding his head.

"The white T-shirt is 'in' this season," Alex agreed, tilting his head to the side like he was trying to get the perfect angle.

"Is this an invitation?" Henry asked with a completely straight face. "I'll come to the party."

I gritted my teeth at their teasing and crouched down carefully at my purse, fishing through the side pocket for my tongue ring. As soon as it was in my hand, I raised it to my mouth and secured it on my tongue.

"No," I said huskily, rising as I turned back toward

them. "Bram just asked me to put in my tongue ring." I shrugged and stuck out my tongue, making their eyes widen. "He likes it on his dick."

Both guys groaned as I laughed.

"I think she just schooled us," I heard Alex say from the living room as I got to my bedroom doorway.

"I think I just came," Henry bitched back.

I giggled, glancing behind me as a strong hand reached through the doorway and pulled me inside.

* * *

"Shit," I murmured groggily the next morning as my phone rang on the nightstand table.

"Whose phone is that?" A voice startled me from the floor, making me jerk back into Bram's warm body.

"What the hell?" I asked, leaning over the bed to find Alex and Henry asleep on my floor.

"It was cold in your living room," Alex mumbled, turning his head away from my glare. "You need new windows."

I just got new windows. *Ugh.* My phone stopped ringing, then started up again.

"Hello?" I answered quietly. I didn't want to wake Bram up, but I was naked under the blankets. There was no way I was going to get out of bed before Thing One and Thing Two left the room.

"Anita?" a woman's voice asked.

"Yep. This is her. Who's this?"

"Hey, um, it's Beth. Bethy. Your sister?"

I stopped breathing.

"Yeah, Bethy. I know who you are, kid. What's up?"

I hadn't talked to her since my birth mom had called to tell me Bethy was pregnant, and I so badly wanted to rip her a new one for being so stupid—but I didn't. The milk was spilled at that point. The only thing left to do was try and clean it up.

Bram's hand slid around my waist as he sleepily curled closer, his palm resting on my stomach.

"Well, um, Mom told you that I'm pregnant, right?" she asked tentatively.

"Yeah, dude. She did." *Why the fuck didn't you make him put on a condom?*

"Well, I'm almost due. You know, with the baby." Her last words were sort of muffled, and in that moment, I fully understood how very young and immature my fifteen-year-old sister was.

"Oh, yeah?" I asked, wondering where she was going with the conversation. I sent presents to her and my brothers on their birthdays and Christmas, and I tried to call at least once every couple months but none of them had ever called me.

"I-was-wondering-if-you-could-take-it," she rushed out.

She said it so fast that, for a moment, I didn't understand the words, but when I did, my world narrowed down to just me and the phone in my hand.

"What?" I rasped out.

"I was hoping you could adopt it."

"What?"

"Stop saying 'what.' Just tell me no if you don't want to," she snapped. "I can find someone else."

"I—" I swallowed hard. "You dropped a bomb here. Can I have a second to process?"

"I need to know soon. I'm due in two weeks so it could be coming out at any time. Someone needs to be here to take it home." She sounded so detached from the whole thing that it made my stomach churn with nausea. It? She kept calling the baby *it*.

"Can I call you back?" I asked, pressing my fingertips to my forehead as my head started to ache.

"Yeah, let me know."

She hung up without saying good-bye and before I could ask any more questions.

"Who was that?" Bram asked, his beard brushing my shoulder as he kissed it softly.

"My little sister," I replied, relaxing as he pulled me tighter against him.

"The one that's having a baby?"

"Yeah." I rested my hand on his and changed the subject. "Do you know that Alex and Hen are on the floor?"

"Yeah, idiots came in after you passed out last night, drunk as shit and freezing. Told them they could sleep on the floor." His sleep-roughened voice was amused, and I couldn't help the way my lips twitched in response.

"I hope you kept me covered up," I whispered lightly.

"Yeah." His hand smoothed up my torso and crossed over my chest, his forearm hiding one breast and his hand covering the other. "Like this," he chuckled. "You sleep hot so, when they came in the door, the blankets were pushed down to our waists."

"Great," I mumbled, making his body shake with laughter.

"They didn't see anything," he whispered, kissing my ear softly, then taking the lobe between his lips. "Wish they'd wake up and get out so I could fuck you."

"Henry! Alexander!" I yelled loudly, making Bram jerk behind me and the guys on the floor moan. "Get the fuck up and get the fuck out!"

Bram laughed as Henry pushed himself up on his hands and knees, crawling out of the bedroom and dragging his blanket with him.

"Go ahead. We're brothers. I'll just pretend I'm not here," Alex said, pushing his head farther into the throw pillow he was sleeping on.

Bram laughed harder.

"Not going to happen!" I yelled again, making Alex's hand fly to cover his ear. "Get out!"

"Assholes," Alex hissed, climbing to his feet and stomping out of the room, slamming the door behind him.

"Problem solved," I murmured as Bram's hips rolled against my ass.

My stomach was still in knots over the phone call with my sister, but I wasn't going to get any thinking done with my house full of hungover men. Instead, I closed my eyes and arched my neck as Bram's fingers pinched my nipple, then moved farther south. Then my mind went completely blank.

Chapter 9
Abraham

Y ou good?" I murmured to Ani, setting my hand at the base of her spine.

"Yeah, just taking it all in," she replied with a small smile as she looked around the room.

We were standing in my parents' dining room, watching as our family crowded in around the table. Shane and Katie's big kids were setting out silverware and drinking glasses while the little ones got set up in their high chairs. Alex was arguing with Trevor about something, and the longer he talked, the madder Trevor got, while Henry watched in amusement. Shane was helping Katie with the kids, following her around like a puppy while all the grandparents watched, talking amongst themselves while they got to their seats.

"Nice having everyone home," I said with a nod, rubbing my thumb back and forth over her soft tank top.

"Yeah...loud," she said with a laugh.

"Why don't you go get a seat? You want a beer?" I asked, giving her a little push.

"Yeah, Hef if they have it, soda if they don't," she replied with a wink over her shoulder as she stepped away from me.

I walked through the kitchen and out the back door to the cooler on the back porch, and that's where my mom cornered me. I knew it was coming, but I was still startled when I turned around and she was standing behind me.

"You and Ani?" she asked, raising one eyebrow.

I'd done a lot of thinking over the past couple of days. When we'd spent that first day at my parents' when everyone had just gotten into town, I'd been nervous as fuck that someone was going to pick up on what was going down between me and Ani. I'd been like a fucking long-tailed cat in a room full of rocking chairs.

But when Alex had actually figured it out? I was oddly relieved.

As one by one the kids had figured out what was going on, I felt more and more comfortable—which surprised the hell out of me. I hadn't wanted anyone to know. I honestly hadn't. The pressure of that was a little too much to deal with when we were nothing but fuck buddies.

But over the past few days, I'd liked being able to touch her when people were around. I *liked* going out to the bar with Ani and my siblings and cousins, being able to kiss her when I wanted and knowing that she was headed home with me when she was shitty drunk and bouncing off the walls.

But I'd known that the parents were going to pick up on the difference between us, and I wasn't wrong. Now I was going to hear about it.

"Yeah," I said quietly, scratching at my beard. I glanced at my mom out of the corner of my eye as she laughed softly.

"You know, people have *always* read you and Alex wrong," she said with a shake of her head. "I probably did too, for about twenty minutes or so." She laughed again, stepping under my armpit to wrap her arms around my waist as we looked over the backyard.

"Alex is so outgoing. He's a people pleaser, no doubt about it," she said with a fond smile. "And you're so quiet. You bluster and bang around like you're pissed at everything."

I grunted. Yeah, I'd heard all the comparisons before.

"So it's not surprising that people assume Alex cares what they think." I looked at her in surprise as she squeezed my waist. "He doesn't. He doesn't give two shits what anyone else thinks. You, though? You've always cared—maybe too much."

"Mom—"

"Zip it, Abraham," she scolded. "You, my son, have always worried far more than your brother did about what Dad and I thought. Ever since you were little."

"Yeah, probably," I said hoarsely.

"No probably about it. But when Dad and I took you in? You were ours from that moment. Didn't matter what you did or said, we were in it for the long haul no matter what came. You need to remember that—it's an absolute truth."

"Okay—"

"And Ani?" Mom cut me off. "She's a lot like you.

Oh, I know she's rough around the edges. Growing up the way she did made sure of that. But she cares what we think, she worries about how we perceive her. Hell, she's had her tongue pierced and that god-awful thing in her nose for ages, and she's still trying to hide it." Mom chuckled. "Bottom line—we don't care if you two are together. You didn't grow up side by side. Ani came to us as practically an adult already. Your relationship with her is your business."

"Thanks, Mom."

"But Abraham?"

"Yeah?"

"Something goes wrong with you two?" she said as she pulled away and moved toward the back door. "You don't bring that shit to my table, you hear me?"

"I hear you."

Mom left me on the back porch, staring at the beer in my hands. That had gone a lot easier than I'd envisioned.

I set the warming beers back in the cooler and grabbed a couple new ones to take inside.

"All good?" Alex asked as he passed me on his way to get drinks.

"Yep."

I found Ani sitting with an empty chair beside her and grinned as I sat down. I was pretty sure Alex had been sitting there before I came in. He was going to be irritated as shit to sit between Gavin and my aunt Ellie in the only spot left. Gavin couldn't keep his food on his plate, and Aunt Ellie kept asking Alex when he was going to find a nice girl.

"Your brother's going to kill you," Ani said with a smile as I set her beer in front of her.

When she looked at me, my tongue got stuck to the roof of my mouth. Shit, she was pretty. Her hair was crazy around her face, and she wasn't wearing any makeup since we were only having family dinner before we headed back to her place. She wasn't even showing any skin in the concert T-shirt she was wearing. But shit, was she pretty.

Ani went still as I leaned forward and raised my hand, gently nudging her septum ring down until it hung beneath her nose.

"Bram," she said quietly, her eyes darting around the table as my thumb swept over her cheek.

I leaned closer.

"They already know it's there, baby," I teased, watching her eyes grow wide. "Might as well flaunt it."

I kissed her softly.

I knew then that something had shifted. Hell, I'd known it the minute Henry slapped her ass and I'd wanted to choke him to death with his own hands.

Even if I said it a thousand times, I wasn't just fucking Ani. It never could have been that, and I was an idiot for assuming it could. Our lives were intertwined. I cared too much before we'd started sleeping together. There was no way I was going to be able to shut that off once I'd been inside her.

We liked the same things. Liked each other. There wouldn't be any talk of kids or pressure to move her into my place when she had her own cool-as-fuck house. She was pretty much perfect for me, and knowing that was almost a relief. I could stop fighting it. My body actually relaxed at the thought.

"We're together, yeah?" I asked, leaning my forehead against hers.

"I think once we started sleeping in the same bed most nights, we were together," she replied quietly.

"I'm a little slow on the uptake."

"That's okay." She wrinkled her nose and grinned at me, and my stomach flipped.

"Gross, Uncle Bram!" Keller yelled as I leaned in to kiss her again.

The table grew loud as everyone dug into their dinners. Fifteen conversations were going on at once, but I could barely pay attention to any of them because Ani's hand was resting on my thigh underneath the table. She wasn't trying to turn me on—she wouldn't do that in my parents' house—it was more of a comfort thing.

She finally had permission to touch me whenever she wanted, and she was using it.

"Ani, I think your phone's ringing," Alex called from down the table. "Did you leave it in the kitchen?"

"Oh shit," Ani mumbled, her hand sliding off my leg as she jumped to her feet. "Sorry, I have to get that."

She left the room, and conversation started up again at the table, but I couldn't focus. Who was calling her on the weekend? Everyone she talked to was already here. I watched the door, but it was almost twenty minutes before she came back in, looking completely shell-shocked.

"Ani?" my Aunt Ellie asked as I got slowly to my feet.

"What's wrong?" Kate got up from her seat as well.

"Uh..." Ani looked around the table, then stopped with her eyes on my mom. "I'm going to be a mom."

"What?" my mom whispered as she pushed herself up out of her seat.

"I'm adopting a baby." Ani's eyes watered as her face broke out in the biggest grin I'd ever seen, and everyone surged up from their places at the table and started talking all at once.

They were asking her the specifics, when she was getting the baby, who the baby was, and how it happened.

All I could do was stand there, my fingers clenching against the edge of the table as I watched her, white noise filling my head.

It was over. Jesus Christ, it had just started, and it was already fucking over.

And I was such a fucking idiot for letting any of it happen in the first place.

* * *

Dinner after that was filled with talk of Ani's new baby.

A fucking baby.

What the hell was she thinking?

I knew from bits and pieces of her conversations with the people around the table that she was going to take her sister's kid in. Apparently the girl had called Ani and asked her if she could, then called back a few hours later demanding an answer.

So many things could go wrong.

Ani's hand fell lightly into my lap again, and I didn't move it. My mom had asked me to keep our shit from her table less than an hour before, and I'd told her that I would.

I didn't want to.

I wanted to drag Ani out of the house and fucking shake her.

That kid could come out with a whole host of medical problems. Her little sister could change her fucking mind. The baby's dad could step in and say he wanted it. If she did this, she'd never escape her birth mother. She'd always be there in the goddamn wings, reminding Ani of how she'd thrown her own daughter away.

It was the most ridiculous plan I'd ever heard in my life, and I was practically vibrating with the need to start laughing as the shit show at the dinner table played out.

She didn't even know if it was a boy or girl. Her house was a fucking disaster. She had zero experience with taking care of a baby and had a goddamn full-time job.

"Hey, you okay?" Ani asked, turning to me as my brother and Shane started clearing the table. Her eyes were shining, and she couldn't seem to keep a smile off her face.

"Fine," I answered with a nod, clearing my throat. What the hell was I supposed to say?

"I think I'm going to head home," she said with an overwhelmed sigh. "Oh shit. I rode with Alex."

"It's all right, I'll take you," I said, the words flowing out of my mouth before I could change my mind.

"Ani," my dad called as we stood from the table and started saying our good-byes. "You clean out a bedroom. Me and Dan'll bring all the boys by tomorrow and get it finished up for you."

"Are you sure?" Ani stuttered through her words. "It needs to be painted and the floors done and everything."

"Well, we'll get the walls done tomorrow. Come back the next day for the floors," Uncle Dan piped in with a smile.

"Okay," Ani said, her voice high. "That would be rad. Thank you."

I ushered her out of the house before they could waylay her with anything else. I needed to get the fuck out of there before I blew. Now I had to go to her house for the next two days to prepare for a baby that I thought was a really fucking bad idea? There was no way my dad and Uncle Dan would let me out of it without giving me a huge ration of shit. I clenched my teeth hard as we climbed in my truck and drove back to Ani's place.

I'd talk her out of it once we were alone and she wasn't surrounded by offers of help and congratulations.

"Hey," Ani called as I rounded the hood of my truck, jumping into my arms like a spider monkey. "I don't know if being able to touch each other during family events is any better than not touching," she said with a small laugh. "I've wanted you all day."

She leaned in to kiss me, and I inhaled deeply. She always smelled so good. I'd miss that.

"Let's get inside," I said gruffly, grabbing ahold of her ass so I could walk us to the front door. "Keys?"

As soon as we were inside, it was like the floodgates opened.

Ani danced around the house, cleaning up Henry's mess from that morning and racing around to pick up random dish towels and shoes. She was talking about the baby—some shit about her sister and how soon she'd go into labor—but I swear to God I barely heard a word she said.

She was so happy. I'd never seen her so bubbly and excited, and I hated that I was going to have to stop all that. When I finally couldn't keep my mouth shut any longer, I grabbed her by the hand and wrapped an arm around her waist.

"You really think this is a good idea?" I blurted out, no buildup whatsoever.

"What?" Ani laughed nervously, pulling away from me. "What do you mean?"

"This whole—" I threw my arm out to the side. "—baby thing."

"Do I think it's a good idea?" she asked incredulously. "Uh, yeah. Or I wouldn't be doing it."

She took a couple steps away from me, and I clenched my hands into fists at my sides.

"You're just going to take in some baby that you know nothing about? Just like that? No thinking it over or planning ahead?"

"It'll be a newborn, Bram," she said slowly. "No one knows anything about it yet."

"What if your sister's a cokehead?"

"That's a shitty thing to say."

"She got pregnant at what, fourteen years old?"

"You are such a dick!" she hissed. "Sometimes I forget that, and then you open your mouth and I'm reminded all over again."

"Oh, I'm a dick?"

"How is this even any of your business?" she shot back, crossing her arms over her chest.

"I'm your man!" I yelled, so fucking frustrated I wanted to pull my hair out. I'd been listening to baby shit for over two hours, and I was done. "You didn't say shit to me about this, and then you're just announcing it at the fucking dinner table?"

"I just found out today!" she yelled back. "And when she asked me, you were still maintaining the illusion that we weren't in a relationship!"

"What, so now I'm supposed to play daddy to your kid?"

"I didn't expect you to do anything," she said quietly, her face twisting into a grimace. "Don't worry, Bram, Maury says you are *not* the father."

"This is so fucking insane," I ground out, shaking my head. I ran my hands through my beard and then up over my head. "The whole reason we started hooking up was because I could fuck you without having to deal with baby drama."

I knew the words were shitty the minute they rolled off my tongue, but I had no chance to take them back.

"Get out," she whispered, her voice cracking. "Get the fuck out of my house."

"That came out—"

"Get out of my house, Abraham," she said a little louder.

I stared at her for a long moment, wondering what the fuck I could do to make her change her mind. We were good—just the two of us. At least for as long as whatever it was between us lasted. We had fun together. Made each other laugh. Got into fights and made up between the sheets. She was the best lay I'd ever had.

A baby would change all that.

Chapter 10

Anita

Henry came flying in the door less than ten minutes after Bram left my house. I was still standing in the center of the room, my arms wrapped around my chest and my heart racing. But I wasn't crying. I wouldn't.

"Honey, I'm home!" Henry called out cheerfully as he saw me. "Where's Bram, little mama?"

Hen's face fell when I didn't immediately answer him.

"Anita Bonita?" he said gently. "Where's Abraham?"

"He left," I said with a humorless laugh, shrugging my shoulders. "He's not ready to play the Mike to my Carol."

"What?"

"Brady Bunch reference," I said distractedly, walking toward my hallway. "Obviously."

"Right," Henry said slowly. "Not sure how I missed that one."

The bedrooms in my house were tiny. At one point, there had been four and a bathroom, but sometime in the

'70s, the previous owners had remodeled the front two bedrooms into a master with a connected second bathroom. So I only had two bedrooms to choose from for the baby's room.

I knew without even looking which bedroom I would choose. It was bright, with two tall windows that I'd have to get child locks for at some point, and was directly across from my bedroom. There was no closet, but I didn't think that really mattered. If he or she needed one at some point, I knew Trev would help me frame one in. He was good with shit like that.

I wondered what Trev thought about me adopting a baby. He'd been kind of quiet lately, and he hadn't even discussed the whole Bram scenario with me yet—but I knew he would. As soon as we had a chance to talk without fifteen people butting in, he'd corner me.

"This one, huh?" Henry asked, stepping into the room behind me. I'd forgotten he was even in the house as I'd looked around the baby's room, imagining where I would put everything. "Cool windows."

"I know, right?" I said, smiling up at him.

"So...you wanna talk about it?" he murmured, glancing down at me.

"Not even a little bit."

"You want to drink beer and clean out this room and *not* talk about it?"

"Yes, please."

"Then I'll go get beer." He wrapped a clumsy arm around my head and kissed the top of it before ambling back out of the room.

I took a deep breath and let it out slowly, trying to form a game plan in my head for clearing out the room—but I couldn't. I couldn't think about anything except the way Bram had stared at me incredulously as I'd made the baby announcement earlier that night. The way he'd picked apart the decision, echoing my own thoughts with every word out of his mouth.

He was right. I didn't know if the baby would have health problems. Adopting a baby from a family member was a huge gamble normally, and it was even more of a gamble when you took my history into account. I was jumping into something and I had no clue how far I'd fall. I was terrified.

But this was my chance. The chance I'd never thought I'd have. I had to take it.

* * *

I was up and ready early the next morning as the guys started showing up at my house. I'd already sent Hen to get some donuts and coffee, so we were all set to get painting as soon as I'd actually bought the paint.

"Uh, we overlooked a small detail," I said to Dan as he hugged me hello. "I don't have any paint."

"I figured that," he said with a chuckle, patting me on the back. "The rest of 'em will start taping off around the walls while we head in and get some. You know what you want?"

"I have no idea."

"Well, you've got about ten minutes to figure it out."

I grabbed my purse off the table and followed Dan out to his truck just as Bram was parking in front of my house.

What the hell was he doing there?

He looked good, wearing a ratty old gray T-shirt and blue jeans with holes in the knees. Work clothes. The kind of work where you knew you were going to get messy so you put on the oldest shit you owned. I swallowed hard, running my gaze from his messy hair covered in a baseball cap to the worn boots on his feet. As he turned toward me, I jerked my head to the side and hurried to the passenger door of Dan's truck.

Dan didn't seem to notice his son was there so I climbed into the cab of his truck and didn't mention it as we pulled away from the curb. I'd deal with Bram...later. Much later. Just looking at him hurt at the moment, and I wasn't about to let that show.

"Wanted to apologize to you for yelling, but I didn't have the chance until now," Dan said as we pulled up in front of the local hardware store. "Didn't mean to scare you or make you feel bad."

"No." I shrugged off his words, extremely uncomfortable with the conversation. I thought I'd gotten away with never talking about that day with him, but apparently Dan had a good memory. "It's fine. I'd forgotten about it."

"All right," he said with a small nod, shutting off his truck and hopping out.

See, that's what I dug about Dan. His wife could talk the ear off a statue, but Dan was more reserved. He didn't push for answers or nag to get what he wanted. If I said we were fine, he took that at face value and let the subject drop. Thank God.

I'd been on emotional overload for the past twenty-four hours, and I wasn't sure how much more I could take.

It was weird. I'd been spending so much time with Bram that, even though I was super pissed at him for being such a jackass, I still wanted to text him a picture of the paint swatches I'd found and ask for his opinion. I'd gotten used to discussing shit with him. Nothing life altering, but small things. What I should get for dinner. Where I should get my oil changed. If he thought a bug bite on my thigh was from a mosquito or a deadly spider.

"I like the green," Dan said quietly beside me, somehow sensing my complete indecision.

"You think?"

"Yep. Went with yellow when we had Katie—back then you didn't know what you were having until they came out—and her room was damn near blinding." He laughed. "Green's better. Works for a boy or girl."

"Yeah, okay." I nodded in relief. "We'll get the green then."

We were back at the house with my freshly mixed paint within twenty minutes, and by then the entire family had descended like a pack of wild dogs.

"Let's get painting," Dan said with a smile as he parked behind my Toyota.

* * *

"You're here!" Katie yelled as we walked back in the house.

"Well, I live here. We considered heading for the border but decided against it. Painting's easier than living on the lam," I replied drily, making Dan chuckle.

"Okay, well the boys are all ready to paint so we're going to leave them to it and go get furniture!" Kate said excitedly, throwing her purse over her shoulder. "Shane's got all the kids at my parents' house. I have the whole day!"

"Uh—" Frankly, I'd rather paint.

"No arguing," Liz ordered, coming down my hallway. "Take that bandana off your head, and let's go."

I reached up and pulled my painting bandana from my hair. "Okay, well I need to show them where the trim paint is. I figured we'd just use the stuff left over from the living room. It's white, so—"

"Bram already got it out," Kate said cheerfully. "Let's go!"

I gritted my teeth at the sound of his name.

I let them usher me out of the house without argument. It wasn't like I'd wanted to spend the day with Bram anyway. Hopefully the guys would be done by the time we got back.

* * *

For as much as I'd dreaded the shopping trip, by the end of the first hour at Ikea, I was as excited as Katie. We'd found a crib and a changing table that were thankfully much less expensive than I'd been imagining, and I'd let Aunt Ellie and Liz pick out a bunch of small stuff like towels and baby spoons.

"You're not paying," I argued with Liz as she pulled out a credit card. "No way."

"Well, you didn't get a baby shower so this is my gift," she said with a sunny smile, swiping the card before I could stop her.

"I can pay for this stuff," I said in exasperation as Katie pulled out a reusable bag from her purse and started loading up the purchases.

"I know you can," Liz huffed. "I'd kick Dan's ass if you couldn't."

I snorted. She wouldn't need to be kicking anyone's ass. Dan and Mike paid me well over what any of my office manager counterparts were making. I'd argued when I first started, but they hadn't budged, and each year they gave me a cost-of-living raise that was way more than average.

"Okay, now we need to go get a car seat, diapers, clothes, and stuff like that," Kate announced as we walked the big cart out to the truck. "Sound good?"

I looked at my phone to check the time. The guys were going to be at my house for hours still, and the thought of seeing Bram made my stomach knot up.

"Yep. Sounds good to me."

"Since we don't know if the baby's a boy or girl yet, I figured we could just buy some gender-neutral stuff— just enough to get you guys home from the hospital,"

Aunt Ellie said with a grunt as we lifted the box of crib parts into the truck bed. "We can get you more clothes and things after we know."

"Good idea." I nodded my head.

"Have you thought of any names?" Liz asked as she closed the tailgate and we walked around to our doors.

Names? *Shit.*

I hadn't even thought about it. Whenever I thought of the baby, I still considered it Bethy's. I'd unconsciously assumed that she would name the baby, and I guess there was a chance she still might.

But I was adopting the baby. I would be his or her parent forever. If I wanted to pick a different name, I could do that.

"I hadn't really thought about it," I said as I buckled up. "I guess I probably should."

"Do you have any ideas?" Katie asked, checking her phone and then stuffing it back in her purse.

"Not really."

"Well, I think you should use an *A* name," she said, dropping her purse on the floorboard as Liz pulled the truck out of the parking lot. "Since you and Abraham are both *A* names."

"Katie." I drew out her name, sighing. "Bram's not a part of this."

"Of course he is. You guys are together and—" she argued.

"He doesn't *want* to be a part of this," I said flatly, cutting her off. "So it's just me, okay?"

The inside of the truck went completely silent, letting

me know that Liz and Ellie had been listening to our conversation.

"You'll do just fine on your own," Liz said with a nod. "Bram or no Bram, you'll do just fine."

"Thanks, Mom," I said with a small smile.

"Hell, Mike didn't help with our boys until they were about ten, and we didn't even deal with the baby stage. All our boys were older when they came to us," Ellie grumbled, making us all laugh.

"Dan was pretty good," Liz murmured, her lips tipping up.

"Shane didn't help at all until Iris came along," Katie scoffed. "I mean, I'm not sure how much he helped Rachel, but I don't think it was much."

Rachel was Shane's first wife, and when she died in a car accident a couple years before, Kate had stepped in to help with the kiddos, and the rest was history. They were crazy about each other.

"I'm a little nervous about going to work," I said, leaning back in my seat.

"I'll keep him or her," Liz said immediately. "I mean, if you want me to."

"Really?"

"Of course! I'm not doing anything but crafting and going places with Ellie. I can take the baby with me."

"God, what a relief. I wasn't sure what the hell I was going to do."

"Well, you wouldn't have had to worry about it for a while yet—you'll be on maternity leave for at least six weeks."

"What?" I asked, sitting straight back up.

"Mike and Dan decided already," Ellie warned, turning to look at me over the seat. "You'll get the six weeks—paid. If you want more than that, you'll have to discuss it with them."

"Just because you're not carrying the baby doesn't mean you shouldn't get the six weeks, Ani," Katie said with a roll of her eyes. "Just wait. You're going to be exhausted. You'll be up all night and tired all day, and you'll have this little person begging for attention all the time."

I couldn't stop the smile that spread across my face. I couldn't freaking wait.

* * *

The next two weeks went by in a blur.

Katie, Shane, Henry, and all the kids went back home to California.

The guys finished up the baby's bedroom, and it looked incredible.

Alex went back to Missouri.

I worked like crazy to get ahead of the game before I took time off.

Life was going pretty well, and there seemed to be this thick layer of anticipation in the air, but when I'd crawl into bed at night, my entire body ached.

I missed Bram more than I'd ever thought possible.

We saw each other at work, of course, and at family dinners, but we barely spoke. Not even to argue. It was as if he'd completely forgotten I existed. I told myself that we were being adults about the whole thing. That this was how adults dealt with their breakups.

It sounded like bullshit every time I said it in my head.

I couldn't understand what happened. No, that wasn't true. I understood it. Bram didn't want kids. He'd never wanted kids.

And now that I was about to have one, he no longer wanted me.

I was a mess of emotions every single minute of every day. I was angry, then sad, then determined, then sad again. I wondered if I was doing the right thing—if I should have told Bram about the baby before I'd announced it to everyone. If it would have even mattered when I told him.

I missed Bram so badly that it made me nauseous.

But I refused to cry about it. Instead, I stomped down the anger and hurt until it festered like a sickness in my stomach.

Having a family was my dream for as long as I could remember. It was something that would be distinctly mine. A family that I could mold and lead in the exact opposite way my mother had. When I'd agreed to the hysterectomy, that dream seemed dead but I hadn't let myself mourn it. I'd pushed it deep down into the recesses of my mind and carried on. Just like I did with everything else that I'd lost. Just like I was doing with Bram.

Growing up in the system meant that I rarely had anything that belonged to me alone. Sure, I had a backpack full of stuff that I'd managed to take from home to home until I'd aged out, but the bedrooms I'd lived in were never decorated especially for me. I'd never had my own bike. My clothes had always been hand-me-downs, and my coats almost always came from the coat drives that a mattress store in Portland had every year.

When I grew up, I knew that I would never live like that again. That's why I'd bought a house instead of renting one. Why I'd paid for my car in cash once I'd saved up enough money. Why I didn't shop at thrift stores or vintage shops.

I shook my head as I climbed out of my Toyota, stretching my arms up high. I'd been working long hours to make sure everything was ready for the temp to come in, and I was tired as hell. I'd been talking to Bethy almost every day, and it seemed like she'd be having the baby soon, which meant that I slept so light waiting for a phone call that, when I woke up in the morning, I didn't even feel rested.

My phone rang in my front shirt pocket, and I almost dropped it on the pavement as I scrambled to answer it.

"Hello," I said, disappointed.

"Sorry, I know you're waiting for a call," Trevor said, chuckling. "Just wondering if you wanted some company. I'll make dinner."

"If you're cooking, you can come over anytime," I answered, smiling as I walked to the front door.

"Okay, good. I'm here."

I turned as Trevor's truck pulled in behind me and parked.

"You ass!" I called out, laughing as he climbed down from the cab. "What if I'd said no?"

"You'd never say no to dinner," he called back with a smug smile.

I unlocked the door while Trev unloaded the groceries, then left it open behind me as I went into the house.

I'd been trying to get things fixed up as much as I could, and the entire place was looking better than it had since I'd bought it. Furniture and a baby swing in the living room, a table and chairs I'd found on clearance in the kitchen, and baby paraphernalia anywhere I could store it.

It finally looked like a home instead of somewhere I crashed when I had nothing else going on.

"Place is looking good," Trev said, echoing my thoughts as I followed him into the kitchen.

"Thanks. It's a work in progress."

"Who knew getting a baby would put a fire under your ass?"

"Who knew I'd ever have a baby?" I chuckled.

"Eh, I knew you would eventually," he said quietly, emptying ingredients for tacos all over my countertop. "Wasn't sure how you'd do it, but I knew you would."

"Really?" I asked in surprise, grabbing a soda out for each of us. "I didn't."

Trev nodded, pulling out the ground beef and a frying pan. "Tunes?"

"Sure." I turned on the stereo on my kitchen counter.

"So, yeah," Trev said. "I always figured you'd be a mom. Get me a spatula? You love kids, and you've always said you wanted a family."

"Yeah, but after this hysterectomy stuff—"

"There's more than one way to skin a cat."

"Ew!" My face twisted. "Why the fuck would anyone skin a cat?"

"Shut up," Trev chuckled. "Adoption is a good choice."

I was silent for a few moments. "Did you ever look for your parents?"

Trev glanced at me in surprise. "You worried about that? Wait. Get a knife. You can help me cut shit up while I'm spilling my guts."

He set me up with a couple tomatoes and a cutting board before going back to browning the meat. "Yes," he said with a slow nod. "When I was nineteen, I looked them up. I probably shouldn't have."

I glanced at him but didn't say anything.

"My dad was fine. Had a family with his wife and wasn't interested in anything I had to say."

"Ouch," I replied, slicing through a tomato.

"Eh. I got it. I have parents." He shrugged. "I didn't need him for anything, more just curious, you know?"

I nodded.

"My mom was dead."

"Oh, shit." The knife in my hand slipped, nearly taking off the end of my finger.

"Whoa, careful," Trev warned. "Yeah, she overdosed when I was fourteen."

"Do you ever wish—" I stuttered, shaking my head. "I feel like I'm stealing their baby or something."

"Seriously?" he asked incredulously.

"I don't know. It's just—she's my little sister. Like,

what if this isn't what she wants to do and I become this monster that takes her baby?"

"She called you, right?" he asked, draining a can of olives.

"Yeah."

"And the dad is out of the picture?"

"No, I think he's around. But he's like sixteen."

"Look, you have to—" He paused as if gathering his thoughts. "She came to you, Ani. She wants you to raise her baby because she's not ready to do it herself. That doesn't make you the bad guy. That makes you the lucky guy."

"Yeah, I guess."

"The baby isn't going to resent you," he said gently, draining the hamburger grease into the empty olive can. "Being adopted—shit. At first, yeah, maybe you might get into fights with him. Okay? Like around thirteen when he wants to go shoot paintball but he got a bad grade so he's grounded. He's going to say shit that breaks your heart. But underneath all that? You *chose* him, Ani. He wasn't an accident or a mistake. You actually chose to take him in and make him yours. He'll know that."

"Did you do that stuff?" I asked, my eyes watering.

"I was an asshole," he said with a snicker. "But probably not as bad as Henry."

"I'm just nervous."

"I think that's probably normal."

"What if she changes her mind?" I murmured, sticking some tortillas into the microwave.

"Then you won't be a mom yet. Yet, Ani. Because you will be. If not this baby, then the next one. Or maybe you'll adopt a five-year-old. Who knows? But you'll have a family. I'm sure of that."

"Thanks, Trev." I smiled at him and grabbed a couple plates out of a cupboard.

Trevor always seemed to get to the heart of the matter, but he didn't bullshit me. He never had. When I talked to him, I always had the feeling that he was going to tell me something I didn't want to hear, but by the end of the conversation, I'd feel better about whatever we'd talked about.

"So, Bram," he said as we sat down at my new table.

"Shit, I'm going to need booze for this," I bitched, standing up to get us a couple beers out of the fridge.

"What happened?" he asked as I sat back down.

"He doesn't want kids," I answered simply.

"And?"

"And he dropped me when I said that I was adopting Bethy's baby."

"That's it?"

"That's it," I replied with a nod. "He hasn't talked to me in two weeks."

"What an idiot."

I just shrugged my shoulders. It was what it was. Did I want to be with Bram? Yes. Did I want to be with Bram if he had one foot out the door? No way in hell.

"Are you hoping he changes his mind?" Trev asked, watching me closely.

"Do you think he will?" I asked, holding my breath. *Maybe I should hold out. Maybe I should—*

"I don't think so, sweetheart," Trev said gently, making

the air rush out of my lungs in a whoosh. "Bram's always said he didn't want kids. He's adamant about it."

"Yeah," I said under my breath, fiddling with the taco that was falling apart on my plate.

"I know that Katie waited for Shane," Trev said, leaning forward to rest his elbows on the table. "And it worked out for them. But I'm not sure that waiting for Bram to get his head out of his ass will ever give you the results you want."

"It's okay to not want kids," I murmured, not meeting Trevor's eyes. "Lots of people don't want kids."

"True," Trev said, nodding. "But Bram's good with kids. He likes kids. His absolute refusal to ever even discuss having some of his own just doesn't fit. Not that I think he'll change his mind. I just think there's probably more going on there than just not being interested in being a parent."

"Why didn't you become a shrink?" I asked teasingly. "You seem to notice shit other people wouldn't think twice about."

"I like playing with wood," he teased back, flexing one large bicep.

"Yeah, *your* wood," I snickered.

"That too."

I laughed hard at the smirk on his face.

"You'll do good, Ani," he said after my laughter had died down.

"Yeah. I got this," I replied with a nod.

That night, as I lay in my bed, I put my thoughts of Bram to rest. Trevor was right. He was always right.

For whatever reason, Bram didn't want kids, and I did. Eventually, it would have come down to that fact, and we would have broken up anyway. I was lucky that I hadn't been in any deeper with him.

At least that's what I told myself.

And I kept telling myself that for the next three days as I passed him in our small office every day at work. Our breakup had been inevitable.

I almost believed it.

Chapter 11
Abraham

I was drunk.

Again.

I knew that I should be out doing something. Hell, it would have been less pathetic if I were out at the bar getting drunk, but I wasn't. I was sitting on my leather couch in front of the TV, drinking beer like it was water.

My phone started ringing somewhere in between the cushions, but I ignored it. I was too lazy to search for the damn thing. I breathed a sigh of annoyance when it stopped ringing and then started up again. I didn't look away from the TV or set my beer down as I pushed my other hand into the cushions, finally dragging the phone out.

"Hello, Alexander," I answered.

"Why aren't you answering your phone?" my twin bitched.

"I just did."

"I've been calling you for two days."

"What's up?" I grabbed the remote and shut the TV off, leaning my head back on the couch.

"Look, I was giving you time to get your shit together—"

"What shit?" I cut in.

"I know you and Ani broke up. Hard not to notice that shit when I was there—but I thought you'd have fixed it by now."

"Nothing to fix," I replied, digging my fingers into my eye sockets. Shit, I was tired.

"She loves you—"

"No she doesn't. It wasn't like that."

"And you love her, you idiot."

"Nope."

"Stop being an asshole," Alex snapped.

"Did you seriously call me to bust my balls? Because I'm in the middle of something."

"I know you're sitting on the couch watching reality TV and drinking beer," Alex said drily, making me sit up and look blearily around the house. *How the hell?*

"Actually, I'm at the bar," I argued, sitting up straighter.

"No you're not," Alex scoffed.

"What do you need, Alex?" I said, pushing myself to my feet. I needed to get to bed. I was tired as hell. Who knew that avoiding your office manager was so much fucking work?

"You're being an idiot," Alex said, sighing. "Why are you so hell-bent on not having kids?"

"Just don't want them," I mumbled, trudging up the stairs to my room.

"Really? That's your answer?"

"That's all I've got."

"And you're willing to give up Ani so you don't have to have any?" he asked gently.

"It's already done, brother," I told him, stripping out of my jeans and crawling into bed.

"You'd be a really great dad, Bram. You know that, right?"

"Probably not, but that's irreverent—irrevelant—irrelevant."

"Jesus Christ, you're plastered."

"Had a few beers," I slurred, starting to fall asleep.

"She's not going to wait for you, man. The longer you wait, the less chance you have of getting her back."

"Don't want her back."

"Bullshit," Alex growled in frustration. "I'm not talking to you like this. Call me when you're fucking sober."

"All right, good talk," I said, tossing the phone on the bed before completely passing out.

* * *

"Good morning, good morning!" Trevor called cheerfully the next day as I was climbing out of my truck. My head was pounding, even after three ibuprofen, so I shut my door carefully, wincing as Trevor slammed his.

"Hey," I said quietly, scratching at my beard.

"Rough morning?"

"Late night."

"Oh, yeah? Where'd you go?" Trev asked as he walked beside me to the front door of our office.

"Bar in town."

"Oh, yeah?" he chuckled, looking at me sideways. He went in the office ahead of me and I cursed under my breath. I didn't need Trevor putting in his two cents, too. I vaguely remembered the conversation with Alex the night before, and he'd been all up in my business, I didn't need any more bullshit.

"I was in Portland," I called as I stepped in behind him. "That's why you didn't—"

My words cut off sharply as Trev turned toward me, and I caught sight of Ani.

She looked good. She looked so goddamn beautiful.

Her short hair was pulled back in two tiny pigtails by her neck, and she was wearing a light blue shirt that clung in all the right places.

"Hey, Bram," she said. "You look like shit."

"You look gorgeous," I replied without thought, my mouth snapping shut as soon as the words were out. *Fuck.*

"She does," Trev said, smirking. "New haircut?"

"Shut up, Trev," Ani replied, elbowing him in the gut.

"I've got shit to do," I said, moving around them to get to my office.

"Hey, Bram?" Her voice was tentative, and I hated it. Ani was bitchy. She didn't take anyone's shit, and she was never fucking nervous.

"What's up?" I asked, turning as Trevor passed me, giving me a slap on the shoulder.

"It doesn't have to be weird," Ani said, a little of her attitude showing as she put her hands on her hips. "You're making it weird."

"I'm making it weird?" Yeah, I was making it weird. I hadn't had sex in two weeks, and even as she spoke, I was imagining how I'd bend her over the desk and pull her jeans over her ass so I could fuck her from behind. I wasn't sure how I could ever not be weird around her when I knew I'd never fuck her again no matter how many times I imagined it.

"Yeah. You can talk to me, you know. Say hi, fuck you, where's my paperwork from the mill, *anything.*"

"I don't want kids—" I blurted, making her eyes narrow.

"Are you shitting me right now—"

"But if I did, they'd be with you," I finished quietly, making her shoulders slump.

"That doesn't really mean anything," she snapped. "God, what the fuck is wrong with you?"

"I just wanted you to know—"

"What, Bram?" she said sharply. "You just wanted me to know that you love me? Is that what this is?"

I opened my mouth to speak, but nothing came out. Did I love her? Probably. I'd probably loved her before we'd ever started sleeping together.

"It doesn't fucking *matter,*" she hissed, dropping her hands to her sides. "I have a baby waiting to be born. Okay? I'm adopting a baby, and that's not changing. So I *will* be a parent. The end."

"Ani," I murmured as she reached up to wipe at her face.

"Stop it," she cried. "Just stop, okay? You made me choose, and I didn't choose you."

I rocked back on my heels, feeling like I'd been punched in the chest.

"Can we just be friends?" she said tiredly, shaking her head. "Can we just—I don't know. I just want to go back to normal."

"So sniping at each other over dinner and bitching at each other at work?" I asked, my entire body tightening as she wrapped her arms around herself.

"Yeah, Bram."

"Fine." I spun and walked toward my office without another word.

What had I expected, that she'd just change her mind because I loved her? I hadn't even said it, she had.

I'd never thought about loving Ani. It had never been a conscious decision that I'd made. Somehow it had morphed into that though. I'd always cared about her, and it probably would have taken months for me to figure out if we hadn't stopped seeing each other. But now that I didn't have her? I knew I loved her.

Shit.

I sat down at my desk and tried to focus on the bids in front of me.

"Hey, Bram?" Ani called softly from the door to my office an hour later.

Her face looked like she'd been crying, and I had to fist my hands on my lap to keep from rounding the desk to get to her.

"Yeah?" I asked, my heart thumping hard in my chest.

"If"—she drew out the word, looking down at her feet before her eyes rose to me again—"if you changed your mind?" She bit the inside of her cheek and I wanted her to stop. Just stop what she was doing.

I didn't want to see her like that. Begging. I didn't want her fucking humbling herself in front of me. I broke up with her. If I decided to grovel, that's what I should do, but it pissed me off that she was acting like every other woman I'd ever known. Making herself weaker for me. *No.*

"Stop talking," I ordered, getting to my feet. My anger was irrational and overwhelming.

"If you wanted to change your mind, I'd—"

"Get the fuck out of my office," I yelled, the words burning my throat.

A sob left her as she startled, and her eyes met mine for just a second before she ran. A few seconds later, I heard the bells ring as she completely left the building.

"You stupid motherfucker," Trevor hissed as I dropped back down into my chair, staring blankly at the papers on my desk.

"Get out of here, Trev," I mumbled, reaching up to smooth my beard.

"She just—"

"I mean it, Trev. Get the fuck out of here."

"You don't deserve her, you fucking prick," Trevor snarled, stepping farther into my office. "I get it, man! You don't want kids. Fucking good for you."

"I'm not doing this with you," I warned, pushing to my feet again.

"*Ani* just came in here, handing you another chance, practically begging—"

"You think I want her begging?" I bellowed, my chest heaving.

"You want her!" Trev yelled back, looking at me like I was an idiot. "What the fuck are you so afraid of?"

"I don't want kids!"

"Nice excuse, fucker. Now why don't you cut the bullshit?"

"I'm done," I said quietly, shaking my head. I reached forward and scooped the paperwork on my desk into a pile, stuffing it back into a file folder.

"Ani's not like Kate," Trev said after a moment.

"Obviously."

"Kate gave Shane a million chances, and thankfully he finally got his shit together."

"What's your fucking point?" I snapped, picking up my thermos and wallet from my desk drawer.

"Ani just gave you another chance, man, which surprised the fuck outta me," Trev huffed and shook his head. "She's not going to give you another one."

He turned and walked out of my office without another word.

"Fuck," I yelled, throwing my thermos so hard against the wall that it put a huge hole in the Sheetrock.

I hated that she'd come in here making my day go to shit and my head throb. I hated that Trevor saw through me. I hated that I couldn't go home because I had actual work to do.

I hated that I was so fucked up that I'd given her an ultimatum, essentially asking her to give up her happiness for mine, and she was still looking at me like she loved me.

* * *

My phone rang late that night, pulling me from a restless sleep. "Mom, is everything okay?"

"It's time, Bram," she sang happily. "Get up. We need to get to Seattle."

"What?" I sat up in bed, trying to wake myself up. Seattle?

"Ani's baby is on its way."

"Oh, uh—"

"Abraham Daniel," Mom said sharply, making me silently groan. She and Dad had changed my and Alex's middle names when they adopted us—with our permission—and whenever she used it I knew she meant business. "This is what we do. When someone in this family is having a baby, we go to the hospital."

"Not sure that's a good idea, Mom," I said quietly, even as I climbed out of bed.

"Son," she sighed, "I don't know why you're so adamant about this, but I'll respect it."

"Thank you."

"But if you don't go meet Ani's new son or daughter, you'll never forgive yourself, and neither will she."

I swallowed hard.

"I'm on my way. Give me fifteen."

"Good boy." She hung up, and I tossed my phone on the bed, going to my dresser to grab some clean clothes.

When I got to my Mom and Dad's, every light in the house was on, and Uncle Mike's truck was in the driveway.

"Oh, good, you're here. Let's go!" my mom called as I

opened the front door. I took a step back onto the porch as the entire family came pouring out of the house. Uncle Mike and Aunt Ellie, my dad, Trevor, and Ani, and then my mom, locking the front door behind her.

"I'll ride with Ani," Mom announced.

"Me too." Aunt Ellie gave Uncle Mike a kiss and then headed toward Ani's SUV.

"Catch you on the flip side," Ani said to Trevor, her voice shaking.

"You're going to do great," he assured her, pulling her into a tight hug.

She passed me on the porch on her way to the car but didn't look my way once. I almost reached out to stop her, but I met Trev's eyes and fisted my hands by my sides instead.

"I'm going to take my truck so I can drive back down in the morning," Trev said.

"I'll ride with you," Mike replied, walking away.

"Looks like it's me and you," my dad said. "Take my truck?"

I nodded and followed him to his truck, climbing into the passenger seat.

The ride was long as we followed Ani all the way up to Seattle. Dad was quiet as we listened to country music playing from his stereo, and I was really glad for that. I wasn't sure I could choke out anything resembling actual words. My hands were sweating so badly that I left a damp spot on the thighs of my jeans by the time we arrived at the hospital, and by the time we parked the truck, I was shaking.

"Hey," my dad called as he opened his door, but I stayed rooted to my seat, not even bothering to take my seat belt off. "You okay?"

"Yep." I nodded jerkily, staring at the cement wall in front of the truck.

He shut his door again and leaned back on the seat, shooing someone away from his window with a shake of his head.

"You wanna tell me why you're pretending to be a statue?"

"I'm fine."

"You know," he said after a minute, settling more comfortably into his seat, "when Katie was born, I was a mess."

I didn't reply.

"I was shaking and sweating like you would not believe. One of the nurses finally had to give me one of those scrubs tops because my T-shirt was soaked all the way through," he chuckled.

I stayed silent.

"Normal to be nervous."

Still nothing.

"It's going to be all right, Abraham," Dad said gently, making my throat tighten.

"If something happens, it'll destroy Ani," I finally choked out, still staring out the windshield.

"Nothing's going to happen."

"You don't know that," I said so quietly that I wasn't sure if he heard me.

"Okay, say it does," he mused, making my head snap

toward him. "You wanna be out here when it does, or you wanna be inside with her?"

I fumbled with my seat belt and threw open the door, barely hearing his "That's what I thought," before slamming the door behind me.

"Where do I go?" I asked in confusion, looking around the garage.

"Come on, elevators are over here." I followed him to the elevators and then through the hospital and to another elevator, finally ending up on the maternity floor where everyone was already waiting.

I searched the room for Ani, but she wasn't there.

"Ani went back to the room to be with her sister," my mom informed us as she came to give my dad a kiss. "No baby yet."

I didn't say a word but moved toward the far wall, dropping into an empty seat and clenching my shaking hands in front of me as I tried to block out the room.

* * *

It was hours before we heard any news. According to my mom, first babies usually took a while.

At some point, another family came into the waiting room and sat down in a little cluster. It looked like it was a mom, a dad, and their teenage son. They didn't ask the nurse to see anyone, just sat down silently and seemed to be waiting.

Then finally, Ani came walking down the hallway, looking at the floor.

Everyone in our family surged to their feet.

She was almost on top of us when she finally lifted her face, and the expression she was wearing made me want to drop to my knees.

"It's a girl," she announced, tears falling down her smiling face. "And she's beautiful."

My mom stepped forward and wrapped Ani in a tight hug, whispering something as Ani nodded against her shoulder. Then Mom let go, and the rest of the family swarmed in, hugging and laughing.

Ani glowed.

Finally, when everyone else had gotten their hugs, she turned to me.

"Thanks for coming—"

She didn't get another word out before I'd pulled her into my arms, lifting her off the floor as she hugged me back.

"Congratulations, Mama," I choked out, inhaling the scent of her neck.

"Thanks, Abraham," she replied, running her hand over my hair.

"Everything's okay?" I still wasn't letting her go.

"Everything's perfect." She continued to run her fingers through my hair, settling me. "You're shaking."

"No I'm not," I lied, setting her back on her feet.

"Can you call Alex? I think Mom's calling Katie, and Trev texted Hen."

"Sure," I said with a completely awkward nod.

She laughed a little as she took a step back and ran her hand over her face before giving me a wide smile. Then she turned away and looked around the waiting room, finally coming to a stop when she found the family that had come in an hour after we had.

"Marcus?" she asked, taking a step forward.

"Yeah," the kid replied, his eyes wide as he and his parents came to their feet.

"Hey, I'm Bethy's sister, Anita."

"O-oh," he stuttered, standing up straighter.

"Everything went really well," she told him gently as he fidgeted. "Bethy's asking for you now."

The kid swallowed, then looked at his parents. At their nod, he raced away.

"Room 422!" Anita called out as he practically ran down the hallway.

"You're Anita?" the boy's mother asked quietly, looking intently at Ani.

I took a step forward, but my mom's hand on my arm stopped me.

"Hi," Ani said, lifting her hand to shake the mom's.

"I'm Sue, and this is my husband Richard," the woman replied, making no move to take Ani's hand.

"It's nice to meet you," Ani replied, dropping her hand back to her side.

"Thank you so much," the mom whispered, her eyes welling up with tears. "We just—I'm a professor and Richard owns his own IT company. We're just—we're too old to take care of another baby."

The dad wrapped his arm around the mom's shoulders as she sniffled.

"I understand," Ani said quietly.

My mom passed me and went to Ani's side. "Hi, I'm Liz, Ani's mom."

"Hello," Sue said. "But I thought—" Her eyes went to Ani.

"My foster mom," Ani clarified.

"Oh," Sue breathed.

"We're big believers in adoption," my mom said, her implication clear. "It's really nice to meet you, Sue."

Sue watched my mom for a long moment, then looked around the room, her eyes stopping on me and then Trevor. When her eyes went back to my mom and Ani, she gave them a tentative smile. That's when Richard's shoulders dropped a fraction, and he reached out his hand. "Nice to meet you, Liz and Anita. I'm Richard."

A few minutes later, I pulled my phone out of my pocket and called my brother as I watched Ani and my mom get to know the baby's grandparents.

"Hello?" Alex answered gruffly.

"Hey, Ani wanted me to call you—"

"Baby?"

"A girl. Healthy and beautiful," I answered distractedly as Sue gave Ani a hug.

I pulled the phone away as Alex whooped in my ear.

"Congratulations," he said happily.

"I'll tell Ani."

"Nah, man. That was for you."

"What?" I asked, irritated that I was talking to him when it looked like Ani was going to head back into her sister's room.

"I'm telling you congratulations."

"Shut the fuck up."

"Nah, man. A little boy? You might have been able to hold out. But a little girl? You're toast."

* * *

"Do you think we'll get to see the baby soon?" Trevor asked over an hour later as he dropped into the seat next to me.

"Don't know," I answered, messing with a loose thread on the inseam of my jeans.

"I need to head out soon."

I nodded. I wasn't really up for conversation.

Ani seemed happy. She'd been flitting in and out of her sister's hospital room, coming out to talk to my mom and Aunt Ellie before skipping back in to be with her sister and the baby. I wasn't sure what was taking so long, why we hadn't been able to see the baby yet, and the longer it went the more nervous I became.

Trevor elbowed me hard in the side, and my head snapped up to see him nodding toward a woman who was walking down the hallway toward us.

"Holy shit," I muttered as she came closer. Her hair was long and curled, and she had on a pair of the tightest jeans I'd ever seen, but that wasn't what made my stomach clench.

She looked just like Ani.

She was doing something on her phone, but when she made it to the waiting room, her head came up, and she glanced around. Her face screwed up like she'd smelled something foul, then moved toward where my mom was still sitting with Sue and Richard.

"I'll knock the bitch out," Trev said under his breath, scooting forward in his seat.

My stomach rolled as I realized that she wasn't just getting to the hospital. She had come from Bethy's room, which meant Ani had been locked away with the woman for hours.

"Hi, I'm Anita and Bethy's mom, Carol," Ani's mom said cheerfully as she got to Sue. "You must be Marcus's parents."

"Hello," Sue said flatly.

"So I think Marcus wants to stay with Bethy, but you guys can head on home if you want," Carol said, oblivious to Sue's pinched mouth. "It's not like he can get her into any more trouble!" Carol laughed, and I saw my mom put a warning hand on Sue's forearm.

"I think we'll stay," Sue said, making Richard nod. He didn't say a word, but his nostrils were flared as he looked down his nose at Carol.

"Okay, well, I'm going to head home!" She completely ignored my mom as she spun on her heel.

"Cunt," I murmured as she walked out the door.

"No way is she that oblivious," Trevor scoffed.

"She knew exactly who we were."

"Can you believe how much she looked like Ani? Her dad must have had some weak genes."

"No shit." I leaned back in my seat and gave my mom a small smile as she met my eyes across the room.

"Well, at least you know what Ani will look like in twenty years. Not bad."

"Shut the fuck up." I closed my eyes and rested my head against the wall.

Fifteen minutes later, I was on my feet, my palms once again sweaty as Ani came walking carefully down the corridor, a little wrapped bundle in her arms. If I hadn't already known that she was a girl, the baby's gender would have been a complete mystery in the unisex blanket and hat she was wrapped in.

She needed something pink. Pronto.

"This is Arielle Elizabeth Martin," Ani announced as she reached us.

"Oh," my mom breathed, "look at her."

"Seven pounds even and twenty-and-a-half inches long," Ani said, meeting Sue's eyes. "Do you want to hold her?"

"Can I?" Sue asked nervously.

Ani nodded, then kissed the top of little Arielle's head before handing her to her grandmother.

Everyone was staring at the baby as Sue held her, but I watched Ani. Her hands were loose down at her sides, but her fingers fidgeted against her thighs. I moved in beside her and laid my hand gently at the base of her spine, trying to calm her down.

She'd just handed her daughter to a person who could take Arielle away forever, and I knew she must be so scared.

"Arielle?" Sue asked.

"Yeah." Ani nodded.

"I like it." Sue leaned down and kissed Arielle's head, pressing her nose softly against the baby's skin for a long moment as she sniffled. She looked up at her husband in question, and he shook his head just a little.

I didn't blame him. The idea of holding the sweet little girl and then giving her away made me nauseous.

"Thank you," Sue said to Ani, handing Arielle back to her. "Thank you for everything." Her breath hitched. "We're going to head home, let your family celebrate."

Ani started to protest but Sue shook her head. "Could you let Marcus know that we left and tell him to call us in a couple hours? I know—" She swallowed hard. "He's going to need us, but I think he wants to be with Bethy right now."

"Of course we will," my mom said, pulling Sue into a hug.

They said good-bye to the rest of us, and then Richard ushered a crying Sue out of the room.

Ani's distraught gaze met mine.

"Hard decision to make," I told her quietly.

"Do you think they'll—"

"No," I told her resolutely, knowing what she was going to ask. "They won't change their minds."

Ani smiled tremulously, then looked around at the group. "Who wants to hold her?"

"Bram first," Trevor said, his mouth tipping up. Asshole.

"Yeah?" Ani asked, turning to me.

"Uh." I glanced at my mom, my eyes widening.

I'd held a lot of babies. I'd carried around Shane and

Kate's kids from the time they were just hours old. It wasn't hard—hell, as long as you kept a good grip and made sure their head wasn't wobbling around, you were golden. But I knew, I fucking *knew,* that the moment I held Arielle, everything would change.

"Sure," I finally choked out. "Let me sit down."

My dad snickered, but I ignored it as I took a couple steps backward and landed in a hard chair.

"Here you go," Ani said quietly as the rest of our family moved to the far side of the room.

She laid the baby in my hands.

I couldn't breathe.

This was insane.

I'd held babies before.

Why was I—

Arielle shifted in her blankets, and I inhaled sharply, watching her tiny face.

She was gorgeous. Like no baby I'd ever seen before. Her skin was darker than mine, but not as red as my niece Iris's had been. And her eyes were almond shaped, which made sense because Sue was obviously of Asian descent. Her lips were puckered, but had a definite Cupid's bow shape.

I pulled off her hat and smiled a little at the full head of short, black hair.

"Bethy's half African American," Ani said, crouching down in front of me to run a fingertip over Arielle's head.

"She needs some pink," I blurted out softly, glaring at the ugly hospital blanket Arielle was wrapped in.

"Yeah. Maybe Liz can get her some stuff. Bethy's in

with the social worker right now, and I don't really want to leave the hospital."

I nodded. I wanted to meet her eyes, tell her congratulations and all that bullshit, but I couldn't look away from Arielle's face.

I pressed my knees together, making Ani scoot back a little, and laid the baby down on my legs so I could unwrap her.

"It's cold in here, Bram," Ani murmured as I unwrapped Arielle.

"I'll hurry," I breathed.

She wasn't wearing anything but a diaper, and her little umbilical cord stump was still gnarly looking, but that wasn't what I was interested in anyway.

I lifted one foot and then the other, startling Arielle as I ran one finger over the soles and then counted the toes. Then I counted her fingers, letting the long digits wrap around my index finger.

"She's got long fingers," I said in awe.

"Yeah," Ani said, resting her hand on my knee. "She's got a birthmark too; did you see it?"

I looked Arielle over and finally noticed where her skin was slightly darker from just above her belly button to right below her sternum.

"It looks like Florida," I said stupidly.

"Yeah, kind of," Ani said with a chuckle.

My mom started walking toward us then, and all of a sudden, I felt extremely self-conscious. I wrapped Arielle tightly back up with trembling hands and lifted her to my chest.

"Can I have a turn?" Mom asked teasingly.

I wanted to tell her no.

"Sure," I said, taking one more close look at the baby. Her eyes were blinking open and closed, and my heart thudded hard in my chest. "Here you go."

Mom took Arielle and started cooing as I grabbed Ani by the back of the neck without a word and kissed her forehead. Then I walked away.

"Keys?" I asked my dad, barely able to get the word out. He nodded and tossed me his truck keys, and I got the fuck out of there.

Chapter 12

Anita

The papers were signed and notarized.

I was a mom.

I tried not to act giddy as I sat across from Bethy in her hospital room while she waited for our mom to pick her up. Arielle was sleeping in a bright pink car seat that Liz had brought me that morning, ready to go, but I couldn't bear to leave Bethy all alone on a floor filled with crying babies.

"Do you think you could send me updates?" Bethy asked, watching Arielle sleep. "Not, like, all the time or anything, but once in a while?"

I chewed the inside of my cheek.

Our mother should be there. She should be comforting my little sister in a way that I couldn't. I didn't know her well enough to play the big sister card. Anything that came out of my mouth would sound false.

"Sure," I replied, nodding my head.

"I won't bug you or anything."

"It's fine, Beth," I said gently.

"Okay," she breathed, nodding her head. "Okay."

The door to her room opened, and I glanced up to find Marcus and Richard walking into the room.

"Hey," Marcus said quietly, going straight to Bethy. "I called your mom and told her we were picking you up."

"You can stay with us for a few days, if you want," Richard said in his rumbly voice, "let Sue spoil you a bit."

Bethy's eyes filled with tears as Marcus's arm wrapped around her shoulders. "Thanks," she whispered.

Her eyes came to me, and I couldn't stop myself from climbing to my feet and crossing the room, wrapping my arms gently around her waist. "Take care of yourself, little sister," I said into her ear, smoothing my hand down her corkscrew curls. "You're going to do big things, Bethy. I know it doesn't feel like it now, but you're going to be an incredible woman."

She sobbed once and dropped her head to my shoulder.

"Let me know how you're doing and kiss the boys for me?"

"Sure."

She pulled away and let Marcus lead her out of the room.

"Thanks for taking care of her," I said to Richard as the door swung closed behind them.

"We've been taking care of Bethy for years," he said darkly. "And we'll keep doing it until she doesn't need us anymore."

My throat tightened as I nodded. I'd had no idea that

Marcus and Bethy had been friends for so long, but I was glad for it. They weren't just a couple of kids that screwed up. They loved each other. Maybe it wasn't adult love— there was no way they were mature enough for that yet— but their friendship obviously ran deep.

God, my mother was a piece of fucking work. The entire time Bethy had been in labor she'd played on her phone and napped. Fucking napped, like her fifteen-year-old-daughter wasn't writhing on the bed and bawling her eyes out. She was such a piece of shit.

I shook my head and picked up the bag I'd packed for Arielle.

"Just you and me, princess," I said quietly, lifting up the car seat.

As I left the room, I caught sight of Marcus and Richard leading the way out the front doors, a nurse pushing Bethy in a wheelchair behind them. I stopped in the door and waited for them to leave before I walked into the corridor.

"Ready?" Aunt Ellie called, waving her hands excitedly.

"All set," I answered with a smile as Liz took Arielle's bag from me.

All the guys had left the night before, but I didn't blame them. Someone had to keep the company running while I was out on maternity leave, and they'd already stayed all night waiting for Arielle to be born. Ellie and Liz refused to go though—they wanted to ride home with me and Arielle.

As I climbed in the back of my Toyota, clicking Arielle's car seat into the base that someone had already tightened into the middle seat, I couldn't stop the giddy laugh that left me, startling the baby before she drifted back off to sleep.

I was a mom. I had a daughter.

Those might have been the most beautiful words in the English language.

* * *

"This is where we live," I cooed, pulling Arielle out of her car seat. "It's not much, but by the time you're old enough to notice, it'll be much nicer."

Liz came in behind me, laughing at my speech.

"Well, it's true," I said ruefully, walking farther into the house.

"Your house is fine," Liz assured me. "When we had Katie, we were living in a crappy old single-wide trailer while we waited for the house to be built. Babies don't care where you live as long as they're warm and clean and fed."

"You care, don't you?" I asked Arielle as she slept through our conversation. "Let's go see your room."

I walked down the hall while Liz and Ellie groaned about sore muscles from sitting in the car for so long. What should have been a four-hour trip turned into close to six hours thanks to traffic and my little princess. I wouldn't be driving back to Seattle anytime in the near future. I didn't know how Kate and Shane had driven all the way to San Diego when Iris was a newborn.

"This is your—Mom!" I yelled, my eyes almost popping out of my head. "Come here!"

"What's up?" she asked, running down the hallway. When she got a good look at the room, she gasped.

The walls were still light green and the wood floors were still gleaming in the sun coming through the window, but the room looked nothing like I'd left it.

Underneath the crib was a large pink and purple woven rug. The white sheet that I'd left on the mattress was gone, replaced by a pink one with little hearts all over it. There was a large pink wooden *A* hanging on one wall and a princess crown on another. In the corner, a short curtain rod had been hung about waist high, and hanging from it were a bunch of pink and purple and yellow frilly dresses that I couldn't imagine Arielle ever wearing comfortably.

The entire room clashed horribly.

I loved it.

"What in the world?" Ellie asked, pushing past Liz and me so she could walk into the room.

"Little girls should have girl rooms," Liz read, picking up a note on the top of Arielle's dresser—the dresser that now had pink crystal knobs on it instead of the white ones it had come with. "Welcome, Arielle. Love Papa, Uncle Mike, Uncle Trevor, and Uncle Bram."

I smiled as my eyes filled with tears.

"Well, calling him Uncle Bram probably isn't the best idea," Ellie said, snickering. "That'll make things awkward when she gets to grade school."

Liz laughed, and just like that, my tears dried up.

"You do realize, this is why we kept it a secret?" I bitched, walking toward the changing table and laying Arielle on the top. "We knew you'd never let it go."

"What's there to let go?" Liz asked, reaching down to pick up a package of diapers and tearing it open.

"We're not together."

"For now," Ellie said, flitting around the bedroom.

"Forever," I argued, unbuttoning Arielle's little pajamas.

"He won't be able to hold out that long," Liz murmured, handing me a diaper.

"Well who says I want him back?" I asked stubbornly, changing Arielle. "He made his choice."

"Bullshit," Ellie mumbled.

"Language," Liz scolded her sister.

"Arielle doesn't mind, do you, sweet girl?" Ellie cooed, making me laugh as Arielle made a weird grunting noise.

"I can't believe she's really here," I murmured as I picked her up, cuddling her against my chest.

* * *

"You've gotta sleep at some point," I told Arielle a week later, walking around my living room for the forty-fifth time that morning. "I mean, people can't live without sleep. At some point you won't be able to fight it any longer."

I'd been up since two in the morning, rocking and feeding and changing Arielle, but nothing seemed to be working. I'd even laid her down in her bassinet thinking that she could just be awake for a while on her own while I fell asleep, but the minute I'd set her down, she started squawking like a chicken, and I'd had to pick her back up.

I'd learned in the first couple of days that my girl liked to be skin to skin, so we were both stripped from the waist up as I carried her around the living room, a small blanket wrapped over her back.

"Hey, you awake?" Bram called from the front door, making me freeze.

"Uh." I looked wildly around me, but couldn't find anything to cover up. My hair was wild around my head, and I was in nothing but a bra and pajama shorts. *Shit.*

"I used my key in case you were sleep—" Bram's eyes widened as he caught sight of Arielle and me. "I brought breakfast."

I should have known someone would be by. Everyone had been taking turns bringing me meals since I'd brought Arielle home. But I was so tired that I'd completely forgotten.

"Whatcha doing?" Bram asked, grinning.

"She likes to be skin on skin," I answered, starting another lap around the room when Arielle began to squawk.

"She sounds like a bird," Bram mused.

"Yeah, a loud bird."

"You need some help?"

"I've got it," I said, rubbing my hand up and down her little back. "We're fine."

"You look tired."

"Is that your way of saying I look like shit?"

"No." Bram drew the word out as he pulled off his flannel. "It's my way of saying you look tired."

"She's been up since two," I confessed, making Bram wince.

"And she's all fed and changed?"

"Of course," I replied irritably. I could take care of my own daughter. I didn't need him to help, I was doing fine on my—"What?" I asked as Bram pulled his T-shirt over his head and came toward me.

"Hand her over," he ordered, wiggling his fingers at me.

I let him take Arielle and cradle her against his chest with one arm.

"Sit down," he said quietly, nodding at the couch.

I stumbled over and dropped down heavily, watching him in disbelief as he came toward me and pulled my throw blanket from the back cushions over my shoulders.

"Rest."

"You don't have to—"

"It's fine, Ani. I've got nothing going on. Lie down and rest for a little bit. We'll be right here."

"If you're sure," I replied, my eyes already drooping.

"Well, I'm already topless so it's a little late to change my mind," he said teasingly before turning away.

I closed my eyes as he started humming a song I didn't recognize, and fell asleep to his steady footsteps circling the living room over and over again.

* * *

When I woke up a couple hours later, Bram and Arielle weren't in the living room anymore, but I could hear him humming quietly in the kitchen. I tiptoed to the bathroom to pee and grimaced when I caught a glimpse of myself in the mirror. *Nasty.* My hair was sticking out in all directions, and I was pretty sure I hadn't brushed my teeth in two days.

I took care of business, then wet down my hair and brushed my teeth, making myself feel slightly less like a hobo when I pulled a T-shirt over my head. I glanced down at my sleep shorts and decided against changing. They were comfortable, and I wasn't leaving the house anyway.

When I got to the kitchen, my jaw dropped. Bram was sitting at the kitchen table working on some sort of paperwork with Arielle in a sling across his chest.

My sling.

The one with the floral print that I hated but accepted with a smile when Ellie had bought it for me on our shopping trip.

"What are you doing?" I asked incredulously, pausing Bram's quiet humming.

"Getting some work done," he said simply, running his gaze from my head to my toes. "You look better."

"You look like a jackass," I said with a snicker.

"Ah, there's the Ani I know. I thought you were going soft on me."

"Not likely." I took a few steps forward. "You have to be careful with those slings," I blurted, taking a couple steps forward. "If you don't put her in there right, it's hard for her to breathe and—"

"She's fine," he assured me, pulling back the fabric so I

could see Arielle's sleeping face. "I can feel her breathing, and I watched a couple YouTube videos before I put her in it."

"Oh, so that makes you an expert?" I asked, fidgeting.

This was new. This overwhelming need to protect someone. I was protective of my nieces and nephews, and of the Evans and Harris families, but this feeling went so much deeper than that. It was overwhelming and almost feral in its intensity.

"I'd never do anything to hurt her," he replied incredulously.

"Here, I'll take her," I said sharply, reaching my arms out. I knew I was being rude as hell, but I couldn't seem to stop it. I needed to hold her.

"Sure," Bram said, lifting the entire sling so that it was loose around his neck. He handed Arielle over and pulled the fabric over his head, then shuffled the papers in front of him, gathering them up into a neat pile.

She was too hot. Was she too hot? I walked to the couch and laid her down, pulling her out of the sling, only to find that she was a completely normal temperature. *Good.*

"I'm out," Bram muttered, sliding his T-shirt back on and grabbing his flannel off the back of the couch. "She likes the vibration in your chest when you hum, try that."

Then he walked out the front door, locking it behind him.

I sat down heavily on the couch after he was gone, sighing in disgust. I hadn't even said thank you.

A part of me felt like such a bitch for that, but the other part—the dominant part? It kept repeating the same phrase in my head over and over.

Hurt me once, shame on you. Hurt me twice, shame on me.

I couldn't afford to get pulled into some anti-relationship with Bram again.

* * *

My phone rang a couple hours later as I was climbing out of the shower.

"Hello?" I answered, out of breath.

"I hear Bram was at your house for *hours* earlier," Kate sang into the phone, making me curse.

"Jesus, this family is such a bunch of gossip queens," I griped, trying to dry off my hair as I held the phone with my shoulder.

"Well, he left work at like eight and didn't get back until lunch," Kate said innocently. "Trev was just wondering if I'd heard anything."

"You live in San Diego," I scoffed, awkwardly pulling on my clothes.

"Semantics," Kate replied. "So what happened?"

"Well." I drew the word out, imagining the huge smile on her face as she waited for some fairy-tale story to come bursting out of my mouth. "He got here, and I was topless, walking around the living room." My voice grew quiet. "And then he started stripping."

Kate was completely silent on the other end of the connection.

"As soon as he was bare chested, he came to me…and took Arielle so I could have a nap while he did the skin-on-skin shit that calms her down."

"Oh, thank God. I was trying to be a good friend but I was totally skeeved out," she blurted.

"You're such an ass," I laughed.

"It sucks being so far away."

"I thought you loved it down there?" I asked in surprise.

"I do," she said cheerily. "But I miss you guys and I want to meet Arielle."

"You should come visit."

"Yeah, I talked to Shane about it last night. We can't really afford to send all of us up there, so I'm thinking I'll just fly up for the weekend or something."

"That would be awesome," I said, checking on Arielle, who was asleep in her little bassinet.

"What's happening with you and Bram?" Kate needled. "You never tell me anything!"

"There's nothing to tell," I replied, going out to the couch so I wouldn't wake the baby. Or should I try and wake her so she wasn't up all night? None of the baby books I had gave me a straight answer. It was annoying as hell.

"Well, he was at your house—"

"Trev was here yesterday, Ellie the day before that, your mom comes over every day at some point, and I've even seen your dad a few times," I said flatly.

"But still—"

"But still, nothing," I said in exasperation. "He made his decision very fucking clear, Katie. Can you just drop it?"

Kate was quiet for a few seconds. "Okay," she said on a sigh. "For now."

"Have you always been this annoying?"

"Oh, please," Kate replied. "You told Mom I was pregnant before I could—you're way worse than me."

"I was worried!"

"Likely story."

* * *

Two weeks later, Kate came home to Oregon and met Arielle for the first time.

"Oh my God, she's gorgeous!" my foster sister said, stealing Arielle from me the minute she walked through the door. "Iris was a pretty baby, but Gavin and Keller looked like little gremlins."

I snorted as she passed me, pushing her way into the house.

"Good to see you, too."

"I'm not here to see you," she joked back as Trevor carried her suitcase inside.

"Are you staying here?" I asked in surprise.

"Obviously."

"I bet Liz is really happy about that," I said flatly as I shut the front door.

"She'll be here in a little bit," Kate replied with a shrug of her shoulders. "She said she didn't care since I didn't bring the kids with me."

Trevor and I laughed as we followed her into the living room.

"How you doing?" he asked, throwing an arm around my shoulders.

"I'm good," I said, giving him a big smile. "Hey, have you heard from Hen? He hasn't called in a few days."

I'd been talking to Alex, Henry, and Kate almost every day since I'd brought Arielle home. They also made me send photos and videos of Arielle so they could see her. I could tell they were feeling pretty homesick, but they'd all come to visit recently so only Kate was able to come back home to meet her.

"He's doing that training thing he was talking about," Trev answered, rubbing his knuckles over my head before moving to sit next to Kate on the couch. "He won't be back for another week."

"Oh, right." I snapped my fingers, then looked down at my hand in disgust. When had I started picking up mannerisms from Uncle Mike of all people? He was the only person who snapped like that.

"Yep," Trev said, nodding his head as he snapped his fingers.

"Shut up."

"I didn't say a word."

"Children," Kate scolded, "let's focus on what's important here, me holding my new niece. Take a picture for Arielle's baby book, Ani."

I looked at her in horror. "What the fuck is a baby book?"

"It's a little book that you put all their milestones in, like when their favorite aunt held them for the first time," Kate said slowly, like I was an idiot.

"What?" I was so confused.

Trevor started laughing hard, his deep voice filling the room until both Kate and I were laughing, too. I wasn't even sure what was so funny, but his laughter was ridiculously contagious.

"We'll go to the store and buy you one tomorrow," Kate assured me, wiping tears off her face.

"Where's my favorite sister?" a voice called from the front door, making me freeze.

I'd barely seen Bram since he left my house two weeks earlier. He monopolized Arielle when we went to family dinners, but he barely said a word to me. I knew I'd been a bitch to him, but I couldn't make myself apologize. If he was going to be butt-hurt over one comment I'd made, that was fine. It wasn't like he hadn't said much worse things to me over the years.

"Abraham," Kate sang, coming to her feet.

"Hey," he said, stepping into the living room with a sweet smile. He walked toward Katie and hugged her with Arielle between them, leaning down to give my daughter a quick kiss on her forehead. "Where's Mom?"

"What?" Kate asked, pulling away.

"Mom said we were doing dinner here. I've got groceries in the back of the truck," Bram said in confusion, his eyes meeting mine.

"That's news to me," I said drily.

"Shit," he mumbled, reaching up to run his hand through his beard.

"It's fine. Trev, get off your ass and help him unload," I ordered.

"When did you get bossy?" Trevor bitched with a smile, pushing himself to his feet.

"When I became a mother," I replied snottily, raising one eyebrow.

Trevor and Katie both laughed at that, but when I glanced at Bram, he was giving me a soft look, his lips tipped up in a small smile.

That night, my house was filled with noise. Ellie, Mike, Liz, and Dan showed up about a half an hour after Bram, and the women immediately got to work making dinner. They passed around the baby and refused to give her back until I'd finished my meal, then finally let me cuddle her as they ate their own. Everyone stayed late, laughing and joking as Ellie and Liz cleaned the house despite my protests. They even gave Arielle a bath in the kitchen sink, taking a thousand pictures of her disgruntled face.

After everyone had gone, Katie and I curled up on my bed with Arielle between us.

"How's everything going?" Kate asked seriously, playing with Arielle's little hands.

"It's good," I said with a little nod. "I'm tired pretty much all the time, and I usually smell like ass because I haven't showered—but I wouldn't change it."

"I know how that goes," Kate replied, rolling her eyes. "Shane will come up behind me all 'let's get it on' and I'm like, 'Dude, this is day three of not showering. You don't want anywhere near my downstairs.'"

I snickered, my giggles shaking the bed and making Arielle startle with her hands and feet straight up in the air. "Well, I don't have to deal with that, at least."

"Still nothing with Bram?" Kate asked quietly.

"Why do you keep harping on this?" I asked.

"Because I watched him watching you all damn night," she replied. "And when he wasn't watching you, he was watching whoever was holding Arielle like he was going to tear their head off if they made any wrong move."

"You're delusional."

Kate sighed. "I'll drop it."

"Thank you."

"But—"

"Oh fantastic, you have more to say," I said drily, lying down flat on my back.

"Just…don't give up on him yet."

"Kate"—I shook my head—"it's been over a month. That horse is dead, yet you continue to beat it."

"That saying is ridiculous. Why would anyone beat a dead horse?" Kate said in disgust.

"Exactly."

* * *

The next morning, Ellie and Liz showed up bright and early, their hands full of donuts and coffee. Then they shooed Kate and me out of the house with gift certificates to a movie theater and a salon. They kept Arielle all day so Kate and I could get out for a while.

I didn't want to go at first, but as we sat in the salon chairs with footbaths massaging our feet, I realized how badly I'd needed the break. It was hard leaving Arielle for any length of time, but it also felt good to leave the house for a little while and gossip with my best friend. I didn't know how Kate took care of five kids; just one was making me feel like I was losing my mind. I forgot everything, from appointments to the last time I'd brushed my hair.

I cried when Kate left on Sunday, but I knew she was anxious to get back to the kiddos. Shane had already left on his deployment, and while her neighbor was rad about keeping so many kids, Kate was ready to be home. She didn't like being without them, and for the first time, I completely understood it.

Sometimes I wonder if that weekend was God's way of preparing me for what happened after that. A reprieve of sorts so that, when the time came, I would be rested and strong.

Chapter 13

Abraham

I was in love. Flat-out do-anything-say-anything-kill-for-and-die-for love. And the object of my affection was a little girl that weighed less than ten pounds.

I'm not sure how it happened, but from the moment I'd held her in the hospital, it was like something clicked. I loved Katie and Shane's kids. I'd loved them since the minute they were born, and I'd do anything for them, but Arielle was different.

What I felt for her was stronger than all that. It made me change. I waited for any mention of her, made sure I ran into whoever had visited her and Ani that day just so I could hear whatever story they wanted to tell. I had a hard time falling asleep at night, wondering if Ani had gotten her to sleep all right or if she was pulling an all-nighter that I was missing. And anytime I was in the same room with her, I couldn't stop my gaze from landing on her over and over again no matter who was holding her, just to make sure she was okay.

I had a thousand pictures of her on my phone already.

I hadn't wanted any of this. I'd fought it right from the beginning.

When I'd left the hospital that day, I drove around for hours trying to get my head on straight—but nothing seemed to help. She'd worked her way under my skin just by being alive, and that scared the shit out of me.

I didn't want kids. The thought of being a parent made my skin crawl as I remembered my biological mother. She was, well, beautiful. In every single way.

A lot of kids I'd met in the system had really shitty parents, parents even worse than Ani's, but my mom had never been anything but perfect. She was single when Alex and I were born, but she'd worked her ass off at job after job to make sure we had what we needed. When we were really little, she'd had a job at a daycare center so she could take us with her, and once we went to school, she'd joined a cleaning company.

But then shit had started happening, things I didn't fully understand at five years old, and by the time Alex and I hit our seventh birthday, she was dead.

And I'd known that I never wanted to have kids of my own.

I clenched my hands around the steering wheel of my truck and pulled into the garage of my town house. There was no reason to relive all that shit. It was what it was. I still didn't want to have kids, but that decision didn't change my feelings on Arielle in the slightest.

Those two truths were a contradiction I would never understand.

I climbed out of my truck and closed the garage door behind me, taking my boots off at the door to my kitchen. I was filthy.

I'd spent the day overseeing some cutting we were doing, and I was covered in mud and leaves. I'd even found some little branches in my hair on the drive home. I needed a shower before I did anything else.

Twenty minutes later, I was leisurely drying off when my phone started ringing where I'd thrown it on the bed.

"Hello?" I answered in surprise.

"Hey, bud. I need you to come on up to the house." My dad's voice was raspy.

"What's going on?" I asked, practically diving for my dresser where I had a shit ton of clothes folded on top. Something bad had happened, I knew it by his tone, the pauses between the words, even the way he was breathing.

"We'll talk about it when you get here," he said firmly. "I want you to go pick up the girls first, then come straight here."

"Does Ani—"

"I'll call and let her know you're coming, but I don't want her worried and driving up by herself," Dad cut in quietly. "Drive safe, but hurry, all right?"

"Okay," I said, pulling on a pair of jeans, not bothering with boxers.

"Love you. See you soon." He hung up before I could reply.

Less than three minutes later, I was in my truck and on my way to Ani's.

"Do you know what's going on?" she asked frantically as she met me at the door.

Her hair was soaking wet like she'd just hopped out of the shower.

"No idea," I murmured back, setting my hand in the middle of her torso to push her backward into the house. "Go dry your hair."

"It's fine," she argued, pulling on a sweatshirt that was hanging over the couch. "Dan said to hurry."

She moved toward the family room where I could see Arielle sleeping in the baby swing, but I hooked her with an arm around her waist to stop her momentum.

"Go run a towel over your hair, baby," I ordered, leaning down to talk directly into her ear. "I'll get Arie in her seat, and then we'll go."

Ani went still under my hand, sighed heavily, then nodded her head and pulled away from me to walk back down the hallway.

As soon as she was gone, I went to the swing and picked Arielle up. She was getting heavier, and my lips twitched as I had to readjust my hands under her little body.

"Time to go to Nana and Papa's," I said, carrying her over to the pink car seat I'd bought her when she was in the hospital. I found it at a random store I'd stopped in for a phone charger, and I'd known she needed to have it. After I bought it, I'd told my mom to give it to Ani because the impulse buy had embarrassed me. "Mama'll bring you a blanket so you're nice and cozy," I told Arielle as I buckled her in and tightened the straps the way I'd seen done on the local fire station's YouTube channel.

"Here," Ani called, tossing me a light purple blanket. "You get her bundled up, and I'll grab her formula and some diapers."

A few minutes later, we were out of the house, and I was driving Ani's SUV up to my parents' place while Ani fidgeted in the seat next to me.

"Hey," I called, reaching out to grab her knee, "calm down."

"What the hell could be wrong? It must be something huge if Dan made you come get me," she replied, crossing her arms over her chest.

"I would have come to get you anyway," I mumbled, letting go of her knee so I could turn my windshield wipers up. It was raining like hell, and when you added that to the dark sky, it made the road almost impossible to see. "The roads are shit right now."

"I can drive in the rain," she muttered back.

I didn't argue. The last thing I wanted to do with Ani was argue at that moment. I wanted to pull over to the side of the road and pull her into my lap so I could feel her. I wanted her to run her hands through my hair while I stuffed my face into that spot between her neck and her shoulder that always smelled so fucking good.

I was scared out of my mind, and the longer it took to get to my parents, the greater the fear became. I didn't let myself speculate. I didn't want to make a list of all the bad things that could have happened to make my dad order us up to the house in that horrible voice.

"I'll get Arie. You go on inside," I said as we came to a stop in the muddy gravel driveway in front of my parents' house. The rain was still pouring down, and I'd rather I got caught in it getting the baby out of the seat than Ani.

Ani's hand instantly gripped mine, and I turned to face her in surprise.

"I don't want to go in without you," she ground out, her eyes wide with panic.

My throat tightened, and I used my free hand to unbuckle my seat belt so I could lean toward her.

"Okay, baby," I said gently, as her nails dug into my skin. "You scoot over here, and as soon as I have Arielle, you can hop out, okay?"

She nodded jerkily, scooting toward me, but she didn't let go of my hand.

I pried her fingers away and jumped out of the truck, my coat instantly getting soaked as I threw open the back door. It only took a second to get Arielle's car seat unlatched from the base, but by then my entire lower back was soaking wet and I could feel rain dripping down the inside of my jeans. I threw the little car seat cover thing over her and pulled her out of the car, snagging her diaper bag as I went.

Then we all raced for the house.

"Hey, guys," Dad said, opening the front door as we reached the porch.

"What's going on?" Ani asked frantically as I pushed her into the house.

"Let's all go into the living room," Dad replied, his words barely leaving his mouth before Ani was looking at me and then leaving us in the entryway.

"Gimme that baby," Dad teased, a tired, halfhearted smile on his face.

"No way in hell, old man. I just got her." I set Arielle's seat on the ground and pulled her out of it.

I followed him into the living room and stopped dead when I saw my mom's pale, tear-streaked face. She was holding it together—but barely.

"Alex?" I ground out, swinging my head toward my dad.

"Alex is fine," he assured me, squeezing my shoulder.

But then he took Arielle carefully from my arms, and I *knew* we'd lost someone.

"Aunt Ellie and Uncle Mike—" my mom choked out. "They got a visit from the Marines today."

"Shane?" Ani asked, her eyes panicked.

"Henry," my dad corrected in a strangled voice.

It took me a second. I couldn't wrap my mind around what they were saying. I'm not sure if it was shock or if the human brain just takes a minute to process big news, but in the moment that it took for me to understand what they'd just told us, Ani started to go down.

She looked at me as her face went gray, and I barely caught her before she hit the ground.

"What?" she rasped out as I lowered her to the floor, settling her between my knees. "No. I just talked to him two weeks ago. He's *training*."

"Something went wrong," my mom said, her voice warbling. She raised her hands palm up, like she didn't understand what was happening, either.

"What?" Ani cried out again. "He was *training*!"

Mom dropped her face into her hands and began to cry, and everything inside me seized up. It was hard to breathe. Hard to think.

"He was training, Bram. That's all," Ani whimpered. Her eyes begged me to make it better.

"Where's Aunt Ellie and Uncle Mike? Trev?" I asked my dad as he sat down next to Mom and started rubbing her back.

"Mike got Ellie a sedative from her doctor. She's out for the night," he said between his teeth. "Trev took off. Not sure where."

I nodded, tightening my arms around Ani as she began to cry softly.

"Have you—" I cleared my throat, closing my eyes for just a second. Just to get myself under control. "Have you called Alex and Katie?"

"Your aunt and uncle called Katie so they could get a Red Cross message to Shane," Dad said with a nod. "I was waiting for you to get here before I called Alex."

Shit. Katie must be going crazy down in San Diego by herself. She and Shane worked like a well-oiled machine at this point, but no one could plan for something like this. It was the worst possible time for Shane to be deployed. I just hoped that the Red Cross did their thing and got him sent home quickly.

Ani's shoulders hitched as she took a shuddering breath, then she pulled away, climbing to her feet. "You should go call Alex," she said roughly, wiping at her face. She reached for Arielle, but my mom stopped her with a gentle hand on her arm.

"You mind if I hold her for a little bit?" she asked.

"Sure," Ani said with a small smile, her cheek puckered where I knew she was chewing on the inside of it.

Dad and I left the room and stopped at the kitchen counter.

"Come here, bud," he ordered gently, pulling me against his chest.

I'd been taller than him since I was fourteen years old, bigger too, but when he wrapped his arms around my back, I felt like the scared nine-year-old I'd been the first time I'd walked into his house. He was the only dad I'd ever known. And as I'd gotten older, the hugs had become squeezes on my shoulder or quick, backslapping embraces.

It had been years since he'd given me a hug like this one.

"It's all right, boy," he murmured as I shuddered. "It's gonna be all right."

Henry had been with Ellie and Mike for as long as I'd lived with Dan and Liz. We'd joined the family in the same year, and even though he was five years younger and had been a total pain in the ass when we were kids, I'd always loved him. He'd seemed so fragile at first, a four-year-old with blue eyes that looked too big for his face and white-blond hair that was always sticking straight up in the front.

Trevor, Katie, Alex, and I had watched out for the little joker. Taking the fall for him more often than not when he'd do stupid shit and get hurt, and we'd be blamed for not watching him. He was our little mascot. Our motion-sick-prone little tagalong.

I couldn't imagine a world that he wasn't in.

"We should call Alex," I said finally, wiping a hand down my beard as I stepped away from my dad. "Do you want to or should I?"

"That's up to you, Abraham," Dad said. "Your mom and I would never put that burden on you, but we—hell—we thought you might *want* to do it."

I nodded, understanding exactly what he was saying. He didn't want me to have to tell Alex the news, but I knew that it should come from me. We were two halves of the same whole, and even though we were close to our parents, there wasn't a relationship on earth that was closer than ours.

"Hey, bro!" Alex answered after his phone rang a couple times. "It's late here, you know? Time difference and all that." He laughed, and I had to brace myself against the countertop.

"Alex," I ground out.

My brother went completely silent. I couldn't even hear him breathing.

"Who?" he asked simply as I was trying to get my shit together.

"Henry."

"Aw, fuck," he hissed.

I heard something crash, but stayed silent as he cursed.

"Motherfuck!" he yelled, followed by more loud crashing coming through the connection.

I stayed with him, letting him get it out of his system. I hated listening to him lose his shit. It killed me that he was so far away. All alone. So I just waited. I would've sat on the phone all night.

"I'll see if I can get home," he said finally, his breathing heavy and loud. "How are Ellie and Mike doing?"

"Uncle Mike sedated her, so she's asleep for now."

"Christ," he sighed. "And Trev?"

"He took off. Probably out in the woods somewhere."

"Yeah, not surprising. He'll come back when he's ready."

"I wish I knew where he was headed," I said tiredly, staring at my mom's granite countertop as I scratched at my beard.

"If he wanted anyone to know, he would have said something," Alex said flatly. "I'm going to call and see what I can do about getting leave, all right?"

"Yeah. Let me know?"

"Yep. Give everyone a kiss for me. I'll call you in a bit."

"Okay." The word was barely out of my mouth before he'd hung up.

I looked up and met my dad's eyes as I dropped the phone to my side.

He was crying.

"He all right?" he asked, not bothering to even wipe off his face.

No. He wasn't. I didn't know when any of us would be all right again.

"He's going to try and come home," I replied instead.

"Good."

The next few hours were spent gathered in my parents' living room as we fielded phone calls from my brother and sister. Both Alex and Kate were trying to fly home the next morning and were calling my parents as they found their flights.

Neither needed help. I think they just needed the connection to home, even if it was over the phone.

Arielle woke up and had to be fed, then fell asleep again. My mom drifted off for fifteen minutes, then jerked awake when the phone rang. Ani paced the floor.

Finally, around one in the morning, my dad forced Mom to go to bed and get some sleep.

"I should probably get Arielle home too," Ani rasped, glancing at the baby.

"I'll drive," I said as my dad came back into the room.

"You two can stay here tonight," he replied, rubbing his hand over the bald spot on his head.

I used to think he'd gone bald there because he always rubbed it when he was overwhelmed or frustrated with one of us kids. Kate, Alex, and I called it his "worry spot."

"She's finally sleeping through the night," Ani replied, shrugging her shoulders. "I should probably bring her home to her own bed."

Dad nodded, and Ani got ready to go. As we left, we both hugged him good-bye and promised him we'd be back in the morning.

It was both a relief to get out of the house, and hard to leave.

Shock was slowly turning into grief.

We were silent as we made our way to Ani's house. I didn't have anything to say and she didn't, either. I pulled into her driveway, and we were silent as I helped her carry

Arielle into the house. Silent as I kissed Arielle good-bye. Silent as I pulled Ani into a hug and kissed her hair.

Silent as I left.

I drove all the way to my town house, but before I'd even reached for the remote to open my garage, I was throwing the truck into reverse and turning around.

Ani met me at her front door like she'd known I'd be back and led me into her bedroom. She climbed into bed facing away from me, and I stripped down before crawling in and curling myself around her.

We were silent even then.

* * *

When Arielle woke us up at seven the next morning, we got up and went back to my parents' house. We didn't discuss the fact that I'd spent the night or that I'd changed Arielle and given her a bottle that morning before Ani had even gotten out of bed.

We spent the day making phone calls. Telling people that Henry was dead didn't become any easier no matter how many times I did it, though none of the calls I'd made that day hurt nearly as much as the call I'd made to Alex.

I picked him up from the airport at noon, and by the time we got to the house, Mike and Ellie had made their way over. My aunt looked like a zombie as she puttered around my mom's kitchen, refilling coffee mugs and wiping down countertops. She didn't stop moving, even fidgeting as Alex and I went over to give her hugs. It made my stomach churn. She was there, but her mind was far away from us.

Uncle Mike was the opposite. He sat silently on the couch, looking at nothing. He wasn't even pretending to be paying attention to the things happening around him.

"Where's my baby?" Alex whispered to Ani the minute she walked into the kitchen.

I ignored the flash of annoyance that hit me.

"She's in Katie's old room in the playpen," Ani said. "Hey, asshole."

"Hey, pretty girl," he replied, a small smile on his face. He pulled her in against his side as she wrapped her arms around him. "How you doing?"

"Shitty."

"Yeah, you and me both," Alex said on a sigh.

"Has anyone heard from Trev?" I asked, interrupting their conversation.

"He called Ellie a little while ago," Ani said, leaning her head against Alex's chest. "He'll be by later."

I nodded, then turned on my heel. I needed to get away from them for a bit. I needed to get away from all of it. The emotion filling the house was stifling in its intensity, with everyone talking in hushed voices, their eyes hollow.

I made my way back to my sister's old bedroom and quietly let myself inside. On the far side of the bed, Arielle slept in one of those little portable cribs that were so popular, her arms flung out to the sides of her head. I moved closer to her and sat on the edge of the bed, watching her chest rise and fall.

She had no idea what was going on. Her life revolved around bottles and diaper changes and baths. She slept when she was tired and cried when she was hungry and had no clue that the adults around her were falling apart at the seams. I envied her that, but was so fucking grateful that she'd never remember any of it.

I silently slid my boots off and lay down on the bed, messing with the pillow underneath my head until I could see her. I ignored the way my eyes watered as I got comfortable and my body relaxed into the bed. I'd stay with her for a while.

"Uncle Bram," a little voice whispered sometime later. "Uncle Bram, wake up."

I opened my gritty eyes to find my nephew Keller's face just inches from mine.

"Hey, when did you guys get here?" I asked groggily, glancing at Arielle's crib to find her gone.

"Just now," he said solemnly. "Uncle Hen died."

"I know, bud," I said, reaching out to run my hand over his head.

He sniffled a bit and raised his chin.

Ah, hell.

I reached out with one arm and pulled him onto the bed with me, and it was a testament to how shitty he was feeling that he didn't try to wrestle with me. Keller was a scrapper. He liked to wrestle and fight and be physical in any way he could, but right then, he lay down quietly beside me. We stared at the ceiling side by side.

"Mom keeps crying," he said into the quiet of the room.

"Yeah, my mom does too."

"But I don't cry," he said stubbornly.

"I do," I grumbled. "Sometimes."

"Really?" he asked in surprise, still staring at the ceiling. "Yep."

Keller went silent, and a few minutes later, Kate came quietly into the room, crawling into bed with us on the other side of me.

"Hey, sis," I said, kissing her hair as she laid her head on my shoulder.

"Hey," she replied, sighing.

We didn't need to say anything else. The reason for her visit was obvious, and I knew exactly how she was feeling. So instead, we just lay there quietly, lost in our own thoughts.

* * *

The rest of the day went by slowly. The women cooked. The men didn't do much of anything. The Marine chaplain came out to my parents' house to talk to us about how and when they'd send Henry home and explained that some Marines would be around to help us with anything we needed.

We had dinner, but by unspoken agreement, none of us sat at the dining room table. A family dinner would only highlight the fact that Henry was gone.

Katie put her kids to bed for the night.

I held Arielle against my chest, leaning back in my dad's recliner. There wasn't anything for me to do. All of it seemed to be a hurry-up-and-wait game. We waited to hear when they were going to fly Hen's body home. Waited to know when the funeral would be. Waited for my aunt to lose her shit as she grew more and more agitated as the day went on.

* * *

Two days later, I was playing Lincoln Logs with Gavin when I saw Kate go running past us. I grabbed Gavin and hopped to my feet, carrying him outside just in time to see Kate jump off the porch and into Shane's arms.

"Shane," she murmured as she wrapped her arms around his head, burying her face in his neck.

"Daddy?" Gavin asked in confusion, looking at me and then back at the scene playing out in front of us. "Daddy!"

He scrambled to get out of my arms, and as soon as I set him on his feet, he was running barefoot through the muddy driveway.

"Hey, little man," Shane said, letting go of Kate just enough to lift Gavin into his arms.

Someone must have heard Gavin yelling because soon all of the kids were running outside, yelling for Shane.

My throat grew tight as Sage flew out the front door, coming to a complete stop at the top step of the porch and bursting into tears.

"Aw, baby girl," Shane said, kissing the top of Keller's head before striding to his oldest daughter.

Sage was getting too old to carry around, but it didn't seem to matter then because Shane picked her right up.

She wound her arms and legs around him as he climbed the porch steps, giving me a small nod as he brought her into the house.

I wondered if I'd still be carrying Arielle around when she was that big. Then I wanted to slam my head against the door frame.

"Okay," Kate called, wiping at her face. "It's cold out here. Everyone inside!"

The kids went running back in, chattering happily as Katie gave me a small smile.

"I'm so glad they got him home," she said as I wrapped my arm around her shoulders.

"I bet," I murmured, kissing the side of her head. "How long does he have?"

"Not that long." She gave a humorless laugh. "It's going to be ten times harder when he leaves again."

"Don't think about it yet," I said, squeezing her shoulder. "Just deal with today."

"Yeah."

I walked her into the living room where the kids were going nuts over Shane, telling him about the shit they'd been doing since he'd left. Even Iris, who wasn't saying very many words yet, seemed to be babbling on and on, competing with her siblings for Shane's attention. They were so fucking excited that their little cheeks were pink with it.

I looked over and met Ani's eyes as she came out of the kitchen, holding Arielle against her chest as the word *daddy* was shouted over and over again. What was she thinking? Her lips were pulled up in a tired smile, but she seemed frozen to the floorboards as I took a step toward her.

God, even exhausted, she was still gorgeous.

My eyes dropped to Arielle, who was lifting her wobbly head off Ani's shoulder, and my heart thumped hard in my chest.

Then Ani suddenly spun around and left the room, leaving me staring at the empty doorway.

* * *

"Hey, man," Shane said a couple hours later, patting my shoulder as he came into the living room. "She's cute."

"Thanks," I replied quietly, rubbing up and down Arielle's little back. I'd heard her squawking in the playpen after her nap a few minutes before and had raced to go get her before anyone else could. It seemed like I never got to hold her now that the house was full of people.

"You and Ani together now, or—"

"No," I said shortly. I didn't want to think about the shit with Ani. I couldn't. There was too much happening. I had too many thoughts running through my head at every moment to focus on just one.

"Oh." Shane sat down on the couch, leaning back against the cushions. "Why?"

"You seriously asking about my relationship with Ani?" I asked incredulously.

A year before, I could have happily killed Shane when he was being a complete ass to my sister. She'd been pregnant with Iris, and Shane had treated her like garbage. Just the thought of all the shit that had gone down between them made my teeth grind. After a while, I'd learned to get along with Shane again, but I wasn't quite as forgiving as my little sister.

"I figured it out," Shane pointed out.

"If you hadn't, you'd be a dead man," I retorted, my teeth snapping shut as soon as I'd said it.

The guy's foster brother had just died. My cousin, who I'd known since he was four years old, had just died. I closed my eyes and dropped my head to the back of the recliner. *Shit.*

"Don't sweat it," Shane said quietly. "It wasn't the first time you threatened to kill me, and I'm sure it's not the last."

"Bad timing," I ground out, making Shane bark out a laugh.

"Ah, Hen wouldn't give a shit," Shane said, smiling. "He'd be watching us with his head turning back and forth between us like we were in the middle of a fucking tennis match."

"True," I choked out. "And he'd be asking how exactly I planned on killing you. His favorite was the wood chipper, even though he knew we didn't have one."

"Wood chipper. That's a good one," Shane said tiredly, closing his eyes.

"How does this shit happen?" I asked seriously, sitting up in the recliner as I held Arielle tightly against me. "He died during *training?*"

"I've seen guys do some pretty stupid shit when we

were training," Shane said, leaning forward to rest his elbows on his knees. "Maybe Hen was doing everything the way he was supposed to—who knows. They try to plan for every contingency, but fuck, sometimes shit just goes sideways, and there's nothing they can do."

"So fucked up," I said, shaking my head.

"I can tell you this much," Shane said, meeting my eyes. "They did whatever they could to save him. They wouldn't have just let it happen. The men he was with, they would have been working like hell to help him."

"Okay." I swallowed hard.

"And he wasn't alone."

"Okay." I dropped my head down beside Arielle's and closed my eyes as my nose began to sting, remembering Henry as a six-year-old with missing bottom front teeth, yelling at us to not leave him behind as we ran to pick blackberries. Henry as an eleven-year-old, trying to hide in the bed of my truck when Alex and I were going out with a couple of girls from school. Henry sleeping on Katie's floor when we'd lost power for an entire week one winter. Henry asking Ani out over and over again, his fourteen-year-old chest puffed out as he tried to make himself seem bigger. Henry jumping on Trev's back and yelling at the top of his lungs as he tried to take him down, but failing because Trev was built like a shark and Henry was a minnow.

"You all right?" my mom asked, pulling me out of my memories as she set a gentle hand on the top of my head.

"Yeah," I rasped, nodding.

"Love you, Abraham," she said, leaning down to kiss my forehead. "Wish I could take this all away from you kids."

"I'm a grown-up," I argued halfheartedly.

"You're still my son," she said, reaching out to take Arielle from my arms. "Now it's my turn to hold the princess. You've been hogging her."

Chapter 14

Anita

Shit, Trev could carry the fucking thing by himself," I growled in frustration, making everyone grow silent around me. My tone was scathing. I couldn't stop it. "Bram, Alex, Shane, and Trev can carry him; all this bullshit about pallbearers is stupid. You've got four. If you don't want the honor guard to do it, tell them no. The end."

My hands shook as I set them in my lap, the silence growing heavier and heavier as I looked at the floor I was sitting on.

My nerves were fried.

It had been four days since we'd found out Henry was dead, and they were finally sending him home to be buried. We were supposed to go meet the airplane he was on—in the fucking cargo hold, no less—in just two hours, and I was about to lose my shit. I couldn't deal.

Arielle was doing fine. She didn't seem to notice or care about the extra attention she was getting from our family and was still sweet as sugar when it was time for her to sleep. No fussing or anything. Like she knew that I couldn't take it.

But Bram was in my bed each night. I'd let him in that first night because I didn't want to be alone, and I couldn't stand the thought of Bram being alone, either. Now that Alex was in town, I'd assumed that I'd be able to distance myself a bit.

I'd assumed wrong.

Bram was up in my space even more. He kept coming to my house, and I kept letting him in—because how could I not? I loved the jackass, and I knew he was hurting. I couldn't turn him away.

However, each time he rolled into me and wrapped an arm around my waist, I felt even more desperate for some space. I was holding on by a thread, barely making it through the hours I was awake without completely breaking down and sobbing my eyes out. There was shit to do, things to plan, people to see. The first week after a person dies is full of company and appointments and never having a moment to yourself.

I knew that.

When I went home at night though, I should have been able to shut all of that shit away and grieve. I couldn't do that. I couldn't do it with Bram's wary eyes meeting mine as I opened my front door to him over and over again. I couldn't do it when he shuddered against my back, practically trembling until he fell asleep every night. I couldn't do it when I woke up in the morning and he was in Arielle's room, changing her diaper and speaking softly to her about everything and nothing.

There was no time for me. And so, as I sat there on the floor, words had slipped past my lips without thought, and now I felt even worse.

"Jesus Christ, Ani," Shane murmured tiredly.

I swallowed hard.

"That sounds fine to me," Ellie said, her voice trembling. "You boys carried him around on your back for years, most of the time because he'd jumped up there trying to bug you. Makes sense you'd carry him now."

My breath hitched.

"Anita," Liz said, making my entire body tense, "kitchen."

She climbed up from the couch and walked away as I pressed my hands against the floor, pushing myself up to follow her. I'd fucked up. When Ellie had gone on and on about not knowing who should fill the last two pallbearers' spots, I'd completely lost patience, and that was really shitty of me. I deserved anything Liz had to dish out and more.

"What's going on?" Liz asked sharply as I hit the kitchen.

"I'm sorry."

"I didn't ask if you were sorry, and I wasn't looking for a damn apology. Now tell me what the hell is going on with you."

"Nothing," I sighed, running my fingers over my hair. "My nerves are just fried."

"All of our nerves are fried."

"I know—it's no excuse."

"Go home, Ani."

My eyes shot to hers, and I almost stumbled back from her words. She was kicking me out? My throat got so tight it felt like I couldn't breathe as my eyes began to fill with tears.

"You need sleep, baby," she said gently as I stared at her in horror. Then she lifted a hand and ran it through my hair. "You need some time out of this house."

"I'm fine." I shook my head.

"No, you're not. Go home for a few hours. I'll keep Arielle here with the kids."

"We have to go get Hen," I argued stubbornly, chewing the inside of my cheek.

"Henry won't care if you're at the airport," she said quietly. "But *I* care that you look like you haven't slept in a week."

"But—"

"Anita Bonita," she murmured, shutting me up. Only Henry used that nickname. Oh, God. My stomach turned. "Go home and get some rest. I'll have Danny drive you."

I nodded as I braced myself on the table. Less than a minute later, Liz was walking Dan back into the room, his worried eyes on me.

"Come on, kiddo," he said gruffly, wrapping an arm around my shoulders.

I walked back to the bedroom Arie was sleeping in and gave her a soft kiss on her forehead before grabbing my purse. She'd be fine there while I got my shit together. All the adults were going to get Hen that night, but a really nice lady named Heather that Ellie and Liz knew from some club was going to watch the kids at the house.

I walked out the door with Dan on my heels and dragged my weary body into his truck.

"Only two hours, okay?" I rasped as we reached my driveway. "Come get me on your way to pick up Hen."

Dan looked like he was going to argue for a long moment, then finally gave me a small nod.

I nodded back, then climbed out of the truck as he rolled to a stop.

I didn't bother undressing, just took off my shoes and crawled between the sheets of my bed.

Then I finally let it all out. It started out as sniffles, a catch of breath, a hiccup, but soon I was sobbing so hard that my entire body jerked with each cry. I cried freely. Hard and loud. Then I fell into an exhausted sleep.

* * *

I woke with a start, looking around my bedroom blearily and wondering what had startled me awake. When I glanced at the clock, I cursed and scrambled out of my bed. When my feet hit the floor, I stumbled to the side, slamming my hip into my nightstand, knocking the lamp there onto the floor with a crash.

It was an hour past when we were supposed to leave to pick up Henry's body.

No one had come to get me.

My heart raced in panic as I ran to my dresser, pulling out the bottom drawer too far, making it fall to the floor. I ignored the mess and grabbed a pair of dark jeans, throwing them on the bed before I grabbed one of Henry's old boot camp shirts out of my pajama drawer. It was navy-blue mesh, with a little emblem in the chest, silky and shiny, and one of my favorites even though it was way too big for me.

Running into the bathroom, I screamed a little as I caught sight of my face and hair. I frantically wet my hair down and grabbed a beanie off the floor to cover it up, then swiped at my face to wipe off the tears pouring out of my eyes.

"Shit," I sobbed, my beanie falling back to the floor as I stripped out of my clothes quickly. My hands were shaking as I panicked.

I was going to miss it. I wasn't going to be there. *Oh, God.*

I was down to my bra and underwear, scrambling to pull on my jeans, when my name was called from the front door.

"Ani?" Bram asked in confusion, walking into the room as I lost my shit. I was sobbing by then and tripping as I tried to pull the jeans up my legs.

"Why didn't anyone wake me up?" I yelled shrilly. "I said to wake me up!"

My words were garbled with sobs.

"Baby, stop," Bram ordered, hurrying toward me. "Stop!"

His arms wrapped around me tightly as I shook.

"You guys were supposed to come get me!" I screamed, slapping at his chest.

"I'm here," he said, trying to soothe me. "I'm right here."

"You were supposed to pick me up," I sobbed, my entire body going limp. "Dan said—"

"The flight was delayed," Bram said quietly, leaning his face down to mine. "We're leaving as soon as you're ready."

My chest heaved as his words penetrated. I wasn't too late.

I cried in relief then. I couldn't stop it. I couldn't even try. I was so far gone that I could feel my eyes growing tight as they swelled with the force of my tears.

"Come on," Bram whispered, letting go to grab the jeans at my thighs and pull them up my body, gently buttoning and zipping them as I held his shoulders for balance. "I wouldn't leave you."

I wiped at my face as I tried to catch my breath, my chest aching with each spasm.

"This shirt?" he asked, reaching behind him for Henry's shirt lying on the bed. "I remember when he came home with this."

He pulled it over my head and waited while I threaded my arms through the sleeves.

"Everything okay?" Katie asked, coming into the bedroom as Bram grabbed me some socks.

"I thought I'd slept through it," I said achingly, meeting her eyes. "I thought I missed it."

"Shit, Ani," she murmured, coming farther into the room as Bram pushed me gently to the bed and lifted my foot. "I'm sorry. Once we heard the flight was delayed, me and Mom figured we'd give you a little extra time. We didn't want to wake you up if you were sleeping. Damn, your poor eyes."

"Hey, baby," Bram called quietly, kneeling at my feet. "Rain boots?"

I nodded as he reached up and gently ran his fingers down the side of my face.

"I remember that shirt," Kate said softly as Bram left to get my boots. "He gave it to you after I told him he looked like a stripper."

I gave a watery laugh as I glanced down at the T-shirt I was wearing. It had tiny holes throughout the mesh, making it look almost see-through. Good thing I'd be wearing a coat.

Bram carried my boots back in and helped me to my feet so I could step into them, then he held out my coat so I could slide it on.

"Ready?" he asked, handing me my beanie.

"No," I said, pulling the hat on.

"Me either."

"Amen," Kate said, leading us out of the room.

* * *

Airport staff met us and led us to where a group of Marines wearing Dress Blues were waiting on the tarmac. They were reserved. Kind. Solemn. Respectful.

Quiet.

We didn't wait long before another Marine was coming down the steps from the tunnel connected to the door on the plane. His strides were long and purposeful, but he didn't seem to be hurrying. His gaze passed over us, his eyes pausing on Shane before he came to a stop.

"Good evening," he murmured, glancing at each of us, like he wasn't sure who he should be talking to. "I'm Gunnery Sergeant Samuel Monroe. I have the privilege of escorting Staff Sergeant Harris home."

Ellie sobbed once loudly, and Monroe's eyes immediately locked on her.

"Ma'am?" he asked, stepping in front of her.

"Thank you," Ellie rasped out, reaching for Monroe's hands.

"It's an honor," he said gently. "Henry was a good friend."

My throat tightened as Bram's hand came up to wrap around the back of my neck.

"Do you have any questions?" Monroe asked gently.

"No." Ellie shook her head, looking up at Mike.

"The chaplain explained it all," Mike said gruffly.

Monroe nodded, then glanced at Shane, giving him a small nod, too.

"I'll be escorting Staff Sergeant Harris to the funeral home," he said, his eyes going back to Ellie. "A Marine will stay with him at all times until we've laid him to rest."

"He won't be alone," Ellie said, almost under her breath.

"No, ma'am. He won't. I promise you that."

He squeezed Ellie's hands once more, then stepped away from us as the honor guard went under the plane.

I held my breath.

A few moments later, his feet snapped together as the six Marines came back into sight, a flag-draped coffin carried between them.

Our Henry. There you are, friend.

I slapped my hands against my mouth as my knees began to buckle. Then Bram's arm came around my belly, holding me tight against his chest as we watched them carry Henry toward the waiting hearse.

Monroe was completely motionless as Marines stopped in front of him, then he raised his arm and saluted the coffin.

From what seemed like far away, I heard Katie give a small sob.

Then they slid Henry into the back of the hearse.

We followed the hearse back to the funeral home, but I don't remember much of the ride. Bram held me, I know that much. I wasn't sure if it was more for my benefit or his. Alex sat with his elbows resting on his knees, his seat belt pulling tight against his chest as he covered his face in his hands. And for the first time since I'd met Liz, I watched her slide across the bench seat in Dan's truck and ride home nestled against his side, her head on his shoulder.

* * *

"What's that?" I asked the next day, coming to a stop on the sidewalk in front of the church where Henry's funeral was held. Once we got him home, arrangements were in full swing. We weren't sure how long Shane would be able to stay, and Ellie and Liz didn't want there to be any chance that he or Alex would have to leave before we buried Hen. They deserved to say goodbye with the rest of us.

Arielle was asleep in my arms, a dark gray blanket wrapped around her purple dress. I hadn't been able to dress my baby girl in black. I just couldn't do it.

"It's the Patriot Guard," Trevor said thickly, stopping beside Bram and me.

"Whoa," I breathed as I looked down the row of motorcycles lined up around the block. "Did someone—"

"No, they just showed up," Trev cut me off, running a hand down the tie hanging from his throat.

"Henry would dig that," I said, looking over the men who were standing next to their bikes. "Oh, shit," I breathed, leaning into Bram's hand at my back as the hearse pulled up.

The motorcyclists, almost as if it had been choreographed, reached up and pulled bandanas, military baseball caps, and beanies from their heads, holding them to their chests.

"We're up," Alex announced, walking toward us in his Class A uniform, his back ramrod straight. He and Shane were both in full military dress, and I'd never seen either of them look more handsome.

"You good?" Bram asked as he walked me over to where Liz and Katie were holding the kids' hands.

"Yeah, go get him," I ordered, glancing at the hearse.

Our family followed the boys as they carried Henry's casket into the packed church, then we slid into the front two pews silently. Even the kids were quiet as the pastor began to speak.

There were photos near the front of the church, lined up to the sides of the casket.

Henry at eighteen in his Dress Blues. I remembered him telling me that it wasn't even a full uniform they'd made him put on for the photo, just a jacket and cover.

Henry at around seven or eight, sitting on Trevor's shoulders, his face smeared in what looked like blackberries.

Henry at four, his arms wrapped around Ellie's neck as he cheesed for the camera. Her mouth was open wide like she was laughing.

Henry in full camouflage, a helmet on his head and his face dirty, his blue eyes vivid as he smiled widely for the camera.

Henry and Mike, sitting in the rockers on Mike and Ellie's back porch—obviously unaware that anyone was taking their photo.

Henry, with me hanging off his back, the rest of the kids crowded around during a camping trip right before Alex had left for the Army.

The last one was my favorite. It was taken the last time he was home, and Katie and Shane's kids were hanging on him like monkeys. Iris and Gunner were on his shoulders like he was showing off for the camera, Gavin and Keller were sitting on his feet, and Sage was standing with her arms wrapped around his waist, her smile wide as she looked up at him.

It was Hen's life in a series of pictures, and I hated that we couldn't put up any extra. He was more than that. He liked vodka, especially the flavored kind, though he'd sworn me to secrecy on that. He didn't wear underwear, but bought new socks once a month because he said he liked them soft. He carried around one picture—of Ellie—that he'd stolen when he was twelve from one of Ellie and Mike's old photo albums.

He hated Mexican food, but loved Thai. He said drinking milk was like drinking someone else's phlegm and refused to have anything to do with it. He liked the color blue and wore it because it looked good on him. He put more product in his hair than I did. He had a tattoo over his ribs that he refused to discuss with anyone, and one on his shoulder that he called a boot camp scar.

He loved his family. He was abnormally good at Ping-Pong...and beer pong.

I looked down at Arielle as I listened to the pastor read the story of Henry's life that Trevor had written. It was full of facts. The day he was born, the day he'd moved into Ellie and Mike's, when he'd graduated high school, his military accomplishments.

My face felt numb.

Arielle woke up and kicked her feet as Trevor and Shane stood up at the end of the aisle, stepping toward the podium at the front of the church. "Shh," I whispered, unwrapping Arie as she pushed at her blanket. "Gotta be quiet, Uncle Trev and Uncle Shane are talking."

"Thank you for coming." Trev's deep voice flowed through the church's sound system. "My little brother would really like that his funeral was standing room only."

The crowded church broke out in quiet laughs.

"He'd never let us hear the end of it," Trev said with a smile, leaning toward the small microphone in front of him. His voice cracked a little, and he reached up to rub a hand over his face as Shane stepped closer to him.

"Henry was annoying," he said, making the church laugh. "Funny, and charming...and annoying." They laughed a little louder.

Liz reached out and rested her hand on my knee as Trevor continued, and we listened to how Trevor remembered his little brother.

The rest of the funeral went by quickly, classmates and a few of Henry's Marine friends that had flown in for the funeral got up and shared little stories about Hen. Most of them were funny, some were poignant, all were welcome. I didn't get up to speak. I didn't think that I'd be able to do it without making an ass out of myself.

Then all too soon we were on our way to the military cemetery a half an hour away. When Mike and Ellie had found out about Henry, they'd immediately found a spot for him, and since Mike was a Marine veteran, bought the plot next to him, too.

The Patriot Guard escorted us there. It was sweet of them to do, even though Henry's death wasn't exactly high profile. I couldn't imagine anyone giving us any trouble that they'd have to guard us from, but according to Bram, it was more of a respect thing. Either way, it was pretty incredible to watch.

The Marines kind of took over the ceremony as soon as we got there, and I knew it was a relief for Ellie. She didn't have to worry about any of it. She could sit there numbly while the cemetery director and honor guard took care of everything.

They played Taps and folded the flag draped over Henry's casket in quick, precise movements. Then one of the Marines moved to Ellie, dropping to one knee and murmuring to her as he handed her the flag with both hands.

Bram took Arielle from my arms, and I watched in confusion as he braced her head against his chest, covering the opposite side with his wide palm.

I jerked at the first gunshot.

Then I closed my eyes as the other two rang through the quiet afternoon.

"Thanks," I whispered, leaning against Bram's shoulder.

"Didn't want it to hurt her ears," he replied.

I nodded, my chest tightening.

Then, all of a sudden, it was over, and we were just supposed to leave him there alone.

* * *

"I'm glad it's over," Katie said quietly, dropping down beside me on the couch as I fed Arielle.

The last person had finally left Mike and Ellie's house just fifteen minutes before. The funeral had gone well, as far as funerals went, but it had hurt. Bad. It had felt so wrong to leave Henry at the cemetery. I tried to tell myself that it wasn't Henry anymore. That it was just the shell of him, not the boy I'd watched grow up—but it didn't matter. He was there in the cold ground, and I was afraid that, if I thought about it too long, I would start screaming.

None of us had been able to leave right away, and eventually, Dan and Liz herded the kids back into the cars and brought them home while the rest of us watched as the cemetery crew used a small tractor to fill in Henry's grave.

We'd eventually moved away, but Trevor had said he'd be a few more minutes.

He still wasn't back.

"When does Shane have to leave?" I asked Kate, pulling the bottle from Arielle's slack mouth.

"He flies back with us tomorrow," she said, reaching out to take Arielle from me, then cuddling my girl to her chest as she started patting her back gently. "Then he'll leave the next day."

"Are you sure you don't want to stay longer?" I asked, turning toward her on the couch. "Since Shane is leaving anyway, you could—"

"No," Kate said, cutting me off with a small shake of her head. "I'd love to stay for a while, but the kids need to be home." She gave me a sad smile. "They need to be in their own house and going through their own routines. The little ones will snap back, but Keller, Gavin, and Sage are having a hard time."

I nodded. Henry had been living in San Diego for over a year, and I knew that Kate and Shane's family saw him often. It wasn't the same with us in Oregon, only getting visits when Hen was able to take some leave. The Anderson kids were going to have to get used to not seeing their uncle at the dinner table and during birthday parties. He wasn't a distant relative for them—he'd been a significant part of their lives, and on top of losing him, they had to deal with a dad who still had five months left on a deployment halfway across the world.

"Do you want me to come down?" I asked tentatively. "I still have some maternity leave."

"Nah." Kate shook her head. "I think that would push Bram over the edge."

"What do you mean?" I asked stupidly, opening myself up to a host of shit I didn't want to deal with.

"He loves you, idiot," she said in exasperation. "It's bad enough that Shane and I have to be separated. You and Bram don't need to do that shit too."

"We're not together," I replied woodenly, leaning my head on my arm. "It's not the same."

"Isn't he staying at your house?" she asked incredulously. "How much more 'together' do you need to be?"

"It's not like that."

"It's exactly like that."

"He broke up with me, Kate," I huffed, closing my eyes. "How much clearer do I need to be? We're not together. He doesn't want to be with me."

"He loves you."

"So do Alex and Trevor. I'm not with either of them."

"You also haven't slept with Alex or Trevor," Kate retorted, then went completely still. "You haven't, right?"

"Shut up," I snorted, making her laugh. "Look, I get it, okay? Bram and I have this thing between us. But that doesn't mean that it's going to go anywhere. I have to think about Arielle."

"He loves Arielle."

"He does," I nodded. "Absolutely. But he doesn't want to be her dad."

"You don't know—"

"I *do* know that. He's been really clear, Katie. And that's okay. He doesn't owe us anything. But I can't start shit up with him again when I know there's no future in it. That's not fair to me or to her."

"Mom said to call you guys into the dining room," Bram said flatly from behind me, making my entire body tense. I wasn't sure how much he'd heard, but he had to have heard something by the tone of his voice.

I twisted slowly to look at him, but I only met his eyes for a second before he was turning away.

"Shit," Kate groaned, pushing off the couch.

"It's fine," I said distractedly, trying to shake it off. I hadn't said anything that Bram and I both didn't already know.

We weren't together, and we weren't going to be together. I loved him, I may always love him, but that didn't mean that we were going to prance away in a field of daisies and live happily ever after. The real world didn't work that way. People died in training accidents. Husbands left their wives for months at a time to fight in wars that had nothing to do with them personally. Fifteen-year-olds got pregnant and had to give up their babies.

Couples split up because one of them wanted children and the other one didn't.

I followed Kate into the dining room and stopped short as I saw everyone sitting around the table. Apparently, Trevor had come in through the back because even he was there, his arm around Ellie as she spoke quietly into his ear. The kids were back in one of the bedrooms watching a movie, but every single adult was present and seated in a chair.

"Come in and sit down," Dan said from his place at the head of the table.

I moved slowly, watching distractedly as Bram reached for Arielle as Kate passed him.

There were two spots left when Kate sat down, and I glanced to the side to see the kids' folding chairs leaned up against the far wall.

"Here," Bram said quietly, pulling out the chair to his left with one hand. "Sit down."

I dropped woodenly into the seat he'd directed me to, and we all sat for a few moments, staring at each other as we waited for one of the parents to speak.

Finally, Ellie cleared her throat.

"First, I want to thank all you kids for how you stepped up this week," she said with a small sniffle. She raised her chin and clenched her hands together on the table. "I don't know where I'd be if my boys hadn't stepped in and taken care of things the way they have. And that goes for you guys too." She glanced around the table, her eyes stopping on Bram and me before moving to Alex and then Katie.

"Henry was my baby," she said achingly, pausing to swallow hard.

My hand reached out blindly and grabbed ahold of Bram's thigh, anchoring myself as a wave of sorrow seemed to crash into me.

"Henry was my baby," Ellie said again after she'd gotten herself under control. "And I'm not sure where we'll go from here. Hell, I can't imagine tomorrow, much less worry about things down the road."

Bram's hand covered mine on his thigh, and he curled his fingers, lacing them through mine.

"But Liz and I were talking earlier," Ellie continued, looking around at us. "And we were discussing how happy we are that we have children who come home whenever they can. A family that's happy to spend time together and loves each other. Not all people have that, you know? Kids grow up and grow apart—but not you kids. You're as close now as you were when you were little."

Bram's hand tightened in mine.

"None of you have wanted to sit down together like we're doing now," Ellie said. "And I understand it, because I didn't want to either." She sniffled again, and Mike reached out to rub her back.

"But this—sitting down together for a meal—it's always been important, and it might be even more important now. I'm not giving it up. So we're going to sit here and eat all this dessert that people have been dropping off, and we're going to talk, and Alex is going to needle Trevor until he starts gritting his teeth, and Kate's going to try and talk to Ani even though she's all the way at the other end of the table. We're going to get this out of the way now, so the next time we sit down and my baby boy isn't here, it might be just a little bit easier." Ellie finished off her last words with a hard nod.

It was a good speech. I understood the meaning behind

it, and I loved how hard she was trying, but no one moved after she'd stopped talking and leaned back in her chair.

I glanced at Trevor, who was looking down at the plate in front of him, then at Shane and Kate, who were looking at each other. None of us wanted to make the first move. My gaze moved to Alex, and I braced myself when I saw the look in his eyes.

"I get the meaning behind it, and I fully agree with you, Aunt Ellie. But I'm *not* eating Mrs. Nielsen's upside-down cake," he said stubbornly, shaking his head with a scowl. "Last time she brought one over, I had the shits for two days."

Everyone at the table froze.

Mike was the first one to break, and as soon as his raspy guffaw broke the silence, the rest of us began to laugh. We laughed so hard that there were tears streaming down our faces.

After the first few moments, I wasn't even sure if we were laughing at Alex anymore. We were laughing in surprise that we could even laugh in the first place. We were laughing to prove that we still *could*, that maybe we were broken but that we could eventually live and not be so aware of the gaping black holes in our chests. We laughed because Henry would have said something completely inappropriate to Alex's comment, and all of us were hearing his voice in our heads. We laughed because we'd been crying for so long that any other display of emotion was almost a relief.

"I'm not joking!" Alex bitched loudly, making us laugh even harder.

I wiped at my face as Bram's hand squeezed mine, and when I looked back up at Alex, he winked, giving me a small smile.

I smiled back.

"Well, this one goes to the garbage," Liz murmured with a chuckle, standing up to grab a cake off the middle of the table. "The rest should be safe."

She walked the cake into the kitchen, and I made a face at Alex, causing his smile to widen. He freaking *knew* I liked Mrs. Nielsen's pineapple upside-down cake, and I knew for a fact that it hadn't given him diarrhea because we'd shared the last one between us and I'd felt fine.

I would have expected the asshole move from Henry, but not . . . My head jerked up to stare at Alex again as my eyes began to burn.

"Asshole," I mouthed, giving a watery laugh.

"Pretty girl," he mouthed back, blowing me a kiss.

"Cake!" Gunner yelled, running into the dining room, then sliding over the hardwood floor in his socks until he came to a stop.

"We're having cake?" Keller asked, flying into the room behind his brother.

"I want some!" Gavin yelled from down the hall.

I looked at the boys, watching as their eyes darted around the room looking for an ally.

I knew who that ally would have been a week and a half ago.

"Good thinking," I said, hopping out of my chair. "Auntie will get you anything you want. Grab your chairs and belly up to the table."

"Ani," Katie warned in a low voice.

I ignored her. My oldest niece and three nephews had already lost their mother. Gunner would never remember Rachel, and I wasn't sure how much Gavin remembered, either—but Keller and Sage had already felt the loss of the most important person in their lives. They had Shane and Kate and a secure and loving extended family, but that didn't change the fact that they'd had the rug pulled out from under them again.

There was little I could do for them beyond loving them. Soon they'd go back to California, and I wouldn't see them for months.

But I could do this one thing. I could give them back that one person who had their back and spoiled them right under the nose of their parents.

My nephews wanted cake, and it was my turn to spoil them rotten.

"We've got white cake, pumpkin pie, some sort of Jell-O with whipped cream, and what looks like brownies," I said to Keller as he pushed his chair up against the table.

"All of them," he answered decisively, looking at me with a wide grin.

I glanced at a teary-eyed Kate.

"Good idea," I said.

Chapter 15

Abraham

I really hope no one pukes on the flight," Kate said as we said our good-byes the day after Henry's funeral.

Kate and Shane were headed back to San Diego so Shane could fly back out the next day. My little sister was putting on a brave face, but I knew she was one second from falling apart.

Usually when one of the boys deployed, we didn't let our minds drift to the possibility that something bad could happen. It seemed like bad luck to prepare for the worst, and beyond that, it was just plain stupid. There was no way to survive when you're always waiting for something bad to happen—you had to trust that everything would work out.

But none of us felt that way anymore.

How could we think of anything else? Henry had died on US soil. He shouldn't have even been in any danger.

Now Shane was going back into a war zone. The entire family was on edge.

"Oh, please," Ani scoffed, hugging Kate.

"Gunner was bouncing off the damn walls until midnight," Kate bitched, pulling away to hug our mom and dad.

"She'll forget," Ani mumbled, glancing at me. "Right?"

"Probably not," Alex said jokingly, throwing his arm around Ani's shoulders as Kate and Shane herded the kids off the porch and into my dad and uncle's trucks. There were too many of them to ride together.

I shook my head at having so many kids that the only thing you could drive was a minivan. Kate and Shane seemed to have a system but I couldn't imagine having more than a couple.

I froze, glancing down at the sleeping baby girl in the crook of my arm.

I was so fucked.

"Bram? Hello?" Alex called, clapping his hands.

"What's up?" I asked distractedly, looking away from Arielle.

"You're gonna need to hand over the baby," he said slowly. "We said we'd go over to Trev's today."

Ani's arms started waving frantically as the trucks began turning around in the driveway, and I looked away from my brother as I raised my arm in good-bye.

Kate was riding in the middle of the front seat of my uncle's truck, leaning against her husband as tears ran down her face. *Shit.*

I understood that life had to move forward, but I wanted everyone close. I fucking hated that Kate was leaving already, and Alex was headed out the next day. How could I make sure they were okay when they were spread out all over the country?

Kate's only support system while Shane was deployed had been Henry, and now she'd be down in California all alone with five children. The thought turned my stomach.

"Come on, bro," Alex murmured as Ani took Arielle from my arms. "Trev didn't even show up to say goodbye."

"Yeah, what the fuck is that about?" I asked, kissing Ani on the head absentmindedly as she passed me on her way back into the house.

"You're so fucked," Alex said with a small chuckle, echoing my thought from just minutes earlier.

"Yeah, I'm aware," I said ruefully, wiping a hand down my beard.

"We'll be back in a while, Mom," I called as my mom and Aunt Ellie followed Ani into the house. "We're gonna head up to Trev's."

"Good," Aunt Ellie said, squeezing my arm as she moved past me.

We climbed into my truck and backed out of the driveway. Trev's property actually backed up to our parents' property, and during the summer, we could take four-wheelers through the woods to his place. In the winter though, we usually took the truck. It sucked balls to get stuck in the mud on a four-wheeler when it was pouring down rain.

"What's going on with Trev?" I asked Alex as we pulled

out onto the road. I'd been so wrapped up in watching Aunt Ellie to make sure she was okay, and watching Ani and Arielle when I was sure Aunt Ellie wasn't going to lose it, that I'd barely spoken to Trevor.

"I don't know, man. I think he got Hen's paperwork, and something in there freaked him out."

"They're already sending his benefits and shit?" I asked in surprise, glancing at my twin. I was pretty sure that the military took their time with stuff like that.

"No, his will. I think he had it fixed the last time he was here. I don't know why he didn't use the services on base. It must have been annoying as hell to figure shit out when your attorney lives a thousand miles away."

"The kid never did things the easy way," I said with a snicker, turning onto Trevor's long gravel road.

"I wish I knew what the fuck happened," Alex said quietly, glancing out the window. "But they're not going to tell us anything at this point."

"Do you think they're trying to cover something up?" I asked.

"Honestly?" Alex asked as we came to a stop.

"Yeah."

"I think Henry was probably being a dick and was taking chances he shouldn't have been," Alex said through clenched teeth. He turned toward me, and his eyes were bright. "But don't fucking repeat that."

"Course not," I murmured, watching him closely.

"They're careful, brother," he said. "They plan for everything. So if something happened to Hen, there's a good chance he fucked up."

Trevor's front door opened, and he stepped outside wearing ratty old sweatpants and a flannel shirt. He looked like he'd been on a bender, and by the way he was swaying, I guessed he was still riding the drunken wave.

"They don't ever need to know," Alex said quietly, watching Trev.

He climbed out of the truck as I shut it off, and I followed him up onto the porch.

"Want a drink?" Trev said roughly, turning to walk back into the house. "I've got whiskey."

"Nah, man, I'm good," Alex said.

"I'm driving," I answered, following them inside.

The house was mostly dark, but there was a fire going in the fireplace in the living room, and it looked like that's where Trev had been camping out since he'd left Ellie and Mike's the night before. There was a bottle of Jack Daniel's on the table next to a water glass half filled with the brown liquid. Next to it was a pile of papers stuffed haphazardly in a manila folder.

"What's going on, Trev?" I asked as he dropped onto the couch, leaning into a pillow that must have come from his bed.

"Fucking Henry," he spat, shaking his head. "Such a fucking idiot."

I met Alex's eyes in surprise and stepped forward as Trev began to cry. He wasn't sobbing or any shit like that, but tears were leaking down his livid face like he didn't know whether to be angry or sad.

"You got his will?" Alex asked, sitting down in a rocking chair next to the couch.

"Man, he fucked up," Trev said quietly, shaking his head. "Hafta tell my parents, but fuck!"

I sat next to him on the couch and racked my brain for something to say. He was clearly far from sober, and he wasn't making much sense, but something was going on, and by the amount of whiskey he'd gone through in less than twelve hours, it was something big.

"We don't have any clue what you're trying to say," Alex said kindly.

I almost laughed. Leave it to Alex to just jump right in.

Trevor bent his head and used the bottom of his flannel to wipe off his face, then he lifted it back up again and pointed to the papers on the table.

"I went through Henry's will," he said clearly. "Most of the shit is not a big deal. He gave his stake in the company to me—I outrank you both now—and he gave his surfboard to Keller. Shit like that."

"Christ, you're going to be such a pain in the ass to work with," I complained, causing Trev to give me a small smile.

"I'll go easy on ya," he promised drily.

"So what's going on?" Alex cut in. "Why are you drowning your sorrows in whiskey? You don't even like the shit."

"He left all money in his accounts and his death benefits to a woman named Morgan Riley."

"Who the fuck is Morgan Riley?" I blurted, glancing at Alex.

"The mother of his kid, apparently," Trev growled, picking up the glass full of whiskey and downing half of it.

"Henry had a kid?" Alex shouted, his face screwed up in confusion.

"What the ever-loving fuck?" I muttered, my mind racing.

I couldn't remember Henry ever talking about a woman sticking around longer than a night, much less one he'd gotten pregnant. He'd never said a word, never hinted or given any kind of clue.

"Yeah, no shit," Trevor said, setting the whiskey back down. "He planned all his shit out—made sure that *I* got the paperwork so *I* could tell our mom that her youngest was a piece of shit who abandoned his daughter. He even left me a fucking letter."

I inhaled sharply.

The thought of Henry's daughter never knowing her dad made me want to break down and weep. She'd never learn his sense of humor or get picked up in the middle of the school day because he felt like going for ice cream. He'd never teach her how to ride a bike or surf. He'd walked away from all that, and now there was no way for him to change his mind. What the fuck had been going on in his head?

I'd never do that to Arielle.

The thought made my breath catch in my throat. *Jesus.* I wanted to drive back to my parents' house that second so I could hold her. I couldn't imagine never seeing her grow up. Never hearing Ani read her bedtime stories or pull her hair back in little pigtails.

"I need to tell my parents," Trevor said, running his hands over his face. "I should probably go over today while Aunt Liz and Uncle Mike are there."

"You want us there?" Alex asked, rubbing his hands over his thighs like he didn't know what to do with them.

"Nah, it's probably better if you're not," Trev said tiredly. "Bram, can you go take Ani home? Let her know what's going on?"

"Sure," I said, getting to my feet.

"I'll drive you over and then make myself scarce," Alex said to Trevor. "But first you need to shower and shave that shit off your face."

"Uncle Mike and Dad won't be home for at least another half an hour," I reminded my brother.

"Yeah, that works." Alex sighed and got to his feet. "Come on, man, you can't go to your parents' house looking like shit."

I left the two of them shuffling toward Trevor's bedroom and climbed back in my truck, dropping my head to the steering wheel.

I understood Trev's devastation. We were all mourning Henry. I'd give anything to have him back, to hear his voice or see his face.

But now I was so furious at the idiot that I wanted to hit something.

* * *

"Is there a reason you shuffled me out of the house like it was on fire?" Ani asked in annoyance as we drove away from my aunt and uncle's place.

"Yes," I grumbled, my hands fisting on the steering wheel.

Trevor had given me the green light to tell Ani about Henry's daughter, but I had no idea how to even open the conversation. *Hey, did you know Henry had a kid that he had nothing to do with? Yeah, that would go over well.*

"Well? What's going on?" Ani asked impatiently, setting her purse on the seat between us.

"Trev got Henry's will from the lawyer," I began, only to have Ani cut me off.

"Wait, why? Why didn't it go to Ellie and Mike?"

"Because he wanted it to go to Trevor," I answered.

"Okay, and?"

"He had a kid, Ani," I said quietly, glancing over at her.

"What? No he didn't," she scoffed.

"He left Trevor a letter, and he left the girl's mom all of his death benefits and the money in his accounts."

The truck was silent for a long moment.

"What?" Ani finally said, turning her head to stare at me. "What the fuck?"

"I don't know. That's all Trevor told me."

"How old is the girl?"

"He didn't say."

"Well, where is she?"

"Trev didn't tell me that either."

"Well, is there anything you *do* fucking know?" she sniped at me.

I inhaled long and deep through my nose, trying not to snap back at her. I'd felt blindsided, too—I knew she was reeling.

"The mom's name is Morgan. Henry didn't have

anything to do with Morgan or the girl as far as I know. That's all Trevor told me," I finally said, my voice as calm as I could make it.

"Well, maybe he tried," Ani murmured as we pulled into her driveway. "I mean, we don't know what happened. Maybe she—"

"He abandoned his kid, Ani," I shot back incredulously.

"You don't know that!" She hopped out of the truck as soon as I'd shut it off, and climbed into the backseat to get Arielle. "Maybe he was trying—"

"No," I cut her off, taking Arielle's heavy car seat from her hands. "He left them."

"You don't know what you're talking about," she hissed, stomping toward the house. "You have no idea if he tried to see her or not."

I followed her into the house and sat Arielle's car seat on the floor in the living room, checking to make sure she was still sleeping before I followed Ani into the kitchen.

"He never once mentioned a kid to any of us," I said as I reached her. "Why would he never say anything if he was planning on being Father of the Year?"

"Well, he's not here to defend himself so I don't fucking know!" she yelled, her hands fisted at her sides.

"He left his kid!" I yelled back, throwing up my hands. "He never planned on telling us shit!"

"How the fuck would you know?"

"Because if he hadn't died, he'd still be a fucking deadbeat dad, and we wouldn't know anything about her," I ground out.

Ani's hand flew up, and I barely had time to grasp her wrist before she slapped me across the face.

"How exactly do you have any place to judge Hen?" she asked, her words coming out hoarse.

"Are you shitting me?" I asked, taking a step back from her.

"You don't want kids either."

"I also didn't get anyone pregnant!" I yelled.

"No, you just took off when you knew there would be a baby anyway," she said quietly, crossing her arms over her chest.

"This is bullshit," I murmured, shaking my head in complete bafflement.

"You have no room to judge Hen when you have no idea what was going on," Ani pressed. "It's easy to point fingers when the person you're accusing is dead."

I looked at her in complete astonishment. Ani was loyal, no doubt about that, but I'd never known her to stick her head in the sand about something important. She knew she didn't have to defend Henry to me. I loved him. Nothing was going to change that—but that didn't mean I wasn't pissed as hell at him.

She was hurting. I could see it so clearly in the way she held her body. The tilt of her head and the cadence of her breath. I knew her from the tips of her fingers to the ends of her toes. And I knew, without a shadow of a doubt, that our argument was no longer about Henry.

"I love you," I said quietly, watching her as she wrapped her arms around her waist. "I know I'm not good at it, but I'm fucking trying."

"You can't keep—" Her words broke off, and it took everything in me not to step forward and pull her against
my chest. "I can't keep doing this. You made your decision
before we even got together."

"Baby," I murmured as her eyes filled with tears.

I didn't know what she wanted me to do. I'd do anything. How could she not see that I was all in?

"You can't stay here anymore," she rasped, her words
like a kick in the gut. "I'm sorry."

I closed my eyes and dropped my head. I knew I was
an asshole for taking advantage, but since we'd gotten the
news about Henry, I hadn't been able to sleep without
her. I needed her near me. I needed to hear the sound of
Arielle's little sniffles as she slept and feel the weight of
Ani's body against mine, or I couldn't calm down enough
to get any rest.

"Okay," I murmured, opening my eyes again. "Okay."

"Is Trevor telling Ellie and Mike?" Ani asked as I
turned away from her.

I didn't know if she was trying to keep me there or
if she was seriously curious, but I guessed that it didn't
really matter.

"Yeah," I said, not looking back. "I'm sure Mom will
call you later with the news."

I walked away while I still could. I wanted to beg
her to let me stay—but that would make me such a
fucking pussy. She didn't need that. She was already so
overwhelmed with everything that she looked like she was
going to fall over at any moment. I'd laid it out for her. I'd
told her that I loved her—but it didn't seem to matter.

"Arielle's awake," I called as I checked on the baby girl, kicking her legs in her car seat.

I lifted up the entire seat and held it in front of my face, pulling back slightly when Arie's little fingers went for my beard. "I'll see you soon, princess," I murmured, kissing at her feet while she kicked me in the face. She started to cry when I set the car seat back on the floor, but her mom was in the next room so I only froze for a moment before walking away.

I left Ani's house with my stomach in knots and both of my girls with tears on their faces.

* * *

"Are you gonna sleep anytime soon?" Alex bitched later that night, lumbering into my room in a pair of sweatpants.

"Sorry," I replied, tossing another pair of ripped jeans into the pile next to me. When I hadn't been able to fall asleep, I'd decided to get some shit done, and I was currently going through my clothes to get rid of the stuff I didn't use.

There was already a huge pile on the floor, because apparently I was a hoarder.

"Come on, brother. It's three a.m. Go to bed," Alex ordered, coming up behind me to set his hand on my shoulder.

I sighed heavily and dropped my hands to my knees, stretching my stiff neck from side to side. I was so fucking tired.

"I can't sleep without her," I confessed, shaking my head. I reached up to get another pair of pants out of my dresser, but before I could even look at them, Alex was pulling them from my hand and tossing them to the side.

"You gotta sleep. End of," he ordered, pulling on my arm until I followed him to the bed. "Come on, you sleep on one end. I'll sleep on the other."

I chuckled a little and crawled in between my sheets, glad when Alex chose to sleep on top of my comforter. I loved my brother, but I'd rather his bare chest wasn't rubbing all over my legs while I slept.

"What's going on with you?" he asked after we'd both gotten situated. "You broke up with her."

"I didn't want to," I replied, reaching out to shut off the lamp next to my bed. "I just wasn't down for having a kid."

"How'd that work out for you?" Alex asked snarkily.

I huffed, rolling onto my back. "Yeah, I didn't think that through."

"What was going on in your head? I honestly don't get it."

"You remember when we were little—"

"Barely," he cut in.

"You remember when Mami got pregnant?"

"Ah, yeah," Alex said after a minute.

"You ever wonder who the dad was?"

"Not even once," Alex muttered, stuffing his pillow under his neck so he could see me.

"I just remember her going into labor and not letting us call 911."

"I don't remember that," Alex said, leaning up a little farther.

"You don't?"

"Huh uh."

"Fuck, I wish I didn't."

"The baby died, right?" Alex said, his voice almost a whisper.

"Yeah, man. She was crying and praying and trying to keep her voice down for so long, it felt like she was in labor for days."

"I sort of remember that," Alex said with a nod.

"You remember when she fucking bit me?"

"What?" Alex asked, his brows drawn together in disbelief.

"Pretty sure it was an accident. I don't remember how it happened, but I remember her catching my arm. It hurt like hell."

"Holy shit."

"You were there when it happened. I remember you being there."

"I must have blocked it out or something," my brother mumbled, dropping his head back down.

"That whole night was so fucked up, and then the baby came and it was dead. All for nothing." I closed my eyes and sighed, resting my head on my arms.

"She was different after that," Alex said quietly, "I remember that much."

"She completely fucking lost it," I corrected, clenching my jaw against the memory of my mother sitting at the kitchen table staring at nothing.

She'd tried to get her shit together. There had been times that I'd thought things were back to normal, but it hadn't ever lasted for long. She'd still taken care of Alex and me, still worked and provided for our family, still loved us, but it was like she wasn't even there half the time. She'd just go off in her own head, quiet for hours while Alex and I tried to keep our voices down and whispered about why she was so sad.

As I got older, I sometimes wondered if she'd deliberately walked in front of the car that killed her.

"Is that why you've been stuck to Ellie like a burr on her ass?" Alex asked after a few minutes of silence. I'd thought he'd already fallen asleep.

"What?" I asked, leaning up to look at him. "I have?"

"Yeah, you've been watching her almost as much as you watch Ani—though I'm hoping for different reasons or Mike is going to be pissed."

"I didn't even notice I was doing it," I said, feeling like an idiot.

"It's cool, Bram. Everyone's been keeping an eye on Ellie," Alex replied.

"I didn't ever want to be in that position," I said after a little time had passed. I didn't even know if Alex was still awake, but I kept talking anyway. "She lost it, man. Just completely checked out."

"You didn't want kids because you were afraid you'd end up like our mother?" Alex asked, startling me.

"No." I swallowed hard and squeezed my eyes shut even though the room was already dark. "I didn't want Ani to end up like her."

"Apples and oranges, Abraham," Alex said, reaching out to squeeze one of my feet, shaking it from side to side. "Nothing is going to happen to Arielle."

A few minutes later, I knew he'd finally fallen asleep by the soft, rumbling snores coming from the other end of the bed. He was right—Ani and our mother weren't anything alike. Comparing the two was stupid.

But it had made sense at the time. When Katie had Iris, I'd felt a little of the same fears, but they weren't nearly as bad. Maybe it was because Katie was already a mother to the other four by the time Iris had come along. She'd sort of worked her way into that family, first just helping Rachel and Shane out and later becoming the kids' sole caretaker after Rachel passed away and Shane had deployed. It had been a gradual thing, which made the entire scenario easier to accept.

I punched the pillow under my head, then froze, braced on one arm as someone started pounding on my front door.

"The fuck?" Alex blurted, sitting straight up in bed. "Is someone at your door?"

We hopped out of bed in a hurry and stumbled down the stairs as the pounding continued. Nothing good came from someone knocking at your front door at nearly four in the morning. Alex stopped behind me as I unbolted the locks and swung the door open.

My jaw didn't even have time to drop before Ani's small frame pushed past me, Arielle's car seat hanging from her arm.

"Ani?" I asked dumbly, swinging the door shut behind her.

"You can't just do this!" she said shrilly, spinning to face me with her back to Alex.

Her face was pale, and dark circles shadowed her eyes as she railed at me. Her jaw was clenched tight but her lips were trembling.

"Baby, what's—"

"You can't just keep saying you love me when you're the one who left!" she shouted, making Arielle jerk awake with a startled cry. "And now the baby's awake!"

She rocked the car seat a little, trying to calm Arielle down, but it wasn't having any effect on the screaming baby girl.

Then Ani began to cry, too. Big, body-shaking sobs as she tenderly shushed Arielle.

"Why don't I take Arie?" Alex asked, reminding me that he was still in the room. He reached out and took the car seat from Ani and walked away into the kitchen.

"I couldn't sleep!" Ani sobbed as soon as Alex and Arie were gone. "I just laid there and laid there and thought about you all alone, and I couldn't fucking sleep."

"Anita," I whispered, taking a step toward her.

"Why do I even care?" she asked, her eyes wide. "You left me! You made your choice."

"I was an idiot."

"You were honest."

"Maybe at the time—"

"No." She shook her head, her entire body shaking. "You were clear that you don't want kids, and yet I still keep coming back. She's the most important thing, but I still keep waiting for you."

"You're exhausted, baby," I said gently, moving toward her even as she put her hands out to stop me.

"Everything is so messed up," she whispered as her body sank against mine. "And I'm so tired."

"Come here," I murmured into her hair, reaching down to sweep up her legs so I could carry her into the living room.

She was still weeping quietly as I sat down on my couch, cuddling her to my chest. Her face rested against my throat, and I could feel her hot breath against my skin as she hiccupped and sighed.

I rubbed up and down her back with one hand as the other pulled her even closer, holding her tight as she shuddered.

After less than five minutes, Ani's body went limp against mine, proving just how exhausted she was. I didn't move though. I could hear Alex murmuring to Arielle in the kitchen as I laid my head on the back of the couch, holding Ani securely while she slept.

"Hey, I'm gonna run out to Ani's rig and get the diaper bag," Alex said quietly, carrying a wide-awake and happy Arielle into the living room.

"All right," I whispered. "Just put Arie next to me. She doesn't need to be outside in the cold."

"Good call," Alex agreed, laying Arielle next to my thigh so I could rest a hand on her little belly. She wasn't rolling from her back to her front yet, but I wasn't going to take any chances.

"Hey, baby girl," I said quietly as she kicked at me. "What are you doing wide awake?"

Her hands went to her mouth, and she made a loud sucking noise as her little tongue came out to lick at her fingers.

"It's a good thing you're not really touching anything yet," I teased, smiling as she kicked excitedly at the sound of my voice. "Otherwise those hands in your mouth would be pretty disgusting."

"Good thing Ani had her shit together enough to bring the bag," Alex said, rushing back in the front door.

"She was tired," I said, looking over the back of the couch at him. "She wasn't stupid."

"True," he replied with a chuckle. "I'm going to change Arielle and make her a bottle. Hopefully she'll sleep after that."

"Where the hell are we going to put her?"

"Can't I just buckle her back in her car seat?" Alex asked, picking Arie back up off the couch.

"Oh, sure," I agreed with a nod, giving Ani's back a soft rub when she muttered something in her sleep.

"You should probably bring her to bed," Alex said kindly, watching Ani as her knees pulled even tighter to her chest.

"You sure you're good with the baby?" I asked, standing up with Ani in my arms.

"Yeah, piece of cake."

I nodded and carried Ani upstairs to my room. The blankets were already pulled down so I didn't bother with a light as I climbed onto the bed and pulled the sheets and comforter up around us. As soon as Ani was on her back, she rolled toward me, her hands searching and finding my skin before she relaxed again.

I closed my eyes and fell asleep almost instantly with her hot breath on my chest.

The next morning she was gone when I woke up.

Chapter 16
Anita

Y ou and me, kid," I said to Arielle as she sucked on a washcloth. "Mama's going to get it together. I promise."

She didn't reply. Obviously. But I felt better saying it out loud.

We were in the bathtub, and Arielle was resting on my bent knees, both of us waist deep in water. Usually I just gave her a bath in the kitchen sink, but after my little meltdown at Bram's the night before, I needed a relaxing bath. I wondered vaguely if Arielle had peed yet in the water, but figured it didn't matter.

What I didn't know couldn't gross me out.

"I have to go back to work soon," I said, spreading the warm washcloth over Arie's chest like a little blanket while she stared at me. "But you're going to stay with Nana. That'll be fun, right?"

Arielle's foot slid up my belly and pressed against the bottom of my boob. "Hey, now," I said, laughing. "Feet to yourself, miss."

I cupped a handful of water and poured it carefully over her head, laughing when she sputtered. I didn't even get any on her face, the big wuss.

"Just so we're clear, I don't want to leave you," I said seriously, running my fingers through her wispy hair. "But Mama's gotta keep you in formula and diapers, ya know? Have to pay the bills and all that boring stuff.

"It's kind of nice when it's just me and you, right?" I said when Arie grabbed at my hand and pulled it to her mouth. "I like seeing all your uncles and aunties, but they steal you all the time.

"Yeah, I get it." I nodded when she looked at me with wide eyes. "You never have to be put down when they're around. But it's not like I ignore you. Sometimes Mama has to sweep the floors and you have to hang out in your swing. That's life, dude."

I jerked hard when someone suddenly knocked on my bathroom door, my heart beating frantically as Arielle froze at my movement.

"Ani?" Bram called through the door, making my eyes close in dread.

"Yeah? I'm—" The door opened before I could tell him to stay out. "Shut the door," I called, curling my body around Arielle's. It was warm in the bathroom, but I knew it was probably ten degrees cooler in the rest of the house.

Bram quickly closed the door behind him, and I scowled in frustration.

"What are you doing?" he asked teasingly, coming farther into the room.

"We're in the bath," I growled, right as Arielle squawked loudly.

"I see that," Bram murmured, smiling at Arielle as he sat down on the toilet next to us. "Are you having fun, baby girl?" he asked, reaching out to run his finger down Arie's arm.

"What are you doing here?" I asked. I really wanted to cover up my boobs, which were on full display, but the only thing within reaching distance was the washcloth covering Arielle, and I wasn't going to steal it from her.

"Just wanted to see how you were doing," he said simply, leaning forward to rest his elbows on his knees. "You were pretty upset last night."

"Yeah," I replied uncomfortably. "I think I was having a chemical imbalance or something."

"You were exhausted," he said tenderly, reaching out to brush some hair out of my face.

"That too. Hey, can you turn the hot water on behind me?" I asked, desperate to change the subject. The water was cooling off around us, and I wasn't quite ready to stand up bare-assed naked with Bram sitting right there.

"Lean forward," he ordered, turning on the taps. His hand ran across my back as he checked the water temperature, and I shivered at the sensation.

The water was loud, and after a few seconds, Arielle's face screwed up into a ridiculously sad expression. "Oh crap!" I muttered. "Turn them off!"

"What? Did I burn you?" Bram asked frantically, rushing to turn the water back off.

"No, but look at her."

Bram leaned forward after the room was quiet again and laughed as he caught the expression on Arielle's face. "What's the matter?" he crooned, making Arielle look even sadder. "What's wrong?"

She let out a pathetic little whimper, and I laughed as Bram let out a soft chuckle.

"I guess I should get her out," I said finally, once Arielle's face had gone back to normal and she was staring at her hands.

"You guys are looking a little wrinkly," Bram agreed, getting to his feet. He reached over to the counter and snagged the two towels I'd set there.

"Give her to me," he ordered, dropping my towel on the closed toilet lid and opening Arie's wide over his chest. He plucked her out of my arms and set her against the towel, wrapping her up snugly. "Your turn," he murmured huskily.

Shit.

I pulled the plug and stood in the tub, shivering instantly as my wet lower body hit the air. It only took me seconds to grab the towel and wrap it around myself, but I felt every single one of those seconds as Bram stared at my body.

"So you're going back to work soon?" Bram asked as he followed me into my bedroom. I'd set out all of our clothes so they were ready when we were done with our bath, so all we had to do was dry off and slip them on.

Becoming a mother had taught me the importance of planning ahead.

"Yeah, Monday actually," I said as Bram laid Arielle on the bed and dried her quickly.

"Arie's staying with my mom?" he asked, deftly putting on her diaper, then pulling her little undershirt over her head.

"Yep," I murmured, keeping one eye on what he was doing and the other on getting dressed as quickly as I could in a pair of yoga pants and a sweatshirt.

"She'll do good there," he assured me, buttoning up Arielle's little footed pajamas. "Mom's looking forward to it."

"I know," I said, stuffing my feet into some socks. "I just hate leaving her all day. I'm going to miss shit."

"Have you thought about staying home with her?" he asked, snagging a receiving blanket off the end of the bed and wrapping Arielle like a burrito before pulling her to his chest.

"Of course I have," I scoffed. "But the bills won't pay themselves."

Bram nodded as I sat down on the edge of the bed, running my fingers through my hair.

"We need to talk," he said, glancing down at Arie. "She's sleeping. Where should I put her?"

I guess bath time was more tiring than I'd realized. I'd have to remember that the next time Arielle refused to go to sleep.

"Crib in her room," I answered, crossing the hallway to lead him into the nursery. "She sleeps in here during the day, but she refuses to at night."

Bram huffed out a laugh and set Arie in her crib with

a kiss on her forehead before turning to me and gripping my arm to tow me out of the room. He wasn't mean about it, and it didn't hurt, but it sure as hell gave off the impression that he meant business.

"We need to talk," he said again as we reached the living room.

"Eh, I'm good," I mumbled, taking a couple nonchalant steps away from him when his hand slid off my arm.

"You came to my house at four o'clock this morning."

"Temporary insanity."

"Don't act like that, Ani."

"I'm acting like myself."

"Stop."

"Well, that's not very nice."

"Quit."

"I'm feeling a bit tired," I said with a fake yawn. "Let's do this tomorrow—or never."

"Why can't you be serious for one fucking second?"

"I am being serious. I'd rather have this discussion, never."

"I am completely in love with you," he ground out angrily. The words were so incongruent with his tone that part of me wanted to laugh. The rest of me was frozen though, like one of those fainting goats that are all over YouTube, the ones who go completely stiff when they're startled and then fall right over. That was me. I was a goat.

"I love you too," I said back softly, "But that doesn't really change anything."

"It changes everything."

"No, it doesn't. You loved me before. You loved me when you punched Alex in the face when he found out we were sleeping together."

"It's different now," he murmured taking a step forward.

"Bram," I sighed, wrapping my arms across my chest. "It *is* different. You're right. But the difference is that my priorities have completely shifted. Arielle comes first."

"I know that," he replied calmly.

"Then I'm not sure what you want from me. I have a family, okay? And as much as I like you, I can't be with someone that I don't have a future with."

"Why the hell wouldn't you have a future with me?" he asked baldly.

"Because you don't want kids!" I hissed, losing my patience. God, it was like talking to a brick wall. I was trying to go easy, but he just kept pushing like he had no idea what I was talking about.

"I changed my mind," he replied softly, making my jaw drop.

It only took a second. One second for my surprise to turn into red-hot fury.

"Oh, you changed your mind?" I said nastily. I could feel my skin growing warm as I flushed with anger. "All of a sudden you want to be someone's daddy?"

"All of a sudden?" Bram scoffed, wiping his hand over his beard. "Sure, let's go with that."

"Too bad," I said flatly.

"What?" Bram's eyes opened wide in surprise, and I was secretly glad that I'd rattled his composure a little.

"I said too bad. We're not here for your amusement, Abraham. You don't just get to change your mind in a split second and decide that I should be what? Grateful? Jesus."

"A split second?" he asked incredulously, bracing his hands on his hips.

"Oh, hey," I said derisively. "I think I want to play daddy today. That sounds fun. Maybe tomorrow I can be a fireman, and the day after that I'll be an astronaut."

"You've got to be fucking kidding me," he growled, glaring at me.

"Well, thanks for stopping by," I said cheerfully, moving to walk around him to the front door.

"A split second," he said as I reached him, gripping my arm to stop me. "Yeah, I guess that's true."

I felt my little black heart curl into itself at his words.

"But it wasn't a split second today," he said quietly, "It was a month ago."

"Oh, give me a fucking break," I groaned, pulling at my arm. "I'm not doing this with you."

"You're such a fucking bitch sometimes," he said in exasperation, letting go of my arm but not letting me pass him.

"I accept that," I agreed with a nod.

"Knock it off, Anita."

"All right." I dropped all expression on my face and stood still, waiting for him to finish what he wanted to say.

I just wanted to get the entire thing over with. It was pointless.

"I want to be her dad," he said seriously, pointing

toward Arielle's room. "I want to be your man and her dad. That clear enough for you?"

I didn't let him see the way his words affected me. It was what I'd been waiting for, wasn't it? I'd kept going, putting our relationship behind me even though it had been damn near impossible, but in the back of my mind a small kernel of hope had flickered. I'd just never imagined that it would actually happen.

"You can't just decide all of a sudden after thirty-three years of never wanting kids that you want to be a family man," I said flatly, refusing to even consider it. "You're full of shit. What, going through a dry spell? Fine—strip. Arielle's asleep for at least an hour. We've got time."

Bram's chest heaved as he stared at me in disbelief. "You think I haven't thought this through?" he ground out.

"I think you're lonely and upset about Henry, and I'm a safe option," I answered honestly, the words tasting like gravel in my mouth.

"You know what, Anita?" he asked, shaking his head. "You're going to believe whatever the fuck you want to believe—"

"Very true," I cut in.

"But you're fucking *deluding* yourself if you think that I haven't been Arielle's daddy since the minute you handed her to me in the hospital."

"I know you love her, Bram," I said, lowering my voice in response to his rising one. "You love all the kids."

"Aw, fuck you," he sneered, making me jerk back in surprise. "You're so fucking blind."

* * *

"Her bottles and formula are in one side of her diaper bag, and the diapers and wipes are on the other," I told Liz on my first day back to work. We were standing in the middle of her kitchen while I held Arielle to my chest, dreading the moment that I'd have to hand her over. "She's got two extra pairs of clothes in there too. She didn't have a rash this morning, but sometimes it flares up out of nowhere so I put her diaper cream in the side pocket just in case. She usually naps around nine, but if she doesn't fall asleep until later that's fine too, but there's always at least two naps during the day, if she doesn't fall asleep then—"

"Take a deep breath, Ani," Liz interrupted with a laugh. "I've got the basics down."

I opened my mouth to argue, then shut it again.

"But since all babies are different, I'll call you at the office if I have any questions, okay?"

"Okay," I answered with a nod.

It was probably time for me to go. I needed to get to my office and start fixing all the things that I knew the temporary office manager had done wrong, but I really, really didn't want to leave Arielle.

"She'll be fine, I promise," Liz said. "You brought over half your house so she'll have plenty to do."

She was right. I had. I'd loaded Arielle's swing, bassinet, and bouncy seat into the back of my SUV and brought it with us to Liz's. It had made sense at the time, but now it felt a little like overkill. Hell, we'd been over at

Liz and Mike's constantly after we found out about Henry, and Arielle hadn't needed any of her stuff then.

I tilted my head down and gave Arielle a soft kiss on her forehead, running my lips against the smooth skin there. Then, before I could change my mind, I handed her over to Liz.

"Send me pictures and updates?" I asked as I pulled on my coat.

"Absolutely," Liz assured me. "We don't have anything going on today so Arielle and I will just be puttering around the house."

"Is Dan home for the day?"

"He went into the office for a little bit, but I think he'll be home around ten. We're good, Ani."

"Okay." I racked my brain for anything else to talk about to delay my departure, but after a few moments, I sucked it up and nodded at Liz.

I left the house with a sinking feeling in my stomach and had to work really hard to keep the tears at bay while I drove to the logging office. It was silly. I'd left Arielle with Liz before, and I knew she was perfectly fine. Actually, leaving Arie with Liz didn't bother me at all, normally.

But dropping her off so I could go to work was the first step in a precedent I was setting where I would be gone from her for nine hours a day, five days a week. Going back to work was the end of spending every day together. It was the beginning of our new schedule, and I *hated* our new schedule.

I would not cry.

I sniffled.

I would get my shit together.

I shuddered.

I would do my job, and I would not call Liz five hundred times to check on Arielle.

I glanced at my phone.

Stepping into the office a few minutes later was beyond odd.

So many things had happened since the last time I'd been there that nothing seemed familiar anymore. My desk and chair still sat in the front office, my photo of Kate and me was still sitting on the file cabinet against the back wall, and my coffee mug was still on the corner near my monitor, but nothing looked the same. Everything felt different.

For the first time, I didn't want to be there. I'd always loved my job because it gave me a sense of safety. It made me independent, able to take care of my bills and provide for myself. Now, when it should have been even more important to me since I had another person to support, I hated it.

"Welcome back!" voices yelled as I set my purse down on my desk.

"Holy shit!" I yelped, jerking in surprise as Dan, Mike, Trevor, and Bram came out of their offices. I should have noticed that the office was abnormally quiet when I'd walked in. They'd been lying in wait.

"Bram brought donuts!" Trev called as they all lumbered toward my desk. "Dibs on the bear claw."

"Happy to have you back," Mike said sweetly, patting my back a few times as he leaned in for a hug.

"Arielle get all set with Lizzy?" Dan asked, hugging me after Mike had let go.

"Yep," I said with a rueful smile. "She was fine. I was the one having a panic attack."

I glanced at Bram across my desk as he grabbed a maple bar out of the donut box. When his head came up and his eyes met mine, he gave me an uncomfortable smile, taking a bite of his donut. He didn't say a word.

While everyone else was teasing me about being gone so long and asking about Arielle, Bram was noticeably silent. He stayed in the front office with everyone else, but held himself apart.

"All right," I finally said as Mike and Dan started arguing about some reality singing show they watched with their wives. "Everyone out. I have a ton of shit to go through to make sure the temp didn't fuck up my files."

"Nah, he did good," Trev said, grabbing one last donut. "It was a guy who'd worked in an office like ours before."

"Well, I still want to go through it," I replied stubbornly. "Out."

"Here for thirty minutes and she's already bossing us around," Dan complained to Mike as they walked back toward their offices.

"Thank God, someone needs to," Trevor joked, following them.

When everyone but Bram and I had gone back to work, he finally spoke.

"You look miserable," he said quietly, stepping closer to my desk as I sat down in my chair.

"It'll get better," I replied. "First day jitters, probably."

"Did you even sleep last night?"

"Not much." I pressed the power button on my computer and kept my eyes on the monitor. "Was there something you needed?"

Bram made a noise in his throat, then cleared it. "Nope."

He walked away, and I breathed a sigh of relief. We hadn't seen each other since the day he'd stormed out of my house, and I didn't want to deal with our drama while I was at work. He hadn't shown up to family dinner the Friday before, and I'd been glad then because I hadn't wanted to see him, but I should have realized that it would make my first day back at work even harder.

I felt comfortable around Bram. Always. Even when we were fighting, I didn't feel uncomfortable or weird. However, I knew that, the next time we talked, shit was going to blow up. I could feel it in the air, like the sensation you get when you walk outside and just know it's going to rain. The minute Bram and I were able to exchange more than just pleasantries, everything was going to burst wide open. The last three times we'd seen each other was merely a prelude to the battle I knew was coming.

I cursed as my computer finally started running and nothing was where it was supposed to be. It was going to be a long fucking day.

My phone dinged as I tried to figure out what in God's name the temp had done to my files, and I smiled as Liz's name popped up. I opened the text messages to find a picture of a sleeping Arielle, her hands spread wide and a little message written at the bottom.

Nine o'clock nap!

The day wasn't going to be long. It was going to be long and *excruciating*.

* * *

"Did you miss me today?" I asked Arielle later that week as I fed her a bottle. "I missed you like crazy."

I rested my head against the back of the couch and sighed. I was so tired. I'd thought that the first couple of weeks when Arielle woke up every two hours was hard, but it had nothing on waking up with her at night and then still going to work at seven thirty the next morning. Katie was right when she'd said that I needed maternity leave. I wished I was still on it.

"Hey, Ani! Your favorite person in the world is calling. Hey, Ani! Your favorite person in the world is calling."

"Crap," I groaned, leaning over to grab my purse on the other end of the couch. "I don't know when your uncle Alex got my phone but his ringtone is even more obnoxious now."

"Hey, asshole," I answered when I finally found my phone in the bottom of my purse.

"Hey, pretty girl. How's it going?"

"Good, just feeding Arielle. Do you think it's cool if I

just went to bed at seven? Arie goes to sleep at seven so I'm feeling like that would be totally acceptable."

"Tired, huh?" he asked with a laugh.

"Yeah, working all day is kicking my ass."

"You'll get the hang of it."

"God willing," I muttered.

"How's she doing?"

"Great," I groaned, pulling the bottle out of Arie's mouth as it went slack. "She's, like, thriving and shit."

"Isn't that a good thing?"

"Yes, it's a good thing. But I'm missing everything!"

"No you're not," Alex argued. "Moms have been working full-time for fifty years, and they haven't been 'missing everything' or all their kids would hate them."

"Was that supposed to make me feel better?" I groused, lifting Arie up to burp her.

"Yes?"

"Well, it didn't."

"Lots of moms have to work, Ani. You're not doing anything wrong."

"I know that," I snapped, then immediately tempered my voice. "I just wish that I could be independently wealthy or win the lottery or something so I didn't have to leave her every day."

"Yeah, I hear you." He paused. "Hey, have you talked to Bram lately?"

"I see him at the office every day. Why?" I asked, pushing myself up off the couch. Arielle was going straight to bed so I could, too, do not pass go, do not collect a bath or change into pajamas.

"Just wondering when you two will get your shit together," Alex said lightly, laughing when I growled.

"Why is everyone all up in our shit all the time?" I hissed as I laid Arie down in her bassinet. Thankfully, she didn't stir as I threaded her arms into and then zipped up the little sleep sack she slept in. "We didn't work out."

"If you would get your heads out of your asses, you'd work out!" Alex replied in exasperation. "Jesus, Bram's got this shit hang-up that dates back to our mother, and you can't see the forest for the trees. It's ridiculous and annoying as fuck."

I dropped down to my mattress and stared at my bedroom door. "Hang-up that dates back to your mother?" I asked softly, making Alex curse.

"You need to ask Bram about that," he muttered.

"I'm asking you."

"Well, it's not my story to tell."

"I don't care."

"Well, I *do* care. I don't even remember half the shit he remembers, okay, Ani? He's got all this shit floating around in his head, and I don't even know how to talk to him about it because I *cannot fucking remember it.*" Alex's voice grew rough, and I heard his teeth snap shut as he finished talking.

"I'm not even sure what to say to that," I replied, kicking off my shoes and standing up to strip off my jeans. At least the dress code at work was one point in its favor. Jeans and T-shirts were pretty much the uniform.

"I just wish you'd talk to him," Alex finally said as I climbed into bed in my T-shirt and panties. "I don't think he's sleeping, and you sound like shit too. Something's gotta give."

"I'm fine—just getting used to having an infant and a full-time job," I retorted.

"You don't miss Abraham at all?" Alex asked.

I opened my mouth to agree but couldn't do it. Even if I thought I could lie to Alex, which I'd never been able to do before without him seeing through me, I couldn't disregard Bram like that.

"Yes, I miss him," I finally said. "But it is what it is."

"Wrong."

"You're a nosy pain in the ass, but I love you anyway," I said with a snort. "But I'm so fucking tired I'm going to fall asleep on the phone."

"You're in bed already?"

"I told you I was going to sleep at seven. It's seven," I replied, pushing my face against the cool pillow under my head.

"Fine, but I have one more question for you," Alex said seriously, making me tense. "What are you wearing?"

"Fuck off," I laughed, hanging up on him.

I set the alarm on my phone and set it on my nightstand before rolling to my back in the middle of the bed.

What had Alex been talking about when he'd mentioned Bram's hang-up? From comments made over the years, I'd been under the impression that Bram and Alex's mom was one of the good ones. They hadn't had a shitty home life like I'd had. Their mom had actually died, leaving the boys wards of the state. I didn't think that they'd ever known who their dad was—we were alike in that respect—but beyond that, our stories couldn't have been more different.

So what the hell was Alex trying to imply?

I curled onto my side and pulled a pillow to my chest. My eyes were heavy as I looked out the window, but I knew it would be a while before I actually fell asleep. Nighttime was when I missed Bram the most. Throughout the day, I could keep myself busy enough that I didn't think about him as much, but after Arielle was asleep in her bed and the house was quiet and still, his absence in my life seemed to magnify.

He'd been so adamant that he wanted to be with me the day he'd caught us in the bath, but I couldn't trust him. How was I supposed to believe that he'd changed his mind? Our disagreement hadn't been as trivial as where we wanted to live or how we spent our money. Having a child was a huge undertaking. It meant that you were dedicated to that child for the rest of your life. It was an even more binding and important commitment than marriage.

That's the part that I couldn't get past. Abraham wasn't asking me to date him, or if he was, he was completely out of touch with reality. He was asking for a lifetime commitment, if not to me than to Arielle. But he couldn't just decide a few years down the road that we weren't working out. Even if he stopped loving me, he'd still be Arielle's parent. It wasn't something he could change his mind about, and the fact that his decision came out of nowhere made it even harder to believe.

My eyes filled with tears as I thought about the way

he'd been dragging his body through the door of the office every morning, smiling at me tiredly as he made his way back to his office. He wasn't sleeping, at least not as much as he needed to be.

I wiped my face and pressed it harder into the pillow, trying in vain to fall asleep.

I was pretty sure I didn't look any better than Bram.

Chapter 17
Abraham

Y ou told her *what?*" I yelled into my phone, hearing the case crack in my hand.

"I mentioned that you had a hang-up about our mom," Alex answered sheepishly. "It just slipped out! I was irritated as fuck that you two were being such idiots, and I—"

"It's none of your fucking business, Alex," I yelled again, pressing my fingers into my eye sockets. "You really think that telling Ani that I'm still dealing with shit from when we were six years old is going to help the situation?"

"Well, it couldn't fucking hurt!" Alex yelled back.

"She's got Arielle to think about, and you made me sound like I can't get my shit together. How do you think that looks?"

"It wasn't like that, Abraham," Alex replied, his voice back to normal. "We were just talking about why you two weren't together and—"

"Why the fuck are you even discussing my relationship with Ani?" I cut him off. I was livid. I'd known the moment I answered the phone that Alex felt like shit about something, and as soon as he began speaking, I'd wanted to reach through the phone and strangle him.

I was so tired that it was giving me a sour stomach, and my eyes felt like they were covered in sand. The only thing keeping me awake in the warm confines of my truck was the fact that Alex was trying to talk his way out of the fact that he'd completely screwed up.

"Because life is too fucking short," Alex barked. "You two need to get your shit together."

"That's *my* problem," I growled. "*Mine*. If I want to tell Ani shit about our mother, I will tell her. It's not your fucking place!"

"I'm not going to stop talking to Ani because you've got some fucked-up desire to piss on her leg," Alex argued, his voice low. "She's one of my best friends. Just because you're fucking her doesn't mean that's going to change."

"I don't give a shit if you two want to play Call of Duty or paint each other's nails," I replied derisively. "I'm telling you right now to stop discussing me with Ani. I'll take care of this. I don't need you fucking shit up more than it already is."

"Jesus Christ," Alex breathed, barking out a laugh. "Abraham, I'm pretty sure you're fucking this up all on your own."

The line went silent, and I pulled my phone away from my ear to find that the fucker had hung up on me.

I was sitting in my truck in front of my parents' house, and I'd taken Alex's call so I could put off going inside. I'd missed family dinner the week before because I'd fallen asleep on my couch without even taking my boots off. I was barely sleeping at night, and when I did, I still didn't feel rested the next morning.

Things with Ani and me were tense, but I didn't know what the hell to do about it. I'd laid it all out. I'd told her exactly what I wanted, and then I'd waited for her to come to me—but she hadn't.

I'd seen her at work, and I'd gone to my mom's on my lunch break to see Arielle, but Ani still hadn't said a word about our conversation. She seemed perfectly fine with the way things were going, while I was a fucking mess.

I scratched my fingers through my beard and hopped out of the truck, frustration and overwhelming exhaustion making my movements sharp and jerky. I was running on adrenaline, and the crash was going to hit me hard. My conversation with Alex had pissed me off, and knowing that Ani was just inside the house made that anger magnify by a thousand.

How could she just write me off? She said she fucking loved me, but what? I wasn't good enough for her because I hadn't wanted kids before I met Arielle? If that was the case, why did she keep spouting off about how she still loved me?

I climbed the steps and walked in the front door without knocking. The closer I got to Ani, the more frustrated I got, and the minute I heard her laughing voice in the kitchen, any patience I'd had was lost.

"Anita," I growled as I cleared the doorway, making my mom and Aunt Ellie's heads shoot up in surprise.

"Abraham," my mom called in warning.

"Outside," I ordered, ignoring my mom as I herded Ani toward the back door.

She didn't argue with me, just took one last look at Arielle, who was swinging back and forth in her little swing at the edge of the kitchen, before leading me outside.

As soon as we'd hit the back porch and I'd slammed the door behind us, Ani wrapped her arms around herself and lifted her chin. "What's up?" she asked calmly.

The lack of emotion in her voice made me crazy.

"Why the fuck are you discussing me with Alex?" I yelled, making her jerk in surprise. "How the fuck is any of this his business?"

It wasn't what I'd wanted to say. I wanted to ask why she hadn't called. I wanted to know why she didn't want me. Why she didn't even seem to miss me anymore. I wanted to know if she still loved me.

But I wasn't going to actually say any of that. I'd already told her what I wanted. She knew where I was at, and she simply didn't care. I wasn't going to lie back down so she could step over me and walk away again.

"Are you joking?" Ani asked in surprise, her hands fisting.

"Do I look like I'm joking?"

"No, you look like you're going to fall over. Why don't you go get some rest and then we can talk again when you aren't completely losing it."

"I can't fucking rest, Anita!" I hissed, taking a step toward her. "I feel like shit all the time. And you seem to be doing just fucking fine. You don't want to be with me? Then just say it!"

Ani's mouth trembled, and her cheek puckered.

"Just say it," I insisted, taking another step forward. "Because this is absolute bullshit! I know I fucked up! I know that I acted like a pussy, and I ran—"

"Why did you run, Abraham?" she asked tearfully, cutting me off.

"Because I didn't think I wanted kids and—"

"No," she cut me off again. "The truth."

"That is the fucking truth!"

"Not the whole truth," she argued, shaking her head slowly from side to side.

"What do you want me to say, here?"

"I want you to tell me why you had a change of heart," Ani said simply, like the answer was something easily given.

"I just did," I replied stubbornly through my teeth.

"No. You didn't."

"Because I fell in love with Arielle. From the second I held her, I knew. It was different with her. I don't know if she was just supposed to be mine, or if it was because she was yours, but there's never been a moment in her entire life that I haven't felt like her fucking parent!"

"But you didn't come to me then," Ani whispered, tears running down her cheeks. "It wasn't until after Hen—"

"I didn't know if I could do it!" I roared, Ani's tears

making me feel out of control. "What if something happened to her? What would that do to you?"

"Nothing's going to happen to her, Abraham," Ani said, reaching out to touch me, then dropping her arm as I dodged her.

I couldn't take her hands on me then. I felt too volatile, my emotions too close to the surface.

"But what if something did?" I asked, throwing my hands in the air.

"What are you so afraid of?"

"Losing everything!" I yelled, my chest heaving. "If I lost you, I *might* survive. Barely. If I lost both of you? I'd be a fucking dead man."

I clenched my eyes closed against the words and turned away, bracing my hands against the porch railing. Even saying the words out loud caused an almost visceral reaction in my body. Everything pulled tight, from my feet to my neck. I tightened my hands on the railing to keep myself from going down.

"Baby, we're not going anywhere," Ani choked out, coming up behind me.

"My mother lost a baby," I ground out as she laid her hand lightly at the base of my spine.

"Abraham," Ani breathed, dropping her head against my back.

"And it's fucking stupid to bring that up—I'm not a child, and I realize that bad shit happens every day. I know that."

"I know," Ani whispered.

"You should have seen what it did to her, Ani. She just

fucking faded, piece by piece. As I got older, I knew I didn't want that. I didn't want to take that chance."

"Baby—"

"And I sure as fuck didn't want to take that chance with you," I hissed, turning to face her.

She rocked back on her heels, but before she could pull away, I was gripping her head in my hands, pulling her face to mine.

"I'd never want that *for you*," I murmured, resting my forehead against hers. "Honest to God, Anita. If you had listened to me, if you hadn't adopted Arielle, I would have never taken that chance."

"That's the problem," she replied hoarsely.

"No," I ground out. "*No.* I'd never go back. I'd never in a million years go back to that—I got fucking lucky." I swallowed hard, swaying a little. "I'm so fucking lucky that you didn't listen to me."

"Baby?" Ani whispered fearfully as I began to slide sideways. "Abraham?"

"I'm okay," I said, righting myself.

"No," she gasped, pushing my body against the railing and bracing me up with her body. "What the fuck?"

"I'm so fucking tired," I slurred, dropping my head to her shoulder as I tried to bring shit back into focus. I knew I was scaring her, but I couldn't stop the dizziness that hit me like a freight train. "Can't sleep without you."

"Trevor!" Ani screamed as I tried to prop myself up.

"Jesus," I groaned, using the railing behind me to steady myself. "I'm fine. Shit."

"Everything okay?" Trevor asked less than a second

later, popping his head out the back door. "Holy fuck, Bram!"

My vision was going spotty, and I shook my head to try and clear it.

"Trev," I called as I felt my knees begin to buckle.

Then it was lights-out.

* * *

"Ani," I said sometime later, opening my eyes in the dark. I knew immediately that I wasn't home in bed, and I groaned as the smell of my parents' house registered.

I'd passed out in the middle of yelling at Ani. *Smooth.*

I could hear voices speaking quietly somewhere in the house as I crawled out of the bed and stumbled to the doorway of Katie's old room. It always took me a minute to get my land legs under me when I first woke up. It was something that had happened to me since I was a kid, and no matter how I tried to change my habits by staying in bed a few minutes after I'd woken up, I still walked around like a drunk for a full minute after I'd climbed out of bed.

It had made getting up with Arielle a bit of an ordeal as I'd waited to get steady before I'd lift the crying little miss from her bed.

I turned on the light by the doorway and glanced toward the playpen at the other end of the room, immediately shutting the light off again as I saw Arielle sleeping peacefully with her arms flung out to her sides.

Then I swallowed hard and stumbled into the hallway.

The voices stopped when I got close to the living room, and as I stepped into view, I found six pairs of eyes staring at me in surprise.

"Abraham Daniel, you scared the shit out of me!" my mom bitched, coming off my dad's lap and bracing her hands on her hips.

"Bram was just exhausted," my dad said soothingly, reaching out to tap Mom's butt with the back of his hand.

"Why the hell are you awake already?" my mom snapped, not ready to let go of her anger. She wasn't mad, not really, but sometimes when she was scared it morphed into anger.

"I—" My words cut off as I glanced at Ani's worried face. "Just tired," I said as she stood up from the couch. "I'm okay."

She moved fast, and when she hit my chest, we stumbled back a step because I hadn't really grown steady yet.

"Why aren't you sleeping?" she whispered against my chest. "You have to sleep, Abraham." Her fingers dug into my back. "You scared me."

"I'm sorry," I whispered back, ignoring the people staring at us. "I didn't mean to scare you."

"You went down, and I—"

"Shh," I said soothingly.

"I caught you," Trevor interrupted with a smile. "You're welcome."

"Shit," I groaned, making Ani laugh a little.

"What the hell *was* that?" my mom asked as she

dropped back down onto my dad's lap, making him grunt.

"I haven't been sleeping very well," I answered, walking Ani into the room so we could sit on one of the couches. "It must have just hit all at once."

"Well, I've heard some doozies about trying to get out of an argument, but I gotta say, this one takes the cake," Uncle Mike joked, shaking his head.

"I wasn't trying to—"

"Uh-huh," my dad muttered like he wasn't convinced.

"Well, now that we know you're just sleepy, we're heading home," Aunt Ellie said sweetly.

"I told you he was just tired," my dad argued.

"I didn't know you were a doctor," Aunt Ellie retorted, climbing to her feet and pulling Uncle Mike with her.

"Think I know my boy," Dad griped as my mom stood up, too. "He's looked like shit for weeks."

"Thanks, Dad," I replied sarcastically, making Ani snicker.

I wanted to look at her, but I was afraid to see her expression. I'd passed out during the most important conversation of my life, and I was both embarrassed that it happened and worried as hell that everything I'd said had gotten me nowhere.

"See you guys later," Trevor called, following his parents out the front door.

As soon as they'd gone, I leaned back on the couch and closed my eyes.

"Are you two staying here tonight?" Dad asked.

I didn't even open my eyes as I said "no" at the exact same moment Ani said "yes."

"You're not going home," Ani barked.

"You can drive us," I conceded.

"We'll stay here," Ani said to my parents, ignoring me. "See you in the morning?"

I didn't want to stay the night, but hell if I was going to argue with Ani about sleeping in the same bed again, even if we were at my parents' house and I was too tired to do anything but sleep. She hadn't taken off when I'd passed out. She'd stayed.

That had to mean something.

I followed her into Katie's old room and stripped down to my underwear after she'd closed the door behind us. We were both moving quietly so we didn't wake the baby, but I was aware of every noise her clothes made in the darkness as she got ready for bed. As I crawled into bed behind her, I could have cried at the wave of relief that hit me.

"You scared the shit out of me," she hissed as I tried to wrap my arm around her middle.

"I didn't mean to."

"Well, what the fuck? You aren't sleeping?"

"I couldn't ever fall asleep, so I was just staying up until I was so exhausted that I could get a full night's rest," I answered, ignoring the way her body had stiffened as I pulled her closer to me.

We were facing each other on our sides, and I scooted down the bed a little so our faces lined up on the pillows, nose to nose.

"I want to talk," I slurred, trying in vain to keep my eyes open.

"We'll talk in the morning," she breathed against my face, lifting her hand to smooth down my beard. "Go to sleep."

* * *

"I'll get her. You sleep," my mom said quietly when Arielle woke me up the next morning.

I was standing next to the portable crib, trying to calm Arielle down without lifting her up. My legs were still pretty unsteady, and I glanced at Ani's sleeping face as my mom pushed past me and picked Arie up. Then I looked down at myself and felt my face heat. I was standing there in nothing but my boxer briefs.

"Sorry about last night," I whispered, moving behind the bed to try and hide my lower half as my mom grabbed Arielle's diaper bag from the floor.

"You need to sleep, son," Mom scolded. "Get this stuff figured out before you make yourself sick."

I nodded as she turned and left the room, shutting the door behind her. Then I climbed back into bed with Ani, wrapping my arms around her.

"I pretended I was asleep," she mumbled against the bare skin of my chest, startling me. "So your mom would take Arielle."

I chuckled.

"Mother of the Year," Ani joked.

"You're an awesome mom," I replied, kissing her forehead.

"You lost your shit last night," Ani said, tilting her face up to kiss my Adam's apple.

"I'm going to blame that on a mixture of exhaustion and adrenaline from the argument I'd just gotten into with Alex," I murmured back.

"So you didn't mean it?" Ani asked.

"No, I meant it." I leaned back so I could look into her eyes. "The delivery left a lot to be desired."

"Well, you definitely made a statement. It was like the ultimate mike drop." She lifted her hand above us and opened her fingers wide with a shrug, like she was dropping a microphone.

"You're such an ass," I laughed, shaking the bed.

"Well, it's a good story to tell Arielle," she mused, her lips tipping up. "*When your daddy was fighting for us, he got so excited that he swooned like a Victorian maiden.*"

"I didn't swoon. I passed out from exhaustion."

"Same thing."

"Not at all the same thing."

"Tomatoes, tomahtoes."

"You're going to tell Arielle that I'm her daddy?" I asked softly, my smile dropping as I searched her face. "That I fought for her?"

"Do you want me to?" she replied, her lips trembling.

"Yes."

"Then, yeah. I will."

I shuddered, closing my eyes against the emotion that swamped me. I wanted to both scream from the rooftops and pull the covers over our heads to block out the world. The relief was all encompassing.

"Tell me about your mom?" Ani asked after a few moments of silence, running a fingertip over my lips.

I sighed, wishing that I hadn't even brought her up the night before. Using your parents as an excuse for anything was a massive pet peeve of mine. I hated when people tried to blame their parents for the decisions they made as adults.

"She was gorgeous," I began.

"Oh, yeah?"

"Oh, yeah. She looked like Alex—"

"So . . . like both of you," Ani said with a small laugh.

"Not really," I replied with a smile, rolling to my back so Ani was draped across my chest. "She had his wide smile—you know the one. The contagious one."

"You have that smile too," she argued loyally.

"Well, her face wasn't covered in hair," I joked, squeezing Ani as she pressed a kiss to my chin. "And she was really nice. She smiled at everyone. She was just perpetually cheerful."

"Ah, one of *those*," Ani grumbled.

"Yeah." I nodded. "She got pregnant when Alex and I were five. I have no idea who the dad was, because she never brought guys around. I don't even remember her leaving us with a sitter so she could go out. We didn't have any extended family. I never knew where her parents were."

"I bet that was hard for her," Ani said softly. "Not having any support."

"She managed," I said. "She was a good mom."

"Her baby died?" Ani prodded when I grew quiet.

"Ah, yeah," I said, reaching up to scratch at the side of my face. "We didn't have insurance so she had the baby at home."

"Holy shit!" Ani blurted, her eyes wide.

"I don't know if that's why the baby died, or if it was already dead when it came out."

"You were so little," Ani murmured sadly.

"Alex doesn't remember it."

"But you do."

I nodded, clenching my jaw. "Probably because she accidently bit me."

Ani's eyes closed, and her forehead hit my sternum with a thud. "Well, I'm a dickhead," she admitted, making me laugh as I remembered our first night together and her snide remark.

"It's not a big deal," I assured her, lifting her head from my chest. "I don't like the biting sensation, but you do. It's just a preference."

"I was an ass about it."

"You're an ass about a lot of things."

"Hey!"

I laughed, my chuckles shaking Ani's slight body.

"I'm completely in love with you," I said as she scowled.

"I love you too, I guess."

"You guess?"

"You're not very nice."

"If we weren't in my parents' house, I'd be very, *very* nice."

"You're sure about all this?" Ani blurted out, making the smile drop off my face. "Really sure?"

"I'm selling my town house," I announced, watching her jaw drop.

"Wait, what?"

"I'm moving in with you."

"You weren't invited," she replied, her eyes wide.

"You don't want to live with me?" I asked seriously, watching her face closely.

"Uh, I do." She drew out the last word. "But…"

"Here's the thing," I said, pushing myself up so I was sitting and she was straddling my thighs. "You're taking a huge chance on me. I know you're freaked out—"

"I'm not freaked out," she lied.

"I know you're freaked out," I said again, ignoring her. "So I'll make the move."

I leaned forward and brushed my lips against hers, reveling in the feeling of her skin pressed against mine.

"I'll sell my house. I'll move in with you. You don't have to take any chances except being with me. Okay?"

I thought it was a pretty fucking good speech until Ani's lips quirked, and she started to snicker.

"You just know my house is a million times cooler than yours," she sang, laughing harder. "Sell my house? Ha!"

"You're such an ass," I laughed, watching her head tip back as she giggled. "I was being romantic."

"So romantic," she said, nodding in mock seriousness.

I growled and flipped her underneath me, digging my fingers into her sides while she begged for mercy through her laughter.

Chapter 18

Anita

Hello?" I yelped, jumping around on one foot as I tried to pull a sock on the other.

"Finally!" Katie bellowed in my ear, making me drop the phone in surprise.

"Shit," I hissed, fishing my phone back out of the laundry basket as Kate continued to ramble on.

"I knew you'd get back together," she said smugly when I had the phone back to my ear again. "Called it!"

"Yeah, yeah."

"Mom said Bram's taking you out tonight?" Kate asked. "What are you wearing?"

"Leggings and boots and a gray sweater that hangs off my shoulder," I replied, pulling on my boots. Bram was taking me to Jay's bar, and I was a little bit giddy at the sentiment.

"No! Why aren't you wearing a dress?" she screeched. "I'm all about the leggings—but it's your first date!"

"I've had Bram's balls in my mouth. He can deal with the leggings and like it," I said flatly.

Retching sounds came from the other end of the connection. "I don't want to hear that stuff!"

"Oh, you don't?" I asked innocently, "But you've been all up in our shit for months! Don't you want details?"

"Hell no!"

I laughed, grabbing my purse from the end of the bed as I left my bedroom. Bram was going to be there at any minute, and I wanted to be ready when he did. I was excited.

Liz had taken Arielle for the entire night—which freaked me the fuck out—but I was excited to have time alone with Bram.

"So what changed your mind?" Kate asked after a full minute of petulant silence.

"He—" I sighed, dropping down to the couch. "He really meant it."

"And you know that because?"

"Because he looked at me like my words were the only thing that could keep him standing."

"Didn't he pass out anyway?" Katie asked with a small laugh.

"That was after," I corrected her.

"I thought it was when you guys were out on the porch."

"How the fuck do you know all this?" I asked.

"Mom had me on the phone, and she gave me a play-by-play as she watched through the window."

"Jesus," I groaned, making Katie laugh.

"That's what you get. Boom!"

"I already told you I was sorry about spilling the beans when you were pregnant!"

"We're still not even," Kate growled.

"Oh, whatever," I said.

A knock on my front door had my head spinning to look in that direction.

"Gotta go, Kate."

"Ooh, is he there?"

"I'm going to have sex now. Bye." I pressed end as she started making vomiting noises again.

When I opened the door, Bram was standing there in a button-down shirt under a tan Carhartt jacket, his head covered in a gray beanie and his beard neatly trimmed and waxed.

"Well, don't you look pretty," I mused, looking him up and down.

"I brought you flowers," he said with a small grin, lifting his hand to show me a bouquet that still had the grocery store tag on it.

"Wow, fancy," I teased, taking the flowers from his hand. "Thank you."

I turned to bring the flowers into the kitchen, and Bram groaned behind me, making me smile. Hearing the front door shut, I set the flowers in the sink and turned to find Bram stalking me into the kitchen.

"I know I said I was taking you out tonight," he said in a rough voice as he slid the beanie off his head and dropped his jacket on top of the table. "But I haven't seen you naked in a *really* long time."

I laughed as he grimaced.

"Change of plans?" I asked, taking a step toward him.

"If you feel anything for me at all, you'll take off your clothes," he replied seriously, unbuttoning his shirt.

"But I was really looking forward to going back to where it all started," I said, trying to keep my smile at bay.

Bram's hands paused for a second on his shirt, then he dropped his head in defeat and slowly started to button it back up.

"I'm joking," I told him softly, reaching out to catch his hands.

"Oh, thank God," he murmured, his hands going to my hair as he pressed his mouth to mine. "I'll take you out another night."

"But we have a babysitter *tonight*," I teased, making him groan again.

"So I'll take you someplace Arielle can go," he promised against my lips, running his hands down my back.

I sucked his lower lip into my mouth and sighed as his hands gripped my ass, picking me up off the floor.

"No more baby talk," he ordered, carrying me into my room as I moved my lips to his earlobe.

"Are you sure?" I asked, running my tongue along the outside of his ear. "Because I've heard some of the women you've fucked talk, and if you're into that—"

"We're not talking about any other people we've had sex with," he said, dropping me to the bed.

"You scraped the bottom of the barrel with those ones," I needled, making him scowl.

I didn't even know why I'd brought it up, but I couldn't seem to stop the words from tumbling from my mouth.

"You know I love you, right?" he asked, standing

above me, shaking his head with a gentle smile on his face.

"Yes."

"It doesn't matter what you say."

"Okay," I breathed as he pulled his open shirt down his shoulders.

"You can't push me away. It won't happen."

"I'm not trying to—"

"I know you're not," he said seriously.

Then he took off his jeans, and in the quiet, his words sunk in.

I was never going to be lovey-dovey. I was always going to say inappropriate things at the wrong time and in the wrong place. I'd never be the girl that left him sappy love notes in his lunch or gushed to people about how sweet he was.

And Bram was okay with that.

He liked me the way I was.

Tears hit my eyes, but I refused to let them fall.

"I'm going to bring you flowers," Bram said as he yanked off my boots and socks. "I'm going to tell you I love you and spoil Arielle."

I bit the inside of my cheek.

"I'm going to brag about you," he said quietly as he pulled my leggings and thong down my hips and off my legs. "I'll remember anniversaries, and I'll get you cool shit for your birthday."

"I'll get you cool shit for your birthday too," I said stupidly through my clenched teeth.

"And you'll love me?" he asked as he pulled my sweater over my head.

"So much you won't be able to stand it," I murmured as he unclipped my bra.

"Good," he murmured, coming down on top of me to press his mouth to mine.

I slid my fingers into his hair as he kissed me, and pulled the rubber band out so I could clench the hair in my fists as he ground his hips against mine.

"I'm going to give you blow jobs at least once a week," I murmured, making Bram chuckle as his lips moved down my neck.

"And I'm going to cook dinner because I like to, but I promise it'll be good."

His lips wrapped around a nipple, and I arched my back in response.

"I'll probably forget anniversaries, but I'll write them on a calendar to try and remember."

"Thank you," he said, running his hand between us to slide two fingers over my clit.

"And I'll be proud of everything you do, even if I don't go telling people about it." I gasped as he slid those same two fingers inside me. "I'll love you even when you're being an ass."

"Hey, now," Bram said defensively, biting the side of my breast gently.

"Please," I whispered as his thumb rubbed slowly over my clit.

He kissed me as he positioned himself, and my breath caught as he slid inside, locking us together.

"I'll—"

"Shh," he quieted me, pressing his forehead against

mine. "We'll make our promises later," he whispered. "When you're wearing a long white dress and I'm in a tux."

"You want to marry me?" I asked as his hips rocked, my hand moving down his sweaty back.

"I want everything," he answered, snapping his hips forward.

After that, we didn't say much. We were too caught up in the dance of our bodies, the sweat that pooled on our skin, the scents and sounds of our coming together. It was the best sex we'd ever had, and it had none of the acrobatics we'd performed in the past. Straight-up missionary, but the emotion made it *magnificent*.

I still liked that word.

Hours later, I watched Bram as he stumbled around my room.

"Do you want me to just go get them?" I asked, giggling at his attempts to reach the door.

"I got it," he grumbled, wiping his hand down his face. "You stay in bed."

He finally left the room to go grab our phones and I fell back onto my sheets with a sigh. Bram wanted to call and check up on Arielle, but we'd left our phones in the kitchen when he'd carried me to my room.

"Mom texted us both," Bram said as he came back into the room, looking at his phone. "She sent a couple of pictures and said they were going to bed so 'don't call and check up on them.'"

I laughed at the scowl on his face.

"What are the pictures?" I asked as he sat down next to me, sliding his bare legs under the sheets.

"One of Arielle in her swing and one of Trevor holding her," he answered, tipping the phone toward me so I could look at them.

"Has he heard anything from Henry's baby-mama?" I asked as I looked at Trev's smiling face on my phone screen.

Ellie, Mike, and Trev seemed to be getting back into the swing of things again, but it was apparent to everyone that they were still in mourning. I'd seen them laugh, and I'd seen them smile, but they still carried an awful expression on their faces when they thought no one was looking. I was pretty sure I wore the same one.

All of the drama with Bram had distracted me, giving me a little breathing room from my grief, even though it hadn't exactly cheered me up. I wondered if, now that Bram and I were solid, Henry's loss would magnify again, like the day we'd buried him.

"Trevor called her," Bram replied, taking the phone from my hands and setting both his and mine on the bedside table. "She was willing to talk, but I don't know much more than that."

"Well, that's good at least," I murmured as Bram shut off the light and slid down the bed, pulling me with him.

"I think he's going to head down there in the next couple of weeks."

My head popped back up, and I looked at Bram in surprise. "Really?"

"Yeah, he wants to meet her—the baby."

"A little piece of Hen," I murmured, laying my head back on Bram's chest.

"I can't imagine what was going through his head," Bram said, running his fingers lightly up and down my back. "That's his *baby*."

"Some people aren't meant to be parents," I replied with a shrug.

I didn't understand why Henry had done what he'd done, either. I could barely wrap my head around it. He knew what it was like to have parents that didn't care, so the fact that he'd followed in their footsteps baffled me. On the other hand, I'd realized over the past few months that some people just couldn't hack it. If Henry had been one of those people, maybe it was better that he'd walked away from the beginning.

"I want to go get Arielle," Bram muttered, making my lips twitch. "I know we can get her in the morning, and I know she's fine with my mom and dad, but I want her here. In her own bed. With us."

"Let's just enjoy the full night of sleep," I said, kissing his chest. "We're not going to get any again for a while."

I closed my eyes and relaxed against him.

"I was thinking that we could rent out my town house instead," Bram suddenly said after a few minutes of quiet.

"Whatever you want," I replied.

"We could sell it and get a chunk of cash, but the steady income would be nice. Plus real estate is a good investment."

"Sure." I could feel myself falling asleep as he continued to ramble on.

"Then you could stay home with Arie," he said, laughing when my head shot off his chest.

"What?"

"You don't want to work anymore," he said with a smile. "I know you don't."

"But I—"

"Please don't knee me in the balls for this," he said nervously. "But let me take care of you."

"I don't need you to—"

"I know you don't. You've already proved that you can take care of yourself and Arielle," he cut me off, pulling me up his chest. "But you'd rather stay home with Arie. I know you would."

"Yeah, I'd love that," I croaked.

"So, do it. I make plenty of money, baby. We'd be fine."

"But what if—"

"I'm not going anywhere."

"Are you sure?"

"Why do you keep asking me if I'm sure all the time? Yes, I'm sure." He leaned down to give me a quick kiss on the lips. "I'd rather Arielle was home with you every day."

My mouth trembled as he gazed at me happily, the moonlight barely shining enough light for me to catch the expression on his face.

"You're going to have to find a new office manager," I hedged, making his grin widen. "A *dude* office manager."

"Fine," he said seriously. "You have to give me more kids."

"What?" I jerked back in surprise as his eyes searched mine.

"Arielle needs a sibling," he said quietly, reaching out to cup my face in his hand. "I don't think I want to foster.

I'm not sure I wouldn't end up running for the border the minute they tried to take our kids away. But if you want to adopt again..."

"Really?" I breathed.

"No one older than Arielle," he ordered. "So we'll probably have to wait a few years."

"But there are a lot more older kids than there are—"

"It doesn't have to be a baby," Bram said, shaking his head. "Just younger than Arielle. When Kate was little, my parents fostered this older kid." Bram swallowed hard. "He attacked her, and he could have really hurt her if Alex and I hadn't found them."

"I've heard that story," I murmured.

"After that, my parents didn't foster any kids older than us. So I'd just feel more comfortable if we did that. Only kids younger than Arie, okay? They don't have to be babies."

I dropped my head to his chest and shuddered as I tried to hold back the sob in my throat. I was overwhelmed. Excited. Terrified.

Bram just held me like that, letting me get my shit together as he started rubbing his fingers over the top of my shoulders.

"Twice-a-week blow jobs," I finally promised, raising my head. "I'll even swallow."

My lips twitched, and Bram immediately rolled on top of me, laughing hard into the side of my neck.

Epilogue
Abraham

Hey, little sister," I answered my phone as I walked out of the grocery store with a pack of diapers. Apparently Ani had forgotten to pick any up earlier in the day, and Arielle was down to her last one.

I usually didn't step foot in the grocery store—Ani preferred to do all of the shopping since I'd moved in almost a month before—but I didn't mind doing it. It seemed like Ani worked harder once she was staying home with Arielle than she ever had managing the office.

It had only taken a week for me and Trev to hire a new office manager. It was the same guy who'd filled in for Ani when Arielle was born. Even though Ani bitched about the guy doing something to her files while she'd been on maternity leave, she didn't argue when we told her he had things handled. She was so fucking ready to spend her days taking care of Arie and fixing up the house. It was a work in progress, and I hated when I'd come home to find her standing in the driveway sanding kitchen cupboards while Arie sat bundled up in her bouncy seat on the porch, but I didn't complain because she loved it and she was really good at it.

"Did you know Trevor was coming down here?" my sister asked accusingly, stealing my attention from the memory of Ani bent over those cupboards.

"Yeah," I replied, throwing the diapers into the passenger seat of the truck. "He was going to go down a couple weeks ago, but he ended up having to push the trip back. Why?"

"Is he coming to see that woman? Henry's chick?"

"That's the plan, yeah."

"Ugh!" Katie growled. "He refuses to give me her name!"

"That's because he doesn't want your crazy ass stalking her."

"I wouldn't stalk her!"

"Yeah, you would."

"Only on Facebook!"

"I rest my case, Your Honor."

"You guys suck," Kate huffed, and I imagined the pout she'd perfected when she was little.

"How are you guys doing?" I asked, changing the subject. "Everything good?"

"Yeah, this deployment feels longer than the other one, but we're hanging in there."

"Thanks for the shit you sent up for Arielle," I said, pulling into the driveway of our house. "We won't have to buy clothes for the rest of the year."

"No prob. Shit! Gunner, get off the counter!" she yelled

in my ear, making me grimace. "I gotta go, Bram. Have Ani call me."

"Will do."

"Love you."

"Love you too."

I hung up, grabbed the diapers, and hopped out of the truck. The light from the living room lit up the front yard through the windows, and I smiled as I thought about Ani painting the bottom half of the trim on the inside when she should've been in bed. They'd looked like complete shit then, but they turned out all right when she'd finished them.

"You'll probably be taller than me," I heard Ani say as I quietly came in the front door. Her voice was coming from the kitchen, and I could tell by the tone that she was talking to Arielle.

"Your birth mom is taller than me, and so is your paternal grandmother."

I stopped in the doorway as I took in the sight that greeted me.

Arielle was in her swing in the corner of the dining room while Ani talked to her over the little island that separated the kitchen space from the dining space. Ani looked like she was trying to make some sort of dough— probably biscuits that would turn out hard as a rock— and her hands and face were dusted with flour. So was the shoulder of her T-shirt, which didn't surprise me because my woman was constantly on the move, and a little flour on her hands would never stop her from doing fifteen things at once.

"Your daddy is tall, so it's not like you'll tower over us like a giant or anything," Ani said seriously while Arielle looked toward her like she was listening intently while sucking on her hands. "You're going to be gorgeous, I can already tell. You're happy and sweet, and those are the prettiest types of girls."

"Oh, I don't know," I murmured, startling Ani. "I like the sarcastic and rude girls."

"You would," Ani snorted, smiling as she rounded the counter and moved toward me.

"Hey, baby," I murmured into her mouth as she went up on her toes to kiss me.

"Hey, did you get diapers?"

"Of course."

"Father of the Year," Ani teased, sliding her hands into my hair and getting flour everywhere.

"Is there a reason you're discussing birth parents with our three-month-old?" I asked, pulling back a little to look at her face.

"Bethy called today," she said quietly, making my heart thump hard in my chest. The reaction was instinctual, even though Ani was Arielle's legal parent forever and ever, amen. "She asked me to send her a picture of Arie."

"Did you?"

"I waited for you," she said, one side of her mouth tipping up.

"Thank you," I breathed, my shoulders slumping. "I don't care—send her as many as you want—but thank you for asking me."

"Yep," Ani chirped.

"I wish Shane would hurry the hell up and get home so we could get married," I groaned, lifting Ani onto the counter so I could step in between her thighs.

"Only a few more months," Ani laughed, kissing my cheek.

"You feel like kissing someplace else?" I asked as her hand slid down the front of my jeans.

Ani's eyebrows rose, but just as she opened her mouth to agree, Arielle squawked loudly from her swing. After grudgingly helping Ani off the counter, I turned toward our daughter, whose face was scrunched up in a supremely pissed expression.

As I lifted Arielle into my arms, I called over my shoulder, "We're taking a honeymoon, right?"

Did you miss Kate and Shane's love story?

Please turn the page for an excerpt from
Unbreak My Heart.

Prologue
Shane

W hy are we going to this shit again?" I asked my wife as she messed with her makeup in the passenger-side mirror.

"Because it's important to your cousin."

"She's not my cousin," I reminded her, switching lanes.

"Fine. It's important to *Kate*," she answered, losing patience. "I don't understand why you're being a dick about it."

"How often do we get out of the house with no kids, Rach? Rarely. I'd rather not spend our one night alone at some fucking coffeehouse filled with eighteen-year-olds."

"Damn, you're on a roll tonight," she murmured in annoyance. "Kate asked me to this thing weeks ago. I didn't know you'd be home."

"Right, plans change."

"I promised I'd go! I drop everything for you every time you come back from deployment. You know I do. I can't believe you're acting like a jackass because of *one night* that I had plans I couldn't change."

"I highly doubt Kate wants me here," I mumbled back, pulling into the little parking lot that was already filled with cars. "She's going to hate it when I see her crash and burn."

I hopped out of the car and walked around the hood to help Rachel out of the car. I never understood why she insisted on wearing high-as-fuck heels while she was pregnant—it made me nervous. She looked hot as hell, but one day she was going to fall and I was terrified I wouldn't be there to catch her.

"You really have no idea, do you?" she said, laughing, as I took her hand and pulled her gently out of her seat. "How in God's name did you grow up together and you still know so little about Kate?"

"You know I didn't grow up with her." I slammed the door shut and walked her slowly toward the small building. "I moved in when I was seventeen and left town when I was nineteen. She's not family, for Christ's sake. She's the spoiled, *weird* niece of the people who took me in for a very short period of time."

Rachel stopped short at the annoyance in my voice. "She's my *best friend*. My only friend. And she freaking introduced us, in case you've forgotten."

"Not on purpose."

"What's that supposed to mean? What wasn't on purpose?"

"She was pissed as hell when we got together."

"No, she wasn't," Rachel argued. "What are you talking about?"

"Never mind. It's not important."

"Can you please, *please*, just be nice and not act like you're being tortured when we get in there? I don't know what your deal is with her—"

"I don't have a deal with her, I just wanted to take my gorgeous wife out to dinner tonight, and instead we're going to watch her friend sing for a bunch of teenagers. Not exactly what I was hoping for."

I reached out to cup her cheek in my palm and rubbed the skin below her lips with my finger. I wanted to kiss her, but after all the lipstick she'd applied in the car, I knew she wouldn't thank me for it.

"We'll go somewhere else afterward, okay? I think she's on first, so we won't be here long," she assured me with a small smile, her eyes going soft. She knew I wanted to kiss her; my hand on her face was a familiar gesture.

"Okay, baby." I leaned in and kissed the tip of her nose gently. "You look beautiful. Did I tell you that yet?"

"Nope."

"Well, you do."

She smiled and started walking toward the building again, and I brushed my fingers through the short hair on the back of my head.

It wasn't that I disliked Kate. Quite the opposite, actually. When we were kids, we'd been friends, and I'd thought she was funny as hell. She had a quirky, sometimes weird sense of humor, and she'd been the most genuinely kind person I'd ever met. But for some reason, all those years ago, she'd suddenly focused in on me, and the attention had made me uncomfortable.

I wasn't into her, and her crush had made me feel weird,

uncomfortable in my own skin. I didn't want to hurt her feelings, but shit, she just didn't do it for me. She was too clean-cut, too naive and trusting. Even then, I'd been more attracted to women who were a little harder, a little darker, than the girl who still had posters of fairies on her walls at seventeen.

So I began avoiding her as much as I could until she'd brought home a girl wearing red lipstick and covered in tattoos after her first semester in college. I'd ignored the way Kate had watched me with sad eyes as I'd monopolized her friend's time and completely disregarded her hurt feelings. I'd never liked Kate that way, and I hadn't seen anything wrong with going after her new friend.

I'd ended up married to her roommate, and from then on I'd acted like Kate and I had never been friends. It was easier that way.

"Come on, baby," Rachel called, pulling me into the darkened coffeehouse. "I see a table, and my feet are killing me."

Why the fuck did she insist on wearing those damn shoes?

"Can I get you anything to drink?" a small waitress asked us. Like, really small. She was barely taller than the bistro table we were sitting at.

"Can I get a green tea, please?" Rachel asked.

"Sure! The green we've got is incredible. When are you due?"

"Not for a while."

"Well, congratulations!"

"Black coffee," I ordered when the friendly waitress finally looked my way. Her smile fell, and I realized my words had come out shorter than I'd intended.

"Sure thing!" she chirped with a tight smile before walking away.

"Seriously, Shane?" Rachel growled in annoyance.

"What?" I knew exactly what. I'd been a jackass, but I wasn't about to explain that the crowded coffeehouse was making me sweat. People were laughing loudly, jostling and bumping into each other around the room, and I couldn't see the exits from where we sat.

"Hey, San Diego," a familiar voice called out over the speakers. "How you guys doing tonight?"

The room filled with cheers, and Rachel's face lit up as she looked past me toward the stage.

"Aren't you sweet?" Kate rasped with a short chuckle. "I dig you guys, too."

The crowd grew even louder, and my shoulders tightened in response.

"There's a coffee can being passed around, who's got it?" She paused. "Okay, Lola's got it now—back there in the purple shirt with the Mohawk. When you get it, add a couple dollars, if you can, and pass it on."

The crowd clapped, and Kate chuckled again over the sound system. "I better get started before you guys riot."

I still hadn't turned to look at her. Frankly, I didn't want to embarrass her if she sucked. I didn't—

The clear notes of a single guitar came through the speakers, and I froze as the entire room went silent. Completely silent. Even the baristas behind the counter stopped what they were doing to watch the stage as Kate began to sing.

Holy shit. My head whipped around, and I felt like I'd taken a cheap shot to the chest.

Her voice was raspy and full-bodied, and she was cradling her guitar like a baby that she'd held every day of her entire life. She was completely comfortable up there, tapping her foot and smiling at different people in the crowd as they began to sing along with her.

It was incredible. *She* was incredible. I couldn't look away. This wasn't some silly idea she'd had on the spur of the moment. She knew exactly what she was doing, and these kids knew her. They freaking loved her.

And she looked gorgeous.

Shit.

Her hair was rolled up on the sides in something Rachel had attempted a few times. I think they were called victory rolls? I'm pretty sure that's what Rach had called them when she couldn't figure them out. Her skin was smooth, and she wore deep-pink lipstick that made her teeth bright white under the spotlight. She was wearing a T-shirt that hung off her shoulder and ripped jeans that were so tight, I wasn't even sure how she'd managed to sit down.

I blinked slowly, and she was still there.

"I tried to tell you she was good," Rachel said smugly from my side.

"Did she write that song?" I asked, turning to look at my wife.

"Babe, seriously? It's a Taylor Swift song."

"Oh."

"This one's a Kenny Chesney song."

"I know this one," I murmured, looking back toward the stage. "Does she only sing country?"

"Hell no. It's mostly other stuff, but it's usually got a theme. Tonight is obviously about kids... teenagers, since the donations are going to some stop-bullying charity."

I nodded, but my eyes were on the stage again as Kate danced a little in her seat, tapping out the beat of the new song on the front of her guitar. Had Kate been bullied? I didn't remember anything like that, but like I'd told Rachel, I'd only stayed with Kate's aunt and uncle for a little over a year before I left for boot camp. Maybe I'd missed it. The thought made me grind my teeth in anger.

Kate pursed her bright lips then, blowing a kiss with a wink for the crowd.

My breath caught.

Jesus Christ.

I pushed my seat back from the table and grabbed Rachel's hand, pulling her over to sit on my lap.

"What are you doing?" she whispered with a laugh.

"If I've gotta stay here, I'm getting some perks."

"Oh yeah?"

"Yeah." I leaned in and kissed her hard, ignoring the lipstick I could feel smearing over my lips. I slid my tongue into her mouth and felt her nails dig into my shoulder as she tilted her head for a better angle. God, kissing her still felt as good as it had the first time I'd done it. I hadn't known that loving someone so much was even possible before I'd met her.

"Rain check?" she asked against my lips as she reached out blindly and grabbed a couple of napkins to clean off our faces. Her face was flushed, and I wanted nothing more than to leave that fucking coffeehouse and get her alone.

My wife was the most beautiful woman I'd ever known, and it wasn't just her looks. She'd grown up like I had, scrounged and fought for every single thing she'd needed—and I was proud of the family and the life we'd built together. We'd come a long way from our nasty up-bringings.

"Can we go home yet?" I replied with a smirk as I wiped my face.

"Hey, you two in the corner!" Kate called into the mike, interrupting the incredibly sexy look Rachel was giving me. "None of that, I've got kids here."

The crowd laughed, and I glanced sharply at the stage.

Kate was smiling so brightly that she looked giddy. "That's my best friend, right there. Isn't she gorgeous?"

The crowd cheered as Rachel laughed softly in my ear and blew a kiss at Kate.

"I wanna know who the guy is!" a girl called out from across the room, making everyone laugh.

"Eh, that's just her husband," Kate answered flatly, making the crowd snicker. She met my eyes and winked, then grinned before looking away and starting in on the next song as if she hadn't just made my stomach drop.

We watched her for almost an hour as she fucking killed it on stage. Then I ushered Rachel out of the building without saying good-bye, making excuses about wanting to beat the rush of kids.

I had the distinct impression that I knew very little about the woman I'd been avoiding for the past ten years, and I wondered how I'd missed it. She wasn't the awkward girl I remembered, or the sloppy woman in sweats and tank tops that Rachel occasionally invited over to the house when I was home.

The Kate I'd seen on stage was a fucking knockout—confident and sassy. I knew then that I'd continue to avoid her, but for an entirely different reason than I had before.

Kate

Evans Web Design," I answered my phone as I switched lanes on the freeway. God, traffic was a nightmare.

"Is this Katherine Evans?"

"Yes, who's this?"

"Sorry, this is Tiffany from Laurel Elementary School. I'm calling because you're Sage Anderson's emergency contact number—"

"Is Sage okay?" I interrupted, flipping off the car that honked at me. Why the hell would they call me and not her mother?

"Sage is fine, Ms. Evans. We were just wondering if you knew who was supposed to pick her up from school today? Class ended about thirty minutes ago, and no one was here to get her."

"Her mom picks her up," I replied, looking at the clock on my dash. "She didn't call?"

"No, ma'am. We've been trying to reach her, but haven't been able to."

"That's weird."

"It is," she agreed.

"Okay, well, I'll come get her and try to get ahold of Rachel, but it's going to take me at least half an hour." It looked like my appointment downtown was going to have to be postponed.

"That's totally fine. Sage can just hang with me in the office."

"Okay, tell her Auntie Kate will be there soon."

I hung up and pulled off the freeway so I could turn around. Shit, if I tried to go north I'd be stuck in stop-and-go traffic for the next two hours. I navigated back streets working toward Sage's school, calling Rachel over and over. The longer she didn't answer, the more my stomach tightened.

My best friend wouldn't forget to pick up her child at school. She was a second grader, for pete's sake. It wasn't like her pickup time was any different than it had been for the last two years. Something was off.

It took me less time than I thought to get to Sage's school, and I whipped into a parking space with shaky hands.

I had an awful feeling in my gut that I couldn't seem to calm.

"Hey, I'm looking for a girl, short, dark hair, goes by some ridiculous plant name..." I said in my most serious voice as I reached the front office.

"Auntie Kate! I'm right here!"

"Ah, yep. That's the one I'm looking for," I teased, smiling as my favorite girl in the whole world wrapped her arms around me.

"You just have to sign her out," the office lady said with a grin.

"No problem."

I signed Sage out and walked her to my car, popping the trunk to pull out the spare booster I kept there.

"Where's my mom?" Sage asked, bouncing around on her toes. The excitement of riding around in my car had obviously eclipsed the trauma she'd endured by being forgotten at school.

"I'm not sure, kiddo," I answered as I got her situated in the backseat.

"Daddy's at the range today!" Sage informed me as we made our way to her house.

"Oh yeah?"

"Yeah, he's been home for a long time."

"It sure seems that way, doesn't it?" I replied cheerfully. She had no idea.

I didn't mind that Rachel wanted to spend time with Shane while he was home. I totally understood it. But it sucked being the friend who was ignored when someone's significant other came home from yet another military deployment. I practically lived with Rachel while Shane was gone—she hated being alone—but the moment her husband stepped foot on American soil, I was persona non grata again.

It had been happening for years. I wasn't sure why it still bothered me.

"Mom's going to have a baby soon," Sage piped up from the backseat as I turned onto their street.

"I know, pretty exciting, right?"

"Yeah. She's having another brother, though."

"What's wrong with brothers? I have two brothers," I reminded her, pulling into their empty driveway.

I climbed out of the car as she started to answer and looked at the quiet house in confusion when no one came to greet us. Where the hell were Rachel and the boys?

Sage continued rambling on as I helped her out of her seat. "—wanted a sister. Boys stink, and they only play with boy stuff—"

"Kate?" someone called from across the street. "Where's Rachel? She was supposed to pick up the boys like two hours ago!"

I turned to see Rachel's neighbor Megan crossing the dead-end street with Gavin on her hip and Keller skipping alongside her.

"No clue," I answered quietly as she reached me. "The school called because she didn't pick Sage up. I've been trying to reach her for the last forty minutes."

"Where's my mom?" Sage asked, looking between us in confusion.

"Hey, sis, take the boys inside for me, would ya?" I handed her my keys as Megan set Gavin on the ground. "I'll be inside in a sec, and we'll make a snack. You guys want to make some cookies?"

"Yeah!" Keller yelled, throwing his fist in the air.

"No hello for your favorite aunt?" I asked him with a raised brow.

"Hi, Auntie Kate! Cookies!" he yelled, racing toward the door with Gavin and Sage trailing behind him.

I watched as Sage unlocked the door, leaving the keys hanging in the lock as she rushed inside.

"What the hell is going on?" I asked, turning to Megan.

"I have no clue. She said she was going to get her nails done and she'd be back in, like, an hour. It's been well over three now," she replied in frustration, wrapping her arms around her waist.

"That's not like her."

"No, I know it's not." She rushed to add, "I'm not mad, I'm worried. She's usually back *before* she says she'll be."

"Auntie Kate, cookies!" Keller screamed at me from the front door.

"I better get in there," I told Megan, looking over my shoulder at Keller swinging on the open door. "Thanks so much for watching them."

"No problem," she answered with a nod. "Let me know when you hear anything, okay?"

"Sure," I said, already walking toward where my little monkey was trying to climb the door frame.

"Let's go make a mess in the kitchen!" I announced loudly, picking Keller up like a football as he giggled. I forced myself not to panic in front of the kids as we pulled ingredients out of the cupboards and began trashing the kitchen. I told myself that Rachel would call soon, but the longer I was there with no word from her, the less I believed it.

* * *

We didn't hear anything, not for hours.

I tried to call Rachel at least a hundred times but she never answered, and after a while I couldn't even leave another message in her full voicemail.

It wasn't until I was making dinner for the kids that my phone rang, and I almost dropped it in my haste to answer.

"Hello?" I said, walking toward the laundry room for a bit of quiet. "Hello?"

"Can I please speak to Katherine Evans?"

"This is Katherine."

"Hello, this is Margie at Tri-City Medical Center. I'm calling about a Rachel Anderson."

My knees felt like water, and I reached out to grip the washing machine to keep me on my feet. "Is she okay?"

"Ma'am, she's been in an accident."

"Is she okay?" I could hear my voice becoming more shrill with every word, and I clenched my teeth to keep myself from yelling.

"Can you come to the hospital, ma'am?"

The woman's voice was unnaturally calm, and I knew that no matter what I said she wasn't going to give me a straight answer. Hell, it was her job to notify people that their family was in the hospital. She didn't give a shit that I was about to lose my mind.

"I'll—" I looked around the laundry room in a panic. What was I supposed to do? "I'm on my way. Tell her I'm on my way."

"Come straight to the emergency entrance when you get here."

"I will."

The minute she hung up, I bent at the waist and braced my hands on my knees, trying to get my shit together.

Rachel was fine. The baby was fine. I was freaking out

over nothing. I was getting myself worked up over nothing. It was just an accident.

"Sage!" I yelled as I walked quickly through the house. "Keep an eye on your brothers. I'm walking over to Megan's real quick—I'll be right outside!"

As I reached the front porch, I began to sprint, and by the time I was at Megan's front door I was out of breath and on the verge of tears.

"Kate? What's up?" Megan asked as she swung the door open.

"Can you take care of the kids? I have to go—the hospital just called." A painful sob burst out of my throat, and I wiped my hand over my face to try to gain some control. "They said Rachel's been in an accident. I need to get over there."

"Sure, honey. No worries," she answered before I was even finished speaking. "Caleb, get your shoes on, bud! We're going over to the Andersons' for a bit."

"Woohoo!" I heard from somewhere in the back of the house.

"Did you call Shane?" she asked, sliding into some sandals by the door.

"I didn't even think to," I replied with a small shake of my head. "He's rarely here. I forgot he was in town." I felt like shit for not calling him, but I was so used to taking care of things while he was gone that it hadn't even dawned on me. I'd driven Rachel to the hospital when she'd had Gavin, taken care of things when Keller broke his arm, and helped with a thousand other little events over the past few years. I stepped in every time he was gone, and I hadn't thought about him for one second as I'd paced around the house that afternoon.

"We'll be over in a minute. I'm sure she's fine," Megan assured me with a nod. "You better go get some shoes on and let the kids know I'm coming over for a visit."

"I'm not telling them—" I shook my head and looked down at my bare feet. I hadn't even noticed the hot pavement as I'd run across it barefoot. Why didn't I put shoes on?

"Come on," she said gently, pushing me away from the door as her kid raced out ahead of us. "We'll walk you over."

* * *

I'm not sure what I said to the kids about the reason I was leaving, and I don't remember the drive to the hospital or even where I parked that afternoon. I can't recall what the nurse looked like as she searched for Rachel's name in their computer system or the walk toward the room where I waited for someone to speak to me.

The first thing I remember clearly is the white-haired doctor's kind face as he sat down across from me, and the young chaplain's small smile as he chose the chair to my left. Their words became a litany that I would hear in my dreams for years.

My Rachel was gone, but her son was alive and in the NICU.

"Is there anyone you'd like for us to call? Any family or friends that you'd like to be here?"

The question jolted me out of the fog that seemed to be getting thicker and thicker around me. *Dear God.*

"I'll make the calls," I answered, looking blankly at the wall. "Can I have some privacy please?"

"Of course. I'll be right outside if you need me," the chaplain answered, reaching out to pat my hand. "I'll take you up to the NICU when you're ready."

The room was silent after they left, and I fought the urge to scream at the top of my lungs just to hear it echo around me. I understood then why people hired mourners to wail at funerals. Sometimes the lack of sound is more painful than the anguished noise of a heart breaking.

My hands shook as I pulled my phone out of my front pocket and rested it on the table in front of me.

It only took a moment before the sound of ringing filled the room, and I rested my head in my hands as I stared at the name across the screen.

"Hello? Kate? What's wrong?"

"Shane—" I said quietly, my voice hitching.

"What? Why are you calling me?" His voice was confused, but I could hear a small thread of panic in the urgency of his words.

"I need you to come to Tri-City hospital," I answered, tears rolling down my face and landing on the glass screen of my phone, distorting the letters and numbers.

"Who?" His voice was frantic, and I could hear him moving around, his breathing heavy.

"Rachel was in an accident." I sobbed, covering my face to try to muffle the noise.

"No," he argued desperately as I heard two car doors shut almost simultaneously. "Is she okay?"

I shook my head, trying to catch my breath.

"Kate! Is she okay?" he screamed at me, his anguished voice filling the room as I'd wanted mine to just minutes before.

"No," I answered through gritted teeth, feeling snot running down my upper lip as I heard him make a noise deep in his throat. "She's gone."

He didn't say a word, and less than a second later the connection was broken.

I could barely force myself to reach across the table for a tissue as I scrolled down my contact list and pressed SEND again. I wasn't finished.

"Hello!" Her voice made me whimper in both relief and sorrow.

"Mom?" I rasped.

"Katie?"

"I—I—"

"Take a deep breath, baby. Then tell me what's wrong," she ordered.

"I need you and Aunt Ellie to come down here," I cried, straightening my back and wiping the tears from my face. "I'm not—I don't know what to do."

"Okay, we'll find a flight," she answered immediately, like flying from Portland to San Diego was as easy as walking across the street. "Now what's going on?"

"Rachel was in an accident," I ground out, the words like gravel in my throat. "She didn't make it, and I'm worried about Shane."

"Oh, Katie. My sweet girl," she said sadly. "We'll be on the first flight down, okay, baby?" Her voice became muffled as she covered the phone and yelled shrilly for my dad.

"I just, I'm not sure what I'm supposed to be doing," I confessed with a sob. "Shane isn't here yet, and I don't think I can see her, and the baby is in ICU."

"The baby's okay?"

"Yeah, they said they were just keeping him under observation." I rubbed at my forehead, trying to convince myself that it was all just a nightmare. Where was I supposed to be? What was I supposed to do now? My best friend in the entire world was there in that hospital, but not really. I couldn't bear to see her. I couldn't help her. Where the fuck was I supposed to go? "What do I do, Mom?"

"You go see your nephew."

"What?"

"You go to the NICU, and you hold your nephew, and you tell him everything is going to be okay," she told me, tears in her voice. "You go love on that baby. Where are Sage and the boys?"

"They're with a neighbor. They're okay."

"Good. That's good."

"Yeah."

"Dad found some flights. I'm on my way, princess," she told me gently. "We'll be there soon. Now go take care of our new boy."

"I love you, Mom."

"I love you, too. I'm on my way."

I made my way to the NICU as quickly as I could, and within minutes I was holding my new nephew in my arms. The nurses told me that he'd passed all of his tests with flying colors, and I was in awe as I sat down in a rocking chair, cradling him to my chest.

"You sure got a shitty beginning, little man," I murmured against his fuzzy scalp, rocking back and forth gently. "I'm so sorry, buddy. You're probably missing your mama and that warm bubble you've been in for so long. I can't help you there."

I sniffled, closing my eyes as tears rolled down my cheeks. My whole body ached, and even though I had that little boy in my arms, the day seemed like some sort of surreal dream, foggy in some parts and crystal clear in others. I wanted to hop up and take his sleeping little form to Rachel, to tease her about the weird Mohawk thing he was sporting and make joking comments about how men always seem to sleep through the hard parts of life. I wanted to see her smile proudly at the sturdy boy she'd produced and grumble that I was hogging him.

I wanted everything to be different.

I hummed softly with my eyes closed for a long time, holding the baby close to me. It was quiet where we sat, nothing breaking up the stillness of the room until I heard someone open the door.

"There he is," the nurse murmured from the doorway.

My eyes popped open to see Shane's ravaged face just feet from me. He looked like he was barely holding on. I swallowed hard as his red-rimmed eyes took in his son carefully before rising to meet mine.

"Is he okay?" he asked thickly, searching my face. I'd never seen him so frightened.

"He's perfect," I answered, my voice throbbing with emotion. "The nurses said he's a rock star."

He nodded twice, reaching up to cover his mouth with his hand, but before he could say another word, he was stumbling and falling to his knees with an almost inaudible sob.

About the Author

When Nicole Jacquelyn was eight and people asked what she wanted to be when she grew up, she told them she wanted to be a mom. When she was twelve, her answer changed to author. Her dreams stayed constant. First, she became a mom, and then during her senior year of college—with one daughter in first grade and the other in preschool—she sat down and wrote a story.